BORN of SCOURGE

Also by S. Jean

Hymn of Memory

Forevermore

The Devil in the Woods

BORN OF SCOURGE

S. Jean

For Jordan,
We had to say goodbye too soon and I'll always
miss you, but I hope you're happy watching me
carry on our love of stars.

LEGENDS OLDER THAN THE KINGDOM ITSELF SAID when the world grew dark and cold, where even the sun was covered by a veil of darkness and scourge poisoned the land until it choked the life out of it, a star would hear humanity's plight and would fall to the earth.

The skies above the castle turned tonight as Princess Celena of Norian watched the darkness from her balcony. For years now, the stars seldom glimmered out of the inky shroud above, but tonight, they were brighter than ever. Celena couldn't tear her gaze away, especially when the stars became streaks of color, lighting up a sky seldom seen. The world sung, something vibrant down to its core, and Celena knew this was it.

A star had heard humanity's plight.

It was falling right over the castle and someone had to catch it as the legends said. One pure of heart to tame the fallen star's magic.

There was a handmaiden outside now, likely thrust there by Celena's mother to sacrifice her health to catch the star, but the poor girl was terrified. She crouched low to the ground as though to protect herself, trembling all the while. She wouldn't catch anything like that and Celena decided, she wouldn't have to.

Celena would do it herself to see it done regardless of what her mother wished.

Her nightgown was thin against the night's chill and clung to her as she vaulted over the balcony rails. She landed in the dying gardens as spry as ever and hiked up her skirt as she ran, never once taking her eyes off the brightest star falling amongst the streaks of rippling colors. Attendants watching the poor girl shouted at Celena, panicked, and the garden lit up with candlelight from the guardsmen chasing after her to stop her foolishness.

None of them mattered—all that did was the star.

The colors in the sky streaked faster, brighter, leaving glittering trails turning into stars themselves until the entire castle was illuminated. This had to be it. The star at its nascent, ready to be caught. She set her bare feet in the old grass and held her hands aloft like the legends said. The star fell into her palms as a twinkling mass, somehow heavy but light at the same time, and she pressed it close to her chest.

It was like nothing else she'd ever beheld. The star's warmth tingled right through her skin and lit up the heavens with a hum, letting her see it all. The darkness so absolute around them, a great burst of light crowning the sky as a halo, and then a great emptiness yawning beneath her feet as she fell through. But she wasn't scared as her legs gave out beneath her. Nor was she frightened when attendants and guards cried her name. Not even when her mother's voice joined the chorus. She held the star as close to her heart as possible because he would bring back the light. She was sure of it.

✦

CELENA BREATHED IN DEEP AND OPENED HER EYES. Sweat slicked her forehead as though she'd just broken a fever and it left her chilled. Slowly, she pushed herself upright until her hands stung. She brought them close, wincing, and saw the first sign: fine purple lines surrounding her newly glittering nails. Followed the legends to the letter, then. Eventually, even her veins would be bold and purple.

Celena only thought it would take more time.

Wait. She picked her head up. The stars were gone beyond her balcony window. All was dark. She was alone in the bed. No. This was wrong. She shoved her covers back.

"Where is he?" She threw her feet over the bedside before her handmaiden, Alyssa came rushing from the other side of the screen dividing her room. "Alyssa!"

"My Princess—"

Celena pushed off her helping hands and stood on her own. "Where is the star?"

Alyssa's round face steeled into a frown. No doubt she'd borne the brunt of the Queen's ire from letting Celena vault from her balcony, but if some-one hadn't caught the star (and that poor girl earlier was not going to in her state), the darkness would have continued.

And now that Celena was separated from the star *she'd* caught, there was a very real chance they'd lose him. Whatever body he'd made while she'd held him would split apart without her continued touch and he'd die. The legends were very clear on this and while Celena wasn't sure how scholars knew what happened—she'd never heard about a failed star— she could not risk it happening now if he was the last hope her kingdom had at surviving the dark.

Her mother could think herself invincible all she wanted, but Celena knew they were not.

Celena drew herself up to be the princess her mother wanted her to be, matching Alyssa's steel, and Alyssa cast her gaze downward.

"Her Majesty wanted you kept safe," she murmured. "It was supposed to be Jessamine."

"Jessamine was terrified—you saw her." Celena took Alyssa's hands, prompting the handmaiden to stiffen. Her eyes locked on the shimmer across Celena's nails. "Where did my mother put the star? I have to be there."

Easing a soft sigh out of her nose, Alyssa nodded. "Of course, my lady. I will take you at once. Just..." She bit off whatever else she'd wanted to say and instead, retrieved Celena's dressing gown. "Please be warm."

Once Celena threw it on, Alyssa gently took Celena's wrist and hurried her into the hallway. Alyssa's pace was brisk and Celena forced herself to keep up regardless how weak her legs felt after the vault from her balcony. Guards stationed in the hallways let them go, ever the stalwart protectors, and the few servants working in the night quickly minded their own business when Celena glared at them. It didn't matter if they ran to her mother with news Celena was on the move—she was going to finish what she started.

The halls were cold despite the dressing gown; the stone frigid against Celena's feet and the air flushed her skin with goosebumps, but she persevered in Alyssa's wake. Their journey ended at the now seldom used wing on the opposite end of the castle. What was once filled day and night with dignitaries from other countries vying for her mother's attention had been empty since the dark closed in on them. Alyssa took her to the door at the very end and faced Celena.

"Here." Alyssa pressed a key into Celena's palm. "Jessamine is inside."

Frustration flushed Celena all the way through and she bit it down. "I will send her out. Send her home. You never led me here. I came all on my own if anyone asks."

Alyssa curtsied and stepped back, as though giving the door space in case something escaped. Nothing of the sort would happen. Celena readied herself. Her mother had wanted to protect her by sending another handmaiden out if the stars ever fell and have her bear the burden, even when Celena was clearly far more suited for the role. She never would have been afraid. She knew the old legends and songs better than anyone. And now, her mother hoped someone else could help the poor star form a human body.

It had to be Celena.

Staying was the only way to help him stabilize his body because it was a reflection of her wants and desires. Even now, she felt a cry in her own body that was not her own. Echoes of pain and anguish as the star's magic struggled to form a human body without the knowledge how.

Besides, Celena had already caught him—she was now sick as all other catchers had been. It was evident in her glimmering nails. Surely, even her blood would sparkle now if she cut her skin. There was no stopping it now.

With nothing else to lose, she unlocked the door.

Frigid air blew in from the far balcony doors left open, making the sheer curtains flutter like ghosts, and Celena braced herself against the chill. The canopy bed in the center of the room was dressed similarly to hers with curtains draped on all edges barely thick enough to hide anything inside. The rest of the room was left bare, any other furniture covered by a white cloth as though it was still unused.

It wasn't; Celena spied a glowing light from inside the canopy and without any other light in the room, it gave everything a soft, haunting glow. Like a moth, she wanted to go to it immediately, but she forced herself to find the whimpering girl hiding in the room first.

Jessamine was a slight girl a few years younger than Celena and looked even young when she set her terrified, wide eyes on her princess as though she'd expected the Queen. They softened with relief upon seeing Celena thankfully, and Celena helped her out of the room without a word. Once she'd shut the door, sealing herself in with the star she caught, she afforded herself a single breath. This was her decision. She hurried to the side of the bed still alight like a dying flame.

Magic—real magic only stars could bring—rippled across her skin as she neared the bed. It lingered as a hum in her ears, one so soft and melodic, it could have lulled her to sleep. She pushed the curtain aside and a gasp spilled from her lips.

There he lay. The star she'd caught. The one who had shown her the beginning and the end, and all the fleeting moments between which had quickly melted into colors in her memories. He lay on his back, writhing beneath sheets someone had covered his naked form with. Appearing hardly older than her, his dark skin shuddered with white cracks lining his face and limbs, like it struggled to hold itself together. White hair haloed his head against the pillows, shimmering bright like the star he was.

Though shaking, face twisted in pain, somehow

he was sublime in a world grown dark. A lone piece of light blazing bright despite it all.

"Hello," Celena whispered. He stilled and inclined his head toward her. "You told me your name was Sol." He watched her, eyes wide as though to take her in. His gaze should have frightened her—it would have anyone else—but she found it oddly mesmerizing. The sclera was a pitch-black like the night sky, and the irises shimmered an ice blue that almost looked white. The color even twinkled, like there were stars inside them.

"Sol," she repeated, more to herself than anything else, "like the sun veiled in the darkness." She came around to the side of the bed. His gaze never left her. "Would you like me to hold your hand?"

She waited as his eyes darted up and down. Whatever he searched for, he found it and gave her a quick nod. Celena sat at the bed's edge and gently touched the hand nearest—the one gripping the sheets so tightly like he might break otherwise—and spread her fingers around his.

The air jolted between them, like a connection being remade, but it wasn't quite as all-encompassing as it had been when she'd caught him. His skin was dreadfully cold to the touch and the cracks lining the top of his hand all the way through to his fingers felt like ice.

"Ten years ago," she whispered as the breeze blew into the room, trickling down her back. "The scourge grew out of the Barrens, marking the beginning of the Sixth Umbral Cycle. All the years since, I've been locked up without a friend as the world ends around me."

Sol's face softened, his mouth parting with a silent question.

"Could you be that? For now? A friend? Before you're sent away?"

Sol turned his hand and laced their fingers together. His grip was soft, but sure as he squeezed. Something stirred beneath Celena's skin and part of her knew she should have been scared because this shouldn't have been comforting. Except it was. A gift from Sol linking them together.

His body calmed the longer they held hands and the shivering ceased, allowing him to breathe evenly. The cracks thinned and the vibrant glow he'd been giving off was growing dimmer by the moment. He nodded again at her and she smiled. A friend. For now. She laid herself beside him and rested her head on the pillow, letting her brown curls spill across his hair.

"I thought you'd like a friend too."

She studied her hand entwined in his and so did he. His eyebrows folded in worry and he rubbed his thumb against the lines reaching up her hand. He mouthed silent words, a hum of a voice spilling forth, and she shook her head.

"It's fine," she said and Sol looked at her. "It's the cost for bringing light back to the world, right?" She tried smiling, but found tears in her eyes instead.

Sol's lips still worked, sounds trying and failing, until he finally spoke. "W-What is your name?" he whispered, his voice like a melodic hymn, making her shiver.

"I am Princess Celena of Norian." She brought his quilt forward and covered them both with it for warmth. "I won't leave. I promise." She drew his hand to her lips and gently kissed the knuckles.

Shaking, Sol brought her knuckles closer and kissed them in return. There was a smile on his lips as she rested against him and closed her eyes. Exhaustion swept over her like a wave and before she knew it, she'd fallen asleep beside the star she'd plucked right out of the sky.

Her dream was warm as she followed the streaks of light Sol made in the dark. Almost like she was playing with him and it went on and on until she heard birds. She hadn't heard birds since she was little; it was such a shy little song they sang now. She opened her eyes, stirring awake, and found the birds were not a dream. They sat on the balcony railing as though they'd never been gone. What drew a gasp from her lips, however, was the soft, dappled sunlight spilling across the room. A true dawn sky unfolded against the horizon, all the colors long since lost to the veil of darkness in a grand display across the sky.

She sat up, still holding Sol's hand tight, and exclamations about the miracle echoed around the castle. Her mother's voice overrode the others before long, ordering messengers to be sent to all corners of the kingdom, and then the clatter of hoofs against stone paths joined the voices as horses carried riders past the gates.

Messengers to find heroes. Heroes to escort the fallen star to the Onyx Spire in the Barrens so he could return light to an entire world grown dark as the legends said.

Celena looked at Sol and smiled. He'd stabilized into a young man. Honey-hued bronze skin, white freckles dusting it like stardust, and such a soft face. If not for the pale lines still present and the points to his ears, he would have looked as human as anyone else. He was asleep, blissfully unaware, his white hair spilling across his bare shoulders. The cracks of light persisted across his body, but all of them came to the spot on his chest where his heart was. A heart beating so sure and steady as he slept.

She brought his hand close and kissed it again.

Here he was, the world's last hope brought home by a princess of pure heart. And though she smiled as she laid herself beside him once more to watch him breathe, she knew this time was fleeting and she wouldn't live to see the world drenched in light.

"She sought a voice no one hears.
Perhaps it was the motion of the world.
The bones settling in the earth.
The way whispers in the cosmos curled.
Or, perhaps, it was nothing still.
Yet, she was not deterred."

—Fragment of "She, Born of Starlight," Anonymous

𝕿HE VAST CASTLE GARDENS BELOW THE BALCONY IN Sol's room soaked up all the sunlight streaming down from a sky not yet blacked out again. Servants flitted about between rows of flowers and planters as they pruned blossoms past their prime and collected petals for decorations, if Sol had to guess. He wasn't honestly sure. Human machinations were still a mystery to him, even a month after being among them, and he didn't really care.

The sunlight wouldn't last.

Although, Sol considered, perhaps he was being hasty in thinking so. He didn't know *why* the darkness had parted above the castle and the land surrounding it after he'd fallen, just that it had. Regardless if it persisted or not, he wondered why humanity bothered celebrating at all. Farther away, the blue turned to black as dark as ink. A reminder the world was still dying as scourge choked the life out of it.

This good cheer was fleeting, just like this new body of his.

As a star, he'd never had one. He simply was. Yet, now that he had one, he disliked it. Not what he looked like or the pieces therein, but rather the physical sensations. He tired easily, headaches wrapped his head in a vice more times than he could count, and largely, the feelings associated with bodies were unpleasant. Especially when he had to act mystical and all-knowing because humanity viewed him as their last hope. Queen Celeste, the Warrior Queen of Norian, treated him with reverence, as did her entire staff, but it made the whole experience lonely. Kept at an arm's length out of fear of something he couldn't do.

At the same time, however, the Queen treated him as something on the verge of breaking and made sure the guards were never far from him. *Or, Sol thought to himself, frowning, she thinks I'll hurt someone.*

In any case, he couldn't leave—the guards made sure of it—until it was time for him to venture forth and bring light back to the world or whatever the minstrels spun it as. When that was, he had no idea. As soon as he was able to walk on his own without Celena nearby to ground him, he should have departed for the Onyx Spire with a retinue of knights. For a time, he'd expected it every morning he awoke, but he quickly learned humans had no sense of urgency, even when the scourge was literally outside their fortified walls. It was close enough Sol could hear its whispers amongst the breeze, but humans never did.

Humanity feasted, spoke and laughed like the world hadn't been encased in darkness, and now with the sky its brilliant blue again, pretended everything had returned to when the scourge was a dark tale told to frighten children.

Vexing. And they kept up the pretense of misplaced normalcy until Sol walked into the room. Their stark reminder who hushed even the loudest laughter on presence alone. He was proof the world was not right. And yet *still*, the Queen kept him trapped here.

Perhaps it didn't matter; another day spent in the castle, whittling away the hours with Celena or on his own, meant another day closer to humanity losing themselves to the darkness without his doing. They'd be their own end if they didn't do something soon.

It was no wonder Celena had said she was locked up. She *was* and now Sol was as well. The only comfort he found trapped in the castle was knowing her presence was somewhere nearby at all times. The same comforting presence, however, coiled guilt into his newfound heart. It'd been a month since his body stabilized. Since he awoke with her beside him. Since the blood in her veins glittered with scourge because of him. Scourge from catching him in a state before he was truly real.

He shouldn't have felt bad. The stories, even the ones whispered amongst the darkness in the cosmos, always said the one who caught the star—gave it the means to create a body of its own—would die because the magic was simply too volatile and heavy for a human to wield. Upon a touch, it had burrowed itself within Celena's veins to draw from her life to create Sol's body. Had she not caught him, he would have fizzled until no light remained. Until even he no longer remained.

Sobering. Sol hadn't realized how close he'd come to dying after countless eons suspended in the cosmos with the other stars. Yet, the thought of fizzling out didn't quite frighten him as much as it ought to have; in a way, falling at all was a kind of dying. Unfortunately, a human body made the process all the slower and more miserable.

A presence down the hall made Sol shiver as it moved and he picked his head up. Her soft footsteps never echoed against the carpets and she made no noise even as her skirts swept through the halls, but he felt her. Celena. The soft light in his thoughts; the hum helping him sleep at night. As long as he knew she was near, where she was in a crowd of humans who all blended together, nothing like bodies and headaches could bother Sol.

He'd hardly glanced over his shoulder before his chamber doors opened.

"Princess Celena!" the attendant with her announced despite Celena trying to hush him. The words rang throughout the room anyway and she followed after them with a petulant huff ending in a snicker she hid behind a gloved hand.

Celena was as beautiful as the day she'd caught him. Barely into adulthood like his own body, she had soft bronze skin like her mother, a round face with a coy smile, and wide eyes shimmering like emeralds. Her thick brown hair went down the length of her back in bountiful waves tamed with braids, gems, and what smelled of lilacs. She wore purple today—her favorite color, as Sol quickly learned—and one of her favorite dresses. It was a soft lilac shade with embroidered white flowers along the bust. The white ivory sleeves were buttoned tight across her arms until they loosened and became ruffles across her hands. A red sash adorned her waist and with it were glittering clear gems making her sparkle as she walked. The rest of the skirts went down to the floor, layers of lilac and ivory, and she had one side gathered in her gloved hands so she could walk.

Gloves to hide evidence of the scourge burrowed into her skin. Her fingernails would be glittering with a purple sheen and her veins would be bold against her skin as the scourge darkened her blood. It was so similar to the scourge choking the life out of the world it frightened most people, but this was more benign if it could be called such. Out there, scourge ravaged human bodies until only a husk remained that felt nothing but pain as its limbs were forcible reanimated. What Celena's had was soft.

She'd still die—it was too much for a human to have in their veins—and the scourge inside would die with her. Sol took a little solace that his scourge was kind; it wouldn't aim to torture her at all because he wished her no harm.

The scourge outside the castle walls was anything but.

"I can never surprise you," she teased.

Sol smiled and they watched the gardens, side by side. The skies were a soft blue today, clear of clouds. "I think your attendants have more hand in ruining the surprise than anything else," he said, words still unnatural on his human tongue. Stars never needed to speak; it simply *was*.

"One day, I'll surprise you!" Celena leaned into Sol, giggling, and he let her.

At first, Sol had wanted nothing to do with her. He'd been convinced she must have hated him for poisoning her when she had so much life left to live. Her mother certainly expressed her thinly veiled disdain, like it was Sol's own choice to infect Celena personally. Apparently, another girl was supposed to catch Sol and failed, so Celena had made the choice herself.

Sol had tried to keep his distance from everyone in the castle once he could, but then Celena kept coming by every morning insistent she spend time with Sol. Never once was there any malice in her voice. Too good to be true, surely, but over the many mornings, Sol realized she was truthful the night they'd laid together. She'd wanted a friend.

Every morning, she'd take him into the gardens for a walk beneath the sunlight they both knew was fleeting. Afterward, they'd spend much of the day together following one of the many plans Celena made up on the spot. Reading in the castle libraries. Tasting what the cooks and bakers were making for the day. Watching the Queen's knights practice drills in the courtyard. Anything she could think of to fill the empty days.

All of it was rote, normal, and helped her ignore the fact the world was ending around them. Sol didn't mind helping her forget. He liked the way she smiled.

And besides, she harbored the belief the world wouldn't end because Sol was there. He hadn't the heart to tell her otherwise or about the promise he'd made as he'd fallen through the skies. Let her believe he'd save the world if it made her smile so.

"Any word from would-be heroes?" Sol leaned his head against hers. He *could* have made the trek to the Onyx Spire by himself, but the Queen and legends dictated he needed escorts. Danger lurked in every corner because of the scourge, after all. Curiously, none of the Queen's knights were up to the task. Neither were any of her generals or nobles who liked to parade around with a sword at their waist.

Escorts were meant to protect the star, but Sol wasn't naïve. Scourge likely wouldn't hurt him like it would humans. Escorts were simply assurance he'd see the venture through. That he wouldn't doom humanity by disappearing.

Escorts simply meant he had to be careful.

Celena drummed her fingers on the railing. "It's what I came to talk about, actually." She produced a small missive from her sash. The wax seal had already been cracked and she unfolded the paper to show him. "Someone sent us word they were coming."

Something resembling unease coiled in Sol's stomach as his gaze darted across the scrawl. Reading was still difficult for him even with Celena's tutelage, but he knew enough to know she was correct. He gripped the railing, steeling himself, and swallowed. There was no reason to act as such—he *had* to go— except it meant this fuzzy time with Celena was coming to an end.

"How many?"

Celena silently read the missive. "Not sure. Could be any number of people, I suppose. This one has the seal of the messenger that went to the southern border between us and Jarenth Kingdom across the river." She peered at Sol, but he had no idea where that was; the maps she'd shown him early on had quickly been forgotten. "Jarenth stopped talking to us shortly after the scourge encroached. Everyone did, actually. My mother ceased trying."

Sol frowned. Legends Celena had read to him

over the month commonly spoke about kingdoms coming together to face the scourge threat. Not ignoring each other. "Do the other kingdoms not care to help us, then?"

Celena averted her gaze and slipped the missive away. "Our allies, yes… but my mother closed all borders shortly after the sky darkened. She doesn't quite see others as allies, but rather places to conquer when the darkness lifts. That's all. Why ask for aid when you're going to strike later?" She said the last bit so quietly, Sol had hardly heard her.

It made more sense why none of the queen's own guard were up to the task of escorting Sol. She needed them close if her plan truly was to conquer once light spilled across the world. Sol snorted. Typical human arrogance.

Celena extended a gloved hand toward Sol, smiling. "Walk with me?"

As he took her hand, his blood hummed with hers, an acknowledgement she'd never quite under-stand. It was why he could sense her so well even from rooms away. It *was* him and always called to him. And, for some reason, he felt ashamed that this feeling—the one that would one day die with her—made him feel at home.

She took him for their daily garden walk, her attendant and guard not too far away. Sol never minded. They seemed to like Celena and she liked them, although he never bothered to memorize their names. They hardly looked at Sol as it was and he gave them the same courtesy.

Quiet and quaint, the castle gardens were a breath of fresh air away from the castle. It was set inside enclosed ivory walls, but ivy and trees had been planted at the far edges so it never looked like they were trapped inside. The castle overlooked the gardens, its beautiful vaulted architecture on full display out here as this side stretched high into the sky until it became steeples at the very top. The rest of the castle wasn't quite this beautiful; most of it was a mix between this architecture of delicate beauty and the thick stone walls ready to withstand any attack. Large windows and balconies adorned this side, each one watching the garden below.

A soft breeze shivered through the flowers, pulling Sol's attention back to the garden. Fallen petals floated along the wind and the faraway trees rustled. Colors lush and vibrant across all corners. Almost too picturesque. Truly separate from the rest of the starved world outside the castle walls.

In all honesty, the plants and flowers should have long since withered, but they'd stubbornly persisted under what scant light the sun still provided in the darkness and now, with the shroud momentarily taken away, everything flourished anew, proving it would not die quietly.

The earlier attendants had been cleared out for Celena's privacy. Everyone similarly avoided Sol, but it was more out of fear than anything akin to respect. He didn't quite mind; he found them as uncomfortable as they found him.

Celena always took Sol to a particular spot where purple heathers grew in abundance alongside the white daisies peeking out from between them like little stars. Her balcony overlooked them and there was many a morning spent together simply watching the flowers shiver in the breeze. Early on, Celena had told Sol the names of every single plant they grew here, but only these two stood out because Celena absolutely loved them.

Celena peered out over the soft purples and whites and breathed in deep. It was calm simply existing together like this, arms entwined, and Sol wouldn't have minded staying like this the entire day. Celena had other ideas; she eased out a breath after a time, like she intended to speak. Until she didn't and the silence settled around them again. She tried once more, although this breath ended as a flustered exhale like she was about to say something silly. Sol waited, curious, and finally, she eschewed words altogether and bent down to unlace her shoes.

She stepped out of them and settled her bare feet into the grass. Sol saw no reason not to join her and followed suit.

The grass was cold, but soft. It was oddly soothing being connected to the world this way and he would have happily stood beside Celena, wiggling toes in the grass and doing nothing else, if she hadn't had other ideas.

"My mother plans to have a feast when the heroes arrive." Celena walked with featherlight steps as she slowly stripped the gloves from her hands.

Humans liked chances of revelry; there had been a small party when he was stabilized enough to move, although he hadn't attended. A headache had kept him abed and all he'd done was listen to the echoes. It hadn't been for him anyway.

Celena was watching Sol almost mischievously. Like the time she'd sneaked them into the tower housing the messenger birds. The birds hadn't quite minded the intrusion—they must have been used to Celena visiting and giving them gentle pets. She made sure Sol gave them the same as well—but the spymaster had been livid.

She tugged him closer. "There's lots of drinking." She placed one of his hands at her waist. "Eating." She took his hand in hers, bare skin letting the hum grow between them. "And *dancing*." She rested her hand on his shoulder and beamed at him. "Would you like to learn to dance, Sol?"

For some reason, when she spoke his name, it made him want to smile. A curious reaction, but one he never minded and let his lips follow the motion. "I'd love to."

Her steps were fluid and her voice clear as she counted the beats. The flutter her skirts made around Sol's own legs quickly became endearing. She danced him through petals left behind and wildflowers attempting to grow underfoot when no one was looking. The gardens spun in delightful colors as Celena showed him how and when he dared to return the favor, he watched as she became all the colors she was in a gentle spiral. The smiles she graced him with were bright and dazzling and made him forget what he was. What fate held in store for her. For the rest of the world.

Reality choked back the colors with its dull edge as armor clinked together nearby. On purpose, even. The guards in the castle knew how to move as silent as a whisper; this was an entrance. Celena quickly let go, eyebrows high, and as she turned, she swept herself into a low curtsy. Sol mimicked her and deeply bowed because only one person would make her react such.

Queen Celeste watched them like a hunter

who'd caught her prize. So alike her daughter, but an older and hardened version of her. A powerful woman, she was known for both her prowess in battle in her younger years as well as her beauty. Though she hadn't seen a battle since Celena was born, she still trained daily as though one could happen upon her at a moment's notice. Brown eyes as piercing as a sword, a wide nose like her daughter, and full lips painted a vibrant red today. Her thick brown hair fell down the length of her back as carefully maintained waves woven with braids and gems aplenty. Her toned arms showed through sheer white sleeves and her physique was complemented by the form of the red dress she wore. A fur cape swept over one shoulder, white and black from an animal Sol did not know, and gold chains kept it in place.

"You may both rise," Queen Celeste said and watched as they did so.

Celena's eyes remained locked on the abandoned shoes and Queen Celeste's lips quirked into an amused smile as she glanced at them too. Celena quickly hid her bare feet with her skirts, but Sol had no such thing to hide his own.

"Greetings, Your Highness," Celena said with a level voice. "I was teaching our star to dance for the festivities to come."

"I see that," the Queen murmured. "Truly though,

it's too cold to be barefoot. And the lack of a cape, my dear you will catch your death out here." Her voice was teasing, but it came without any real warmth. A performance at best. "You've even stripped your gloves. Are you not cold, my dear?"

Celena nodded meekly, chastised, and covered her hands as quickly as she could. Sol remained silent. Their bodies had been warm as they'd danced across the grass, but now standing still, the rush of blood quieted and a chill crept back into his bones. One of the guards quickly freed his own cape once Celeste glanced at him, and even quicker was it gently placed around Celena's shoulders.

Celeste looked at Sol and he kept his gaze downcast. "Would I be able to steal a moment of our star's time from you?" It was a question, but she needn't have bothered with permission. If she willed it, Sol would be taken to her with or without his or Celena's consent. "I will let you continue teaching him once I have finished."

"Of course." Celena curtseyed again and when her mother nodded, she straightened. The guard who had offered his cape collected her shoes and gently took her further into the gardens to wait elsewhere.

Celeste's gaze never left Sol even as her daughter walked away. Once Celena was out of earshot—once the scourge buzzing through her skin settled against a wooden bench near the heathers she so loved—the Queen nodded pointedly toward Sol's shoes. He quickly tugged them on and only then did Celeste offer her arm which he took. She stood taller than him—taller than most, really—and she led him further into the gardens. Her other guard remained where she'd been, a beacon of shimmering ivory beneath fleeting sunlight.

They stopped before a bench beneath a large trellis, the wood a brilliant shade of white like it had never weathered storm or gust. The flowers grew up and around the trellis' arc and the blossoms were bright reds and yellows. Celeste took a seat on the bench and brought Sol down with her before finally letting him go.

She stayed silent, but unlike her daughter where the silence bored into her until she spoke, Celeste relished in it. Must have come with power; she commanded the silence and therefore, it was wholly hers. It would only break if she allowed it.

Gently, she cupped one of the red blossoms—Sol couldn't remember the name of the flower—and held it close so she could smell it.

"What do you know of the first star?" she finally asked when she let go.

Sol hesitated, searching her. "Not anything

substantial, Your Highness."

Celeste pursed her lips and settled her gaze forward. Through the gaps between flowers and carefully maintained bushes, Sol caught the color of Celena's dress.

"Do stars not dwell?"

Once more, Sol hesitated. The traitor of a heart within his chest stirred and raced, piecing together a million reasons for the question and each one was worse than the last. "I am unsure of what you mean."

Her jaw tightened. "Do you not care for your brethren? Do you not care to know what happens upon the fall?"

Anger sparked deep in Sol, but he kept his face blank. Of course he cared for them. It was why he was *here*, but she didn't need to know the lengths he'd go for them.

"There are whispers," Sol said slowly, "of journeys along the darkened night. Nothing more than that."

She watched him with eyes almost a match for her daughter, but they held no warmth. Sol stared right back, as impassive as possible. She never balked at his stare like much of the castle did. Then again, she was the woman who'd survived the assassination of her father and uncle and the one who'd made it through the kingdom's civil war unscathed as she led victory after victory against every bloodbath splitting the place in two. At least, that was what the minstrels sang. No one was shy about talking about her prowess as the warrior princess who now sat upon the throne as the warrior queen. A pair of eyes would never disturb her.

All in all, she was too clever for her own good and keeping her gaze only reminded Sol of the fact. Careful words and intense eyes to goad Sol into saying something he wanted to keep close. What no one else could know.

"Scholars posit it thusly," Celeste finally continued, "the first star spent years on a journey following a *voice*. No one's been able to quite figure out what that voice was. When she disappeared and we entered the First Umbral Cycle, the next star to fall also searched for a voice they heard." She gently tapped her knuckles against her chin. "Opinion is mixed whether or not it was the first star's voice, our voice, or perhaps the one searched for and now forgotten. Do you think they are all one and the same?"

Hardly, but Sol swallowed the word. "I am unsure."

Her expression soured. "Do you know what happens when a star reaches the Onyx Spire?"

"It seems that light returns, Your Majesty."

The glib way he'd said it made Celeste's eyes

narrow. He wasn't wrong. Time and time again across the Umbral Cycles, stars entered the Onyx Spire in the Barrens and then light spilled across the world again. If heroes returned, they were mum on what exactly transpired within, but every legend agreed: stars entered the spire and light always returned.

Truthfully, the how didn't matter. He'd let Celeste talk until she was out of words. There must have been a reason she was asking him all this now and out of fear of her finding the truth behind his lies, he stayed silent. Suspicion weighed heavy between each question and he would not let any take root.

"You are correct," she acquiesced slowly. "And, afterward, all tales agree to this one fact: once light returns, the dark recedes quickly. All of it from the sky, from the land, anything afflicted bleeds out scourge like it's *retreating*. Then it's all gone as though it never existed. Although there are some rumors it festers where the light cannot reach, but those are merely rumors." She spoke quieter, studying his expression. "I've had scholars scour exactly *how* and what transpires in the Onyx Spire to achieve this feat, but there have been no hard answers. Light returns regardless of what we know and we all hail it a miracle."

"Indeed," Sol agreed.

"Yet your brethren never come back. It's not a secret they disappear. No one's recorded why and heroes never say. Curious, no?"

Sol's throat felt tight. She watched him *so* closely like she expected something damning from his lips. "I am unsure what you want from me, Your Highness."

As if running out of patience, Celeste roughly took his chin and held it still. Her hands were bare, her fingers ice cold as they touched his skin, and he froze. She stared so deeply into his eyes, Sol feared she'd see all the way through to every hidden plan and to the whispers spoken through his thoughts to remind him of his promise. Yet, he dared not turn away and prove he had something to hide.

"I want the light," she said finally and released him. "I want assurance my faith is not displaced, my dear star."

"Is there reason to doubt?"

The words came forth before Sol could bite them back. Celeste raised her eyebrows, amused, and her lips split into a smirk.

"You are curious, you know." She sat back to fold her arms against her chest. "The other stars were said to be brilliance incarnate. Loving everything they were given from the prettiest of fabrics to the lowliest of dolls. Almost like the world and every-thing in it inspired wonder within them." She tilted her head and narrowed her eyes. "Yet, here you are. Dull. Uninspired."

Sol bit down. He hadn't realized how different he was from the other stars. Thinking of forcing a smile upon his lips as he danced for humanity made him sick.

"Until," Celeste continued, "you are with my daughter. Then you are another man entirely." She leaned closer as her voice dropped to a whisper. "And until you're watching the knights spar. Oh, don't think I don't notice it. Your eyes sparkle the way Celena's does with attention, hm? Tell me, which knight is it that makes you smile? It would be remiss of me to send you so dull and uninspired to save humanity and I cannot very well send my only child."

None of them. Sol swallowed as a chill work its way down his spine. It wasn't a secret he and Celena had found scant joy watching the knights train in the courtyard from up on high. It was more for Celena's benefit, really. Sometimes, the knights would notice them and put on a show with brilliant smiles. And while Sol did not deny watching a few knights more keenly than others with their strong arms and chests, no faces came to mind. Humanity all blended together as it was. Fleeting human tainted fancies he wanted nothing to do with.

Celeste was still smiling at him like she'd caught him in a trap. "We expect our heroes to arrive soon," she said. "I will have my staff procure provisions and traveling supplies for you. I want you to see this journey through to the end as all others before you have, do you understand me?"

"You've nothing to worry about, Your Highness," Sol said. A lie. A promise. Something in-between or even neither. Her worries would come to an end, one way or another.

Celeste watched him as though parsing the hidden thoughts and Sol would not look away. Nothing she did mattered. He *had* to go to the Onyx Spire or else the scourge would continue. Even she must have known that despite all she did to keep everyone from dwelling on the dark, castle fortifications would only last so long once the scourge pounded at the gates. If she continued her inaction, her castle and everyone inside it would fall to the scourge or plain starvation once they were truly trapped. Eventually. She must have realized it. Perhaps it was why she allowed heroes to arrive finally and everything leading up to it was a performance for the history books.

She rose without another word. Her guard was

there quicker than Sol could blink and had her arm offered for her queen. She took it and she led her through the cold grass to reunite her with her daughter just past the flowers.

Sol only let himself breathe when he felt the scourge within Celena twist in the presence of her mother.

His thoughts were growing so loud and numerous, Sol had to close his eyes to calm down. No one saw through him. No one saw the lies hidden behind his words. They believed he'd bring light back to the world. If it got him out of the castle, he'd say anything at this point and dance the part. He just had to get to the spire.

When he opened his eyes again, Celena had returned. Still radiated a softness in the world Sol couldn't help but want to hold. He wanted to believe in it despite evidence humanity was not like her. Was too hardened and diseased to save.

Before she spoke, he did, just to chase away the simmering thoughts. "Will you dance with me again?" he asked, hopeful. "I want to learn more."

Celena was so resplendent when she smiled. Sol wanted to memorize it and sought to trace it with his fingers, so he'd never forget. Even when darkness claimed everything that was and ever would be, he'd hold onto this smile. This afternoon as they swept each other through the gardens, their soft laughter mixing together amongst the whispers in the wind.

"Scholars and the common folk alike had no answers.
They were sure: what she heard simply didn't exist.
Even as everyone tried to convince her,
she would not be dismissed."

—Fragment of "She, Born of Starlight," Anonymous

IN A WEEK'S TIME, THE CASTLE HAD TRANSFORMED into one befitting the arrival of heroes. Drapery against tall windows became soft whites and reds to signify rebirth and the sheer curtains had been steamed and hung anew. Carefully arranged flower corsages dotted the hallways, making the castle smell like more than cold stone and gave a pop of color to every corridor. What was once a quiet and morose castle awaiting its eventual demise despite the laughter echoing the halls became what it must have been before: alive, colorful, and welcoming.

All because of supposed heroes.

The day of their arrival came before long and Celena sneaked Sol up into the front hall's overlook where royalty like her could watch people come and go from the heavy main doors in the entryway. It allowed them some semblance of privacy because no one ever thought to look up and there were also heavy curtains they could hide behind if anyone did. Celena wanted to see the heroes without them knowing she was watching and honestly, Sol was curious the same.

A soft rumble of activity from the city came in on the breeze. An eager buzz that was absent before. Sol hadn't been allowed into the city, but the servants had conversed at length how beautiful the streets looked nowadays, decked out for the arrival of heroes. Streets and buildings had been washed and scrubbed, making them gleam anew beneath the sunlight. Flower blossom garlands were run from building to building and hung from them were banners welcoming the heroes. The main road was even said to shine underneath the sunlight. If it was true, it wasn't going to last. As soon as the heroes were gone, the light was sure to follow. Hope would wane with it and they would return to waiting for the inevitable.

A horn finally sounded outside, announcing the heroes' imminent arrival with the procession leading them, and Celena pulled Sol as close as possible to peer over the rail.

Walking between the entourage of the Queen's knights were only three heroes. While the knights shined with polished armor, the heroes didn't. They were dull, dressed in old leathers and cloaks. It didn't dampen Celena's excitement any; she hurried Sol to the other side of their overlook as the heroes strode underneath and they continued watching them pass by below.

Out of all of humanity, only three bothered to answer the end of the world. Two women and one man.

The smallest woman on left had frizzy copper-red hair escaping the confines of her hood and she had a lute affixed carefully to her back. While her cloak was old and mended with care, the lute was immaculate.

Sol leaned on his palm, uninterested. Heroes needed bards to tell their tales as it happened, he supposed. She seemed awfully young, however; no older than Celena.

The second woman to the right was a strikingly tall figure with feathery raven black hair she kept in a long braid down her back. She wore no cloak, instead showing off the thick musculature of her arms, and had a large labrys strapped across her back. A wonder it was allowed in.

The man walking in the center was hardly as tall

as the warrior woman and had thinner shoulders, but looked hero enough. Wavy auburn hair had been tousled across the front while the back was closely cropped. His tawny skin was dark from the sun like the bard beside him. The cloak across his shoulders held an emblem of a flower across the back, but Sol wasn't sure what it was. There was a sword at his side, but compared to the labrys and lute, it wasn't anything special.

Celena cupped her hand to his ear. "He's handsome," she whispered, smiling.

Sol wasn't quite sure how she could tell since he hadn't even looked their way, but she was giddy. Maybe it was the man's shoulders. Sol was unimpressed with the whole of them. They were simply people.

"What is the flower on his back?"

"Oh." Celena glanced again and squinted her eyes. "It looks like a yarrow, I believe."

The man paused, brief enough Sol wondered if he'd somehow heard Celena, and glanced over his shoulder. At them. Celena squeaked and yanked Sol into the curtains with her for cover. They waited, silent and pressed against one another, until the knight at the front announced the heroes' entrance into the throne room. Celena immediately devolved into a litany of giggles and rested her forehead against Sol's.

"See?" she said. "He was handsome."

"I barely got to look at him," Sol insisted.

That made her giggle more and he was glad to see her in good spirits despite the sudden dread in his own stomach. It worsened when her good cheer waned and she peeked around the curtain again. One hand twisted a handful of her skirts mindlessly as her smile faded into a frown.

Sol gently touched her hand. "What is it?" he whispered, his voice almost drowned out from the cheers welcoming the heroes inside.

"Part of me actually hoped they wouldn't come." Celena bowed her head and held Sol's hand. Scourge hummed against the touch, sending a shiver through Sol's entire arm. "So then I'd have more time with you."

The statement struck Sol, making him forget to breathe, and the dread uncoiled throughout his entire body. Time to stars was fleeting, but never ending. The cosmos persisted and so did they. Days became blinks and years the same. But in a human body with finite time, a body that would one day dissolve, time had an end. Distantly, he knew and accepted he'd have to leave Celena, but it had been so far from his thoughts, non-existent.

And now, with the arrival of the heroes, it was

there right in front of him. He didn't want her to be alone. His only friend.

But then she graced him with another smile. "It's selfish of me to say so."

It wasn't selfish, he wanted to say, but his voice caught in his throat. She smoothed her hands over his tunic and righted the ties in the front.

"I am of pure heart," she whispered and stepped away. She breathed out and gathered her skirts again. "I should be there with my mother. The feast is tonight and I've tasked Alyssa with choosing an outfit for you." Her smile turned teasing, but Sol couldn't match it. "She has wonderful color sense. Shall I see you then?"

He forced the smile to his lips. "I'll be there," he said. "And I'll dance with you all night if it pleases you."

They shared the silence for a brief moment before Celena steeled herself with an expression befitting the princess her mother wanted her to be and not the young woman she was. Steady confidence. Her attendants were quick, blending out of the shadows as she descended the steps, reminding Sol they never had any real privacy, and took her away.

Sol watched her go from the railing. Her back straight, not a stiff joint in sight. Practiced poise to cover the scourge building beneath her skin. He picked his gaze off her and peered into the archway that led into the throne room. The three heroes stood before the Queen's throne, just barely visible. Their voices were but echoes, no weight or substance to them, and he watched the man in the middle with the yarrow flower cloak.

For some reason, Sol couldn't bring himself to look away.

✦

ALL THROUGHOUT THE DAY, MUSIC STRUMMED across the castle as bits and pieces of old songs while bards and minstrels tested their instruments, weaving their songs together to entertain everyone to come. The aroma of food from the kitchens wafted through the halls and though Sol had no idea what was being made, it made his stomach grumble. If Celena hadn't been immediately taken to her chambers to prepare, she would have sneaked Sol into the kitchens with her to sample some of the planned delicacies. He couldn't do it by himself; the cooks didn't like him very much. So, after a bath the servants graciously filled for him with shampoos and soaps aplenty, he languished in his room, listening and waiting, until the sun began to set and Alyssa graced his doorway with a bundle of clothes.

She gently laid it across his bed in order of how

he had to dress and wordlessly left him to do the deed himself. Sol never minded; most servants were afraid to touch him. Besides, this had allowed him to get used to his own body all the more.

After he'd stabilized and the Queen had scrutinized him, she'd sent him to the castle seamstress to get measured for clothes. She hadn't wanted him running around in anything ill-fitting; it'd reflect badly on her. Sol wouldn't have cared otherwise. The seamstress had been quick and efficient and it helped he'd had no reason to feel embarrassed. Celena still apologized for what she'd called intrusive and brusque so soon after waking, but Sol honestly hadn't been bothered. All humans had bodies—admittedly, some with different shapes and slightly differently arranged appendages—but in the end, made up of parts so similar, to be embarrassed about it was vexing. Celena had only shaken her head when he expressed this, embar-rassed enough for the both of them.

First went on the thin cotton undershirt and hosiery. Then atop that was the white tunic with loose sleeves tucked into leather wrist cuffs. On next went the dark pants tucked into leather boots made for the journey. Each one had gold fastenings, glimmering against the setting sun slipping inside. The long black linen overcoat with open sleeves went over everything, providing warmth, and the edges of it were lined in a silver filigree trim. Tying everything together was a vibrant yellow sash atop a thicker red one around his middle.

Last to go on was the fur-trimmed snow-white cape. The fur was a dark russet brown and incredibly soft to the touch. It went halfway down Sol's back and part of him hoped the cloak he was given for the journey had the same fur on the inside. The warmth was nice.

All in all, however, the outfit was a far cry from the simplicity of the tunics and trousers he'd been enjoying, but he supposed he looked presentable. A prim young man stared back at him from the mirror, after all.

At first, mirrors had elicited uncertainty in him. Though Sol had no qualms with his body, he'd never expected it to look as it did. Granted, he hadn't expected anything and he wasn't sure if he would have changed it if he'd been given the chance. Over time, that feeling lessened and he could say with certainty yes, the reflection was indeed himself.

His white hair was still soft from the bath and he drew his fingers through to try and settle it down his back. Cutting it shorter to better manage it occurred to him shortly after falling, but Celena had enjoyed drawing her fingers through it, so he'd left it be. As he smoothed it over his shoulder, he caught the aroma of lilacs. Just like Celena's hair. It made him smile.

The door creaked open on the other side of the room and Sol quickly focused on his surroundings. Celena was right there. She really *could* have surprised him this time if the door hadn't been so loud.

Celena came in unannounced, likely already having shushed the attendant with her, and she was smiling as Sol came around the wooden screen giving him privacy. Dressed in soft pinks and reds, her dress complimented the rosy complexion given to her cheeks. Fitted well to her form, the dress had a plunging neckline surrounded in white lace, and the skirts went straight to the floor. Teardrop gems hung from gold chains around her waist, once again making her sparkle. The sleeves were tightly buttoned up the length of her arm, hiding evidence of scourge underneath, and white ruffles cascaded over hands once again covered in a pair of white gloves. The whole of it was almost seamless. No one would know she had scourge inside her at all. Her hair was carefully done with two braids wrapped around the crown of her head while a handful of golden barrettes and pins kept it in place. The rest of it was left to hang as shimmering waves down her back.

It all suited her, especially when she carried

herself with dignity. She considered Sol from head to toe, tapping a finger on her chin.

"You look nice," Sol said, feeling he should say something although it didn't feel like it was enough.

Celena hid her shy smile with a shake of her head. "As do you." She adjusted his yellow sash and then the way the sleeves billowed over his cuffs. Her gaze traveled to his hair and she tucked a lock behind his ear. "Would you like me to braid your hair back?"

She'd done it so many mornings before as they'd basked in the sun and while Sol had immensely enjoyed her fingers combing through his hair, he shook his head. "It might look *too* nice," he said and a laugh bubbled its way out of Celena's throat. "I don't want it to look better than yours."

"Imagining you with a braid around your head like mine is quite the sight," Celena teased and brushed her own hair off her shoulders. "I scarcely think you have enough hair for that and still have any left to hang down!" She extended her arm and Sol let her wrap it around the crook of his elbow. "Are you ready? They'll be announcing guests soon and we're first."

"As long as I am with you," Sol said.

Arms entwined, Celena and Sol headed for the great hall. Celena told Sol a little of what to expect on the way; introductions for them, the heroes, and then anyone prominent in order of their importance. Food and drink would then be served, and after a few courses—Celena wasn't sure how many—there would be dancing until they were too sore to move or until dawn light flitted inside from the great hall's balconies. Queen Celeste didn't care which happened first; it was a feast in the midst of the world ending and she wanted people to forget about the ending part.

The great hall had been decked out for the occasion. The balcony doors were peeled back, allowing their sheer curtains to billow in the breeze. Dusk sunlight streamed inside like liquid gold, casting the place in such warm hues, one could forget all about the dark. The hearth built between the balcony doors was ablaze, the fire making it so the cold breeze coming inside didn't matter. In front of it was the high table dressed in an ivory white tablecloth and it was reserved for esteemed guests and the Queen herself who already sat at a high-backed chair in the center. The other two tables along the sides of the room were bare beyond glass jars with candles twinkling like little stars inside. The wooden floor, once scuffed from meetings and dances of yore, now shined beneath the chandeliers across the center of the room. Up above, the ceiling was made of a mosaic of dark glass and when the ample firelight caught it, the glass resembled the night sky. One of the few things Sol liked about the room.

Guests stood on either side of the great hall doors, watching esteemed guests enter, and a small gathering of nobles awaited just inside for their arrival. Sol's body trembled as Celena proudly strode them through when their names were announced. The crowd hushed, eyes on him and Celena in a sea of vibrant colors of tunics and dresses. Head held high, Celena crossed the room with practiced ease and stopped before the high table where her mother watched with a soft smile. Celena bowed deeply, bringing Sol with her.

Queen Celeste wore the same carefully built façade she'd had in the garden days prior. A powerful woman sat in the throne without fear of the dark closing in on them. Her hair shined a rich brown against the glow from the setting sun outside and almost appeared as gold as the chain circlet she wore across her forehead. Another crown sat upon her head, this one inlaid in rubies and opals, and glittered as she moved. She wore a deep burgundy dress not unlike the one Celena wore, but her sleeves were left open, allowing sheer ruffles to spill across her bare arms.

She smiled at her daughter and raised her hand,

hushing any side conversations still whispering around them. Celena slowly stood and Sol followed her up. The Queen regaled the room with the tale of how her only daughter had valiantly caught the falling star, but Sol was too overwhelmed with everything to pay attention to individual words. Too many faces he didn't know, too many eyes upon him when he'd thought he was used to it by now, and worst of all, there was another hum he could hear. Distant and hushed. Not like the immediacy of Celena's hand tight in his and not a hum he knew.

Before he could gaze across the crowd to find the source, Celena had brought them to their spots at the high table beside her mother and she'd sat down. Sol hurried to as well, drawing his eyes away from the Queen who still watched him curiously. The crowd tittered between themselves and it wasn't long afterward before the first of the heroes was announced.

"Sir Gareth of Norian!" the announcer proclaimed as a man not with the original three marched inside with purposeful strides. "Slayer of Scourge. First of Her Highness' knights! Hero to all the realm!"

The knight was dressed in a rich, black surcoat with a shimmering silver lining that covered his collar and shoulders so he simply glittered beneath the candlelight. The flames even caught the wavy blond hues of his golden hair, making the strands glimmer as it tumbled down his neck. His fair complexion was free of any blemish as far as Sol could see and as a result, nothing took away from his brilliant smile. It sent a tremble of excitement through most of the nobles, but Sol didn't like it. Not with how Celena stiffened upon seeing him. There was a carefully composed smile on her lips, but the scourge within her stirred.

As did something within the man in response.

Gareth bent down in a deep bow before the high table, drawing his white half-cape across himself where the Queen's heraldry had been stitched. A golden sunburst with radiating lines. Only when Gareth straightened at the Queen's behest, did Sol recognize him. One of the knights always by the Queen's side or in the courtyard training others. Not yet middle aged and his beauty hid his age well, although *something* was there that hadn't been before. That distant hum. A resounding buzz like Celena's, but also not. Like a stranger.

Queen Celeste welcomed him, her smile turning warm, and she spoke words lost to Sol's thoughts as he concentrated on the buzz. Gareth soon peered at Sol. Not in idle curiosity like he'd done over the month when he thought Sol wasn't looking, but something intense. Sol's skin crawled, but he didn't look away. He held it until Gareth acquiesced on his own and headed to the seat reserved for him on the Queen's other side.

Celena only relaxed once Gareth was sitting and Sol gently touched her hand. She shook her head and leaned toward him. "It's no matter," she whispered underneath the fanfare the minstrels strummed for the next hero. "I simply dislike him."

There must have been more to it, but Sol didn't have a chance to ask what before the announcer drew his attention.

"Nebora of the Swallows!"

Not as long of an introduction by any means, but the tall warrior woman came in just as proudly as Gareth, no axe in sight. She wore a slim fitted tunic brazenly showing the curves and musculature of her body and she'd had the sleeves carefully taken away to showcase the black tattoos of circles and flowers across her shoulders and arms. The vibrant red tunic was fastened in the middle with a cinched yellow sash, not unlike the one Sol wore. She wore thigh-high boots leaving enough of bare skin showing on her thighs that a few of the nobles quickly noticed and were scandalized. But she was a hero—nonstandard wardrobe aside—and Queen Celeste clapped in approval, prompting others to follow.

Nebora flashed everyone a grin and bowed low before the Queen, although Sol noted she did not bow quite as low as Gareth had.

Sol leaned toward Celena as the Queen and Nebora traded pleasantries. "What are the Swallows?" he whispered.

"It's a stretch of land." Celena tipped her head toward him, but never took her eyes off Nebora. "There was a rumor the ground there could swallow you whole, but I've been told realistically, it's swampland filled with bandits who pillage and make bodies disappear. Hence, the Swallows. My mother decided it was useless to watch and leaves it to its devices."

Interesting choice of hero. Queen Celeste certainly didn't bat an eye and part of Sol admired Nebora's brazenness for showing up at all. She straightened, throwing her braid over her shoulder, and proudly headed off to her seat. It wasn't at the high table beside Gareth, but rather at the long table on the far end of the room. Upon sitting, she immediately pulled another chair beside her and propped her feet up, eliciting a few glares from the nobles likely hoping to sit as near to the high table as they could when all introductions were spent.

"Mira of Yarrow!"

In the midst of watching Nebora, Sol hadn't

noticed the new fanfare sung for another hero to come in. It was the same string instruments the minstrel had used for Nebora, but this one was strummed delicately and slower to match the young woman's stature. Her frizzy red hair was free from its earlier hood and was cut neatly above the nape of her neck while the rest crowned her face. She couldn't have been older than Celena, all round cheeks with freckles splashed across tan skin. She'd donned a simple dress of yellows and whites and the sleeves were cinched at the elbows before billowing out across her arms. A white shawl was tied around her shoulders and there was a yarrow flower embroidered along the back. It absolutely dwarfed her, like it was meant for someone older. She bobbed up to the Queen, eyes wide like a deer ready to bolt, and curtsied as low as she could go.

She was nervous, anyone could tell, especially when she spoke. Soft words hardly heard tripping over themselves. Sol cast his gaze across the room. There were so many older and physically able people simply watching and it never occurred to them to volunteer to go so someone barely into adulthood didn't have to maybe sacrifice her short life to save the world.

None of them cared, so long as it was someone else. Many of them had come with gifts once news of

Sol spread, but none had offered to escort him. Instead, they'd quickly become one of the frivolous many pretending the world wasn't ending. Their money and standing made them believe they were above the end of the world—made them think they were untouchable. They'd all learn just how wrong they were.

Mira's voice continued to be too soft to hear amongst the chatter on both sides of the room, but Queen Celeste nodded appropriately and smiled at her like a mother would to a child. When the Queen dismissed her, Mira hurried to Nebora's side and happily sunk into the chair.

Sol leaned toward Celena as the fanfare started once more for the final hero. "Where is Yarrow?"

Celena shook her head. "I'm unsure," she replied. "I've never heard of it."

Fanfare similar to Mira's tune filled the hall, but unlike the daintiness it had before, it was louder and surer as though befitting the man striding inside as the last hero.

"Loren of Yarrow!"

Without intending to, Sol sat at attention. Loren held himself straight and stoic, although there was a shy smile on his lips as Nebora hooted and cheered, drowning out the nobles clapping for him. He'd been similarly dressed to Gareth, but in white to contrast his tawny skin, and had a rose gold filigree accent lining the tunic from the collar all the way to his shoulders. He'd kept his cape with the yarrow flower over one shoulder, but servants must have cleaned it as it appeared more vibrant now. Sol was drawn to the man's face. Not old, but not as young as Mira before him. He had deep set green eyes, a long nose, and faded freckles across his skin. Dark stubble lined his jaw, but it somehow looked intentional. He bowed low for the Queen, smiling at her as he did so, though Sol couldn't help but think it was a mask.

Celena tugged on Sol's sleeve, jolting him out of his fascination, and as he leaned toward her, he almost bumped their heads together with how quickly she'd bent toward him. What a sight they must have been if all eyes hadn't been on Loren.

"See?" she hissed. "*Handsome*. You're admiring him too."

"Hush!" Sol bit back the smile wanting to match hers and was warmed to find Celena giggling at her own boldness. They quickly sat back up as a few guests glanced at them, amused. Loren was none the wiser as he traded pleasantries with the Queen. He soon stood at her behest and sat at the far side of the table beside Gareth.

The rest of the guests who came in didn't matter to Sol. People across the realm that helped the

Queen keep the kingdom hers. None of them had been bothered to drum up heroes or even go themselves. No matter what finery they were dressed in, no matter how many titles the announcer rattled off, or how many battles they'd lived through, they simply didn't care to stop the end of the world themselves. Queen Celeste must have been keeping her allies close and ready so once the darkness lifted, she could move on to conquering like Celena feared.

It was a waste of time.

The last of the important guests came in, some noble with too much gold on his fingers to count, and he took his seat near Nebora for lack of anywhere else to place himself—he didn't seem happy about the arrangement and pointedly turned away from Nebora once she grinned at him. Queen Celeste stood, the movement hushing all conversations as all eyes turned to her. She held her goblet high, letting it sparkle beneath the light.

"Tonight," she said, her voice carrying easily through the room, "we feast to send off our intrepid heroes who answered the call to save our kingdom and the world." Her tenor was always strong and sure; never had Sol heard a word waver from her lips in the month he'd been in the castle. "And it's a sendoff to our very own star, Sol of Norian."

Sol of the Cosmos, Sol corrected to himself. A few

eyes had settled on him and him alone, but many more were still on the Queen. He was an afterthought, soon to be forgotten when light returned to the world. As have all other stars before him.

"And so," Queen Celeste continued, "I command you: dance. Drink. Be merry. Feast on what we have graciously shared to celebrate the saviors of the world. Forget we're on the cusp of darkness and instead, party like the days of yore. Send our heroes off with confidence!" She raised her goblet and the room followed suit with a raucous cheer.

Celena raised hers, smiling bright, and Sol did too. All to celebrate the saviors of the world. Quaint words meaning nothing because that was the last thing they'd ever be.

"No answers came to her ivory tower,
and so, she decided to leave.
A tearful farewell to those who caught her,
and she sought the voice only she believed."

—Fragment of "She, Born of Starlight," Anonymous

SERVANTS EMERGED LIKE SHADOWS, PLATES OF food balanced upon their arms, and they flitted about the room serving every table without missing a beat or getting in anyone's way as they raised their goblets for the cheer. A roasted bird stuffed with various ingredients and spices came out alongside platters of vegetables for each table, and before Sol had half of his plate finished, the roast boar came out next and plates were quickly filled with hearty slices glazed with honey. The constant flow of dishes and bodies mingling with one another warmed the room and it only grew the longer everyone drank deeply from their cups. Sol could hardly keep up with everything around him, although he didn't want to. All of it was inconsequential.

Still, he hated what the crowd did to his nerves. He couldn't even lift his fork without his hand shaking.

By the time the meal's second course was picked apart, an entourage of minstrels and bards was striding inside with their instruments. Heads lifted, conversations shifted, and there was a twinkle in everyone's eye.

Celena eagerly stood and she snatched Sol's hand. It took him another moment before he realized she wanted to dance and then suddenly they were on the floor with the other nobles excited for the same. Eyes on every side watched Sol's every move, some curious, others too amused for their own good. What Celena had taught him over the week wiped clean and clear from his mind, leaving him blank. The tremble in his hands went up his arms and down his legs, but when Celena took his hands in her sure ones, it felt like stars themselves sung beneath her skin. The world drifted away until only Celena mattered as she led, eyes twinkling beneath the candlelight as she watched only Sol.

The world came back into focus in spurts. The touch of skirts and capes swishing together as others danced around them. The colors the fabrics made as dancers swirled, each garment a seamless tether from partner to partner. Laughter and good cheer intermingled with the jaunty tune the minstrels poured out of their instruments. Everything blended together like it simply belonged.

Celena was fluid and her smile so wide, she was a star that the room revolved around. There was something simply about her, burrowing so deep into Sol that it broke through the walls he'd fashioned to lock himself off. Ever since he'd woken beside her, bit by bit, the wall dissolved and put the damning thought into his head that perhaps, the world wouldn't end. Not while humans like her lived.

Except it *would*. He'd already promised.

The nobles pressing in on all sides remained a mystery to Sol—he didn't care to recall them with any clarity—but he did take notice of the heroes among them. Nebora expertly led a smiling Loren along, as fluid as Celena but with more power behind her strides while Loren struggled to keep up. Gareth swept by too with a noblewoman in a puffy dress that brushed up against Sol when she twirled too close. Mira was the only one of the heroes absent and before Sol could idly glance for her out of curiosity, the song's tune switched to another's.

Sol barely hid his grimace. Celena had warned him beforehand that minstrels liked to play a game of switching songs to make the dancers change partners. It was to facilitate meeting new people. Sol had no intention of meeting new people, but it wasn't up to him. Nebora quickly handed Loren off to a flustered Celena—it must have been planned; perhaps Celena's attraction to him was more obvious than she'd thought—and Nebora took Sol's hands within hers. She had a soft touch, like she feared hurting him, but she led with the same precision as before, never missing a beat. It was all Sol could do to keep up as he stared more at their feet to make sure he didn't trip than at her directly.

When he did finally look up, she was grinning at him, amused. "You're better at this than Loren," she teased and spun him. When the room stopped spinning, smearing colors into continuous streaks around him, he noticed she was eyeing Celena. The princess' face was a deep red; instead of staring at Loren, she watched their feet and guided him the same as she'd guided Sol in the gardens. Except this time, she tripped over her words. Loren listened intently to her all the same, the softest smile on his lips.

The smile made something stir in Sol and he hastened to look away. The motion only brought him Nebora's attention and his cheeks warmed despite his insistence his body behave otherwise.

Nebora's grin turned wide in barely concealed realization as she swept Sol through couples hoping to dance with Celena next the way they crowded her. Miffed, the couples made room for Nebora, clearly annoyed, but the warrior woman didn't care one bit. She happily danced side-by-side with Celena and Loren, making sure to loudly tease Loren. When the song finally switched again, Nebora guided Sol's hands to Loren's and intercepted Celena's own. Celena's shyness melted and she laughed louder, especially as Nebora spun her so fast across the dancefloor, her skirts became a flutter all around her.

And it left Sol's hands in Loren's; he wasn't sure how his body felt about that.

"I don't know *where* she learned to dance like that," Loren conversed, gently leading Sol along. Slow and a little clumsy compared to either Celena or Nebora, but it wasn't like Sol could do better. Rather endearing, if Sol was honest.

It was then Sol realized Loren waited for a reply. Sol cast his gaze elsewhere, unable to think of one. His hands were trembling and his heart thumped too fast, echoing in his ears. It was a much different sensation than what he had with Celena; she was simply right and soothing, but with Loren, he became lightheaded and dizzy. He was glad Loren moved slow; if he'd been moving as fast as Nebora was now, Sol might have fainted.

Eventually, Loren abandoned the need for a reply and drew his gaze above Sol's head. Mira, the only hero Sol hadn't seen dancing, was sitting on the edge of the table and had her lute in her lap. Where she'd pulled it out from was anyone's guess, but her quiet strums quickly grew surer as she matched the noise the other minstrels made around her. As Loren turned his smile on her, warm and familiar, it lit a strange softness within Sol. He quickly brushed it away, staring decidedly anywhere else.

Humans weren't meant to invoke this feeling.

The dancers traded hands again, the original song playing once more, and Sol found himself happily returned to Celena. Her cheeks were flushed and she was absolutely vibrant like she wasn't dying.

After another dance, this one without any partner switching and much more high energy than Sol preferred, Celena's legs were shaking and she pulled Sol back to their seats under the guise of wanting dessert. It had been laid out neatly across the table, their earlier plates gone, and was a cold vanilla treat with a drizzle of warm chocolate and berries atop everything. The sugar must have helped because as soon as she'd finished, she was up and dancing again.

The room's energy thrummed against the walls,

never once waning even as Celena's did. More drink melted inhibitions and augmented the buzz of excitement; it was all Sol could do to keep up. Nebora continued to be a force across the dance floor, inviting anyone sitting too long to dance with her while Loren had his share of partners despite his hesitation and tight smile. He'd tried to get Mira to dance with him, but she'd steadfastly refused and instead, continued strumming her lute between bites of dessert. Gareth made the rounds as quickly as Nebora, much more at ease than all the rest, and nobles happily latched onto his arm for dance after dance.

By the time the stars twinkled across the night sky to peer in on their festivities and a cold breeze blew throughout the room to usher in night's full arrival, Celena stopped pretending she was as energetic as everyone else. She firmly retired to her seat and turned dancers away. Her skin had paled, her eyes were half-lidded as she tried to remain alert, and most of all, her movements had turned so slow. Alyssa had come out of the shadows with water for her, but it hadn't brought the color back to her cheeks.

"Perhaps," she whispered to Sol and Alyssa, barely heard over the revelry, "I should remain seated." She smiled sadly at Sol. "I'm sorry, Sol. I wanted to dance longer with you."

Sol touched her hand, the buzz beneath her skin jumping to his as he tried to soothe it. "I enjoyed the dances we did have," he said. "And I like sitting with you just as much."

"You should dance more." Celena patted his hand. "I like seeing you out there."

She was perhaps the only one. While *everyone* had wanted to dance with the princess who caught and tamed the fallen star, they certainly hadn't wanted to dance with Sol. The two that had were Loren and Nebora. When Celena was pulled away from Sol to dance with some noble or knight, Sol had many times found himself without a partner. More often than not, Nebora was free and came to his rescue. Men were too daunted to dance with her and many women were too shy. The constant rescue was endearing, like she was an older sister, but it grew tiresome.

"More than our hero?" Sol teased and Celena chuckled, brushing him off.

It did prompt her, however, to gaze out at the dancers and Sol followed her gaze until it came right back to Loren in another dance with a pretty girl dressed in blue.

He'd been taken as often as Celena, like the crowd assigned him as *the* hero of the tale being spun about the beginning of their adventure. Loren wasn't any more the hero than Nebora, but Sol still found himself watching the man so he could memorize him with some fascination he couldn't describe.

"Watching isn't so bad for now," Celena whispered and took the tea Alyssa had procured for her when water didn't help.

Watching was what Queen Celeste had been doing the entire night so far. She'd remained seated as an ever-watchful eye over the festivities even when dignitaries surrounded her in attempts to speak about some frivolity. Each visitor had claimed they'd wanted to see the star—their salvation—but they'd hardly acknowledged Sol before they were talking to the queen. She gave them non-committal responses at best and kept her gaze on the dancefloor.

Celena finished her tea, but her color refused to return. The buzz from her blood was so loud now, running through her like a spark. If only Sol could quell it. Give her normalcy back so she could be the girl she'd been before she'd caught him.

It didn't happen; he was too afraid to try.

She sighed and waved Alyssa closer. "I'll be fine," she whispered to him as Alyssa helped her up. "Stay a while and dance some more. Tell me all about it when you retire."

"I promise," Sol said.

Another handmaiden came up swiftly and whispered to the Queen, prompting her to glance once at Celena. Though her brow furrowed with worry, she stayed seated and nodded at her daughter. Permission to leave. Alyssa gently guided Celena around the high table, Celena's arm folded into hers to mask the need for support. The room didn't notice her departure nor how slowly she moved. They were too busy dancing with all the life in the world because they weren't the ones who had caught Sol. They weren't the ones slowly dying for giving the world its only chance at survival.

All of them truly believed they had their whole lives ahead of them because Sol was there. It would be brief. Celena should have been the one with a long life to live and she might have, if she hadn't caught Sol, but he reminded himself that was a lie. Despite the miracle of the darkness parting around the castle, the world was still starved. They were so disconnected from it, no one cared to look and see how dead it all was. The world was on the brink of being but a whisper in the cosmos as it was devoured beneath the dark.

And it was Sol's fault. Both Celena's short life and how dark the world was. He hadn't wanted to fall; he'd held on as long as he could until the cries were too loud to stand.

In the dead of night, alone, he could still hear it when no one else could.

The room was noisy and loud, drowning any meaningful thought to a whisper. Some had begun to brave his icy stare to ask him for a dance, but with a mere shake of his head, they left like they hadn't even asked. There was one, however—the knight whose blood sung over the noise—Garen? No. Gareth—who lingered even after the shake of the head. He leaned on the table at Sol's side, practically brushing up against him.

"Why not?" the knight asked, his low voice slurring. Alcohol wafted off his breath from the many cups he'd already had and his fair cheeks were flushed pink. "The party's for you, is it not?" He made to reach out—for what, Sol didn't know—but the hum grew suddenly louder inside his veins. He stopped short of touching Sol. "Your sendoff. Loosen up."

Sol simply stared at him, waiting for more, but Gareth didn't continue. The charismatic knight running drills in the courtyard was so far gone in a haze of drunkenness, unable to string together enough words without slurring them. Some hero. Gareth glanced away first with a sharp sigh and though he looked ready to say more, someone called his name from the swish of fabric dancing the night away. His scowl replaced itself with a smile and he rejoined the noblewomen awaiting him.

Soon, even he was lost amongst the dancers. A face Sol did not want to memorize, but even as he tried to forget, the hum of his blood reached Sol's ears and it made his skin crawl.

That was enough attention for now. When no one was looking, Sol slipped out the balcony doors for some air. It was deserted—much too cold for anyone to linger—and the curtains dulled the grating noise inside. He breathed in the night air as deep as he could, hoping it would bring his senses back. It was frigid going in, making him shiver all the way down, but it also helped Sol forget about everyone inside.

He drew his cloak tight for some semblance of warmth and leaned against the balcony's stone railing to peer outward.

The stars twinkled so far away. Had he done the same so high above? Had the stars even realized he was gone? He'd hardly noticed the previous star's fall and had barely acknowledged her absence until he heard her whimper beneath the world. Her sadness and anguish had wormed into his every waking thought. The world had been bright and vivid then, ignoring the quiet cry holding it together for them until it could no longer. Sol remembered the way darkness stretched across the land, snuffing out the vibrancy so quickly with sheets of black. For a time, embers burned in the dark, revealing humanity still lived, and then the cry touched him. He honestly never thought it would have been him to fall and he'd resisted for as long as he could until the cry was never ending. Then, he let go and fell.

He missed the other stars. At least there, he'd been nestled perfectly in place amongst the cosmos, warm and fuzzy. Here, it was wrong. Cold and alone in ways he never thought possible.

Sol pulled the fur tighter around his shoulders to stave off another shiver. What he wouldn't give for the oblivion of the cosmos above.

"Cold?"

Sol spun to look beside him. He'd been so deep in his thoughts, he'd blocked out everything else. Loren stood an arm's length away as he rested his elbows against the railing. There was a goblet between his hands, the gold glimmering from the firelight behind them.

"Apologies," Loren said, lifting his eyebrows. "I didn't mean to frighten you. I thought you heard me come out." His eyes caught Sol's and unlike the many, he held his gaze. Silence weaved between them, probably longer than necessary, but Sol didn't know what to say. "It's cold out here, huh?"

"Yes, I heard you the first time." Sol looked out into the stars and Loren chuckled as he sipped from his goblet. It smelled different than what Sol had been drinking. Harsher, somehow, the smell making Sol's nose crinkle.

Loren swallowed and tilted his head, jaw muscles working like he wanted to say something. The torches ablaze against the balcony pillars lit him in flickering oranges, highlighting the planes of his face and the stubble along his jaw. Part of Sol had the sudden urge to trace Loren's face with his fingers like he'd done with Celena's so he'd remember it, but he refrained, keeping his hands beneath the furs.

"Are you scared?" Loren finally asked.

Sol blinked and glanced at him. "No," he said and Loren watched him again with the same assuredness. Never once hastening to look away like others. Sol never blamed anyone; his eyes were so unlike humans. Black pools with ice-blue irises with what Celena had described as akin to stardust inside.

"Are you?"

Loren shrugged and nodded toward the curtains. Dancing was as lively as ever, especially now that Queen Celeste had put down her cups, shrugged off dignitaries wanting her ear, and joined everyone.

"I thought everyone was," Loren said. "That's

why we're having a feast. Dancing and drinking so loud until we forget how scared we are." He paused and swirled the drink in his goblet, drawing Sol's eyes downward. After another moment, he held it out toward him. "Want a drink? Might warm you up."

All because Sol had been staring at it instead of Loren. He hesitated. The music grew louder behind them and Sol caught the shimmer of Nebora moving across the dancers, leading Queen Celeste along in a bawdy dance. Many of the dancers gave room to the two, deciding instead to clap to the rhythm.

Sol took the cup and sipped, not trusting more given how everyone else acted, and his face contorted as what felt like fire slipped down his throat. Yes, it certainly warmed him, but not quite in the ways he wanted. He handed the goblet back, swallowing the cough as the bitter taste dragged itself downward. Definitely not what he'd been drinking earlier—that had a silky taste to it. This was something else.

"Mira made that face too," Loren said, smiling, and it took Sol another second to realize Loren was teasing him. His heart raced, bloomed warmth into his cheeks, and he looked away to hide the sensation. The motion only made Loren chuckle and he took another sip.

"You know," he said, "with all the talk we heard

as we were coming in, I thought you'd be scary. You really aren't."

Sol gave Loren a weary glance. "I think everyone has a different opinion given the way they've acted all night."

"I mean, yes, your eyes are different," Loren said, "but you've got these freckles." He almost looked like he was going to reach forward to touch them, but stopped before he'd raised his hand. Instead, his fingers tightened around the goblet. "They remind me of constellations."

All over again, Sol's face surged with warmth and his hand betrayed him, gently touching his own cheek. For once truly warm since falling and it was because of superficial feelings he had no control over. He cleared his throat, hoping to move on as he dropped his hand, and Sol spoke the first observation coming to mind.

"I thought heroes were older."

It took the smile off Loren's lips and Sol wanted to take the statement back immediately. "Yeah," Loren said softly. "Me too." He took another drink, this one deeper, and handed the goblet out for Sol again. Sol dutifully took another sip, trying not to make a face this time, and handed it back. "If my father was still alive, he'd be here instead. Maybe with me in tow." A chuckle worked its way out of

Loren's throat, but the smile remained absent. "Gods, he would have answered the missive faster than you could blink. *He* was the hero."

Sol waited silently for more, but it didn't come right away. "What happened to him?" he asked quietly.

Loren fiddled with the cup. "One of the first waves of scourge got him—before anyone even acknowledged another Umbral Cycle was starting. We'd sent messengers—numerous messengers— telling everyone here something wasn't right, but we were ignored. Yarrow was this no-name logging place not far from the Barrens, so we were simply first ignored and first attacked." Loren paused and swallowed, training his eyes downward into his cup. "My father told me to run. Scourge fell over the village, beasts I've never seen before eating anyone they could, and I couldn't even save my mother or any of my sisters. All I saved was Mira and I can barely remember how I managed that. Everyone else died that night, but *I* was the hero because I'd saved one girl."

It didn't surprise Sol that evidence of the Umbral Cycle beginning was ignored in favor of pretending the world was still at peace. It also shook him more than it should have thinking of how many smaller villages had been wiped out before anyone cared.

"My father was the hero—believe me." Loren finished the rest of his drink and sighed. "Slain so many beasts encroaching on the village. Kept out the bandits. Braved storms and fires to help others. They sang songs about him in our village. I'm not a hero."

His voice turned meek and sad, on the verge of something—Sol wasn't sure of what—and Sol waited for more. Except there was nothing more; just the soft flutter of the wind through the faraway trees and the muted sounds of celebration from within. Sol gently moved closer, but stopped shy of putting a hand on Loren's arm.

"But you came," Sol said. "No one else has."

"Yes," Loren whispered. "I did." He cleared his throat and pushed his hair back before he eyed Sol again. There was a quirk to his lips as he did so, like a little smile, and he turned to fully face Sol. "So, tell me—since I think I got you talking—why *aren't* you scary?"

Once more, Sol found himself snorting back a laugh. "Are you complaining?" He drew an arm across himself. "Would you rather something frightening than something appealing?"

The words aloud sounded a bit too bold and Sol's entire body warmed as Loren laughed, trying to hide it as he glanced away; at least Sol knew he could make the man laugh, but he wasn't sure if it was because of any attempt on his part or of what was in the cup.

"Uh. I mean—let me rephrase." Loren cleared his throat again and was still smiling. "I meant: what makes stars look the way they do?" He glanced back, curious this time. "The pictographs of the stars are always pretty. I thought maybe they were embellished, but... here you are."

There was a bold compliment there Sol chose to ignore. Celena called him pretty all the time, but it didn't make his heart flutter the way it did hearing Loren insinuate the same.

"We take the form our catcher wishes us to be," Sol said. "I suppose most of them want us to be pretty because they find stars pretty."

Loren nodded slowly, accepting the answer, but then glanced Sol up and down. There was another question there, one Celena had been curious about as well and insisted it had been pure curiosity on her part when she'd gathered the nerve to ask. Just to understand how close humans were to stars were in their new bodies.

"Likely, my body is made of the same parts as yours," Sol said to save Loren from attempting to ask the question and Loren glanced away, biting back an embarrassed smirk. "Princess Celena wanted a friend and someone to protect her like the old knights in bard tales. Those were largely men. She also wanted me similar to her, so I resemble her age and stature. While I cannot lift a sword as well as you, I'm sure I can still protect her."

It was the easiest way Celena explained what she'd thought when she'd caught Sol. Someone to be her friend. Someone to help protect the world. Somehow, that gave way to the body he now had.

"Could you have looked different? If you'd wanted to?"

Loren's curiosity was refreshing. Most never bothered to learn anything about stars. Though the question stumped Sol for a moment before he shrugged.

"Stars do not have physical bodies before we fall," he said. "We hardly even have a sense of self like humans do. My body now is merely the core of who I am reacting to what the princess needed and wanted. I am not at all displeased with it, for what it's worth, but had I wished to be different, I am sure the magic would have accommodated me."

Even if his traitor of a body now warmed as Loren smiled at him.

"All she wanted was a friend, then?" Loren asked.

"Yes," Sol said, drawing it out, and chuckled as Loren raised his eyebrows at him. The same look many of the handmaidens had given Celena when they first came out of his room together—her in her nightgown and him in a threadbare undershirt she'd found. "I assure you, if she'd wanted an intimate partner, I would have come out looking far more like you."

This made Loren's face flush and he laughed. It was such a happy and ridiculous sound, Sol found himself laughing too, although his was a much quieter affair. It was almost like he was with Celena. There was a carefree air between them Sol had only ever been able to find with her. Maybe he'd made a friend.

Eventually, their laughter petered out, letting silence descending across them like a blanket, and Sol struggled to find another conversation so they didn't have to part yet.

"W-Why—" He paused as Loren gave him his full attention. "Why *did* you come? If you claim you're not a hero."

It felt unfair to go from laughing to the sad frown spreading across Loren's lips and Sol cursed his inability to predict human reactions.

"Someone had to," Loren said and turned to rest his chin on his palm. "Nebora thought maybe this was what we had to do—we'd been protecting this town along the Swallows for so long and no matter what, the scourge was never ending. The place egged us on, telling us someone had to go since no one was. I don't even know if it's still standing."

The thought sobered Sol and he wished he hadn't asked.

"Although, I *did* think there'd be more of us."

They were due to head out tomorrow. There wouldn't be any more heroes coming in; all of them were likely already dead like Loren's father. Taken down by scourge long before Sol had fallen from the cosmos. Sol ignored the faint part of him that cared and stayed silent, wrapping his cloak tighter around himself.

"The stars are nice tonight," Loren whispered.

"We won't see them on the road," Sol replied. And neither would the stars see them. The darkness from the scourge was so absolute, all they could do was listen at this point.

Loren inclined his head and looked past Sol. "We'll see that one above the spire."

Sol looked, feeling his stomach drop. In the distance, there she was. He hadn't even realized he could see so far in the dark. It was the vestiges of the star before him held above the Onyx Spire in lands everyone referred to as the Barrens.

It was a twinkle at most this far away, but it was no normal star. What remained of her magic had created a phantasm and it masqueraded as something safe for humans to look to. Draw humanity closer for salvation only to swallow them whole with scourge. At least, that was what Sol had heard from some of the darker legends Celena had read to him. The star before him was dead, Sol knew that much, but something like her voice drifted from the phantasm and carried itself on the wind.

A voice he gave a promise to as he fell.

It stole what scant cheer Sol had found, leaving him cold in both body and mind. The sounds inside were in stark contrast to his mood; happy and joyful while Queen Celeste moving as fluidly as her daughter once had among the dancers. It soured his mood even more that Celena couldn't be there too. All because of him. He looked away, his heart aching, and found Loren attempting to say something.

No more. He was done.

"I'll see you on the morrow, then?" Sol said and Loren stopped. "I should retire."

Whatever Loren had wanted to say was still there in his face, but his expression grew soft around it, leaving it unasked. "Yes," he said and drew his gaze back to the curtains. "I should honestly stop Nebora before she makes an ass of herself—she's too drunk to keep dancing like that." This elicited a small chuckle from Sol and Loren smiled as he bowed, drawing his cape across himself like Sol was royalty. "I will see you then."

No more questions. No more dancing. Freedom. When the room erupted into good natured laughter from Loren tempting a tipsy Nebora away from the queen, Sol slipped out through one of the side doors servants used to come and go. Part of his body argued to stay with Loren, especially when he glanced at the man over his shoulder and watched the soft way he spoke to Nebora, but Sol dashed the emotion aside. He didn't need the connection. Especially not when it made his heart light up so.

Once out of the great hall and into the empty hallways, he let himself breathe. The chamber leading to the great hall remained a spark of brilliant orange light, but the rest of the castle was dark, almost like a tomb. Sol didn't mind it. He turned his back on the light and continued into the dark corridors.

Because the castle *would* be a tomb. This *would* be the end. He'd make sure of it. All his wants and emotions be damned. Celena would pass on and then so too would the rest of the world. Only they wouldn't see it coming.

Sol didn't make it to his chambers before Alyssa intercepted him. He envied the way she blended in and out of the dark. "Princess Celena wishes your audience," she said.

Alyssa didn't even give him a chance to consider saying no—not that he would—before she laced her fingers around his wrist and led the way. Candles had been lit here, giving bursts of color to the dark tomb of the corridor. Alyssa paused before the door and for once, looked at Sol directly.

"I will return in the morning to take you back to your chambers before anyone comes to rouse Celena for your send off." She drew her gaze slowly to the door. It looked as though she wanted to forget about bringing him at all, but when she stared at him once more, the emotion was subdued. "Be kind to her, all right?"

It confused him; he was *always* kind to Celena, but he nodded nonetheless and Alyssa let him inside. The room was drenched in warmth from the single candle left lit at Celena's bedside. Celena sat propped against her pillows, dressed in the same nightgown she'd worn the day she'd caught him, and her arms were bare. The scourge glittered below the skin and made her veins bold and purple as it reached past her elbows. If it wasn't going to kill her, it might even have been pretty the way it shimmered beneath the candlelight.

Sol crossed the room and smiled as she gave him her own radiant one.

"Alyssa said she'd sneak me back before anyone else comes in the morning?" Sol raised his eyebrows. "What did you need? I think she may be misunderstanding."

Celena rolled her eyes and set the book she was reading at her side. A tome of fairy tales and legends she'd used to teach Sol how to read scant words. "Oh, I'm sure she'll give me a talking to." She patted her bed and Sol sat down. "I just... this will be our last night together. I wanted what we had the first night you arrived one last time."

Sol took her hand and kissed the knuckles like she'd done then. "If you wish it, I'm sure I could bring that hero in here instead," he teased.

Celena took her hand away to cover her face. "No!" she exclaimed between laughs and shook her head. "No. Not this time." She peeked up at Sol, still smiling wide. "But I appreciate the offer, Sol."

Sol wasn't quite sure what he would have done had she said yes, so he was glad this time would be theirs to share. Especially since she spoke his name as she did. He stood and peeled off some layers and his boots, leaving them neatly nearby, and crawled into bed with her. She snuggled up to him, one arm pulling him close, and breathed out a sigh once they were both settled.

"This is what I like," she whispered, drawing the

fingers of her other hand through Sol's hair. "Even if no one understands it."

And no one would because they had their own notions of what Celena meant to Sol. He took the hand laying across his chest. The scourge vibrated at his touch, a hum he could follow all the way through if he'd wanted to. It had once been part of him, after all. Celena laced their fingers together and held their hands close.

"It doesn't hurt," she said.

A lie.

"I wish it hadn't happened."

"I knew what would happen when I ran to catch you."

Another lie. She hadn't, not the true scope of it, but Sol bit back from arguing. She'd wanted to be the dutiful princess who helped the world. It was the role she'd given herself to ensure light would return. That would be it. The scourge would eat her from the inside out, leaving her the husk of the princess she could have been in the end.

It didn't matter. It was done. Sol couldn't take it back and neither could he undo his fall to save her from her fate. He banished his second thoughts and curled up with Celena. It was soft and warm beneath the quilts and so was she as she rested her head against his chest. Sol drifted off, simply listening to her breathe and the way her blood hummed against him, and part of him hoped morning never came because deep down buried in his heart, he didn't want to leave her.

*"With flowers braided into her pearl-white locks
    and her cheeks dusted with white freckles,
she traveled to find towns bright with festivities
    celebrating her divinity beneath a shower of petals.
Her smile was never said to waver,
    but one must wonder if she enjoyed these spectacles."*

—Fragment of "She, Born of Starlight," Anonymous

WILDFLOWERS FELL ACROSS THE CITY FROM THE very azure sky above for their departure. Morning had gone by too fast; Sol hardly recalled waking up beside Celena before the frost had melted from the gardens and then Alyssa was sneaking him back into his room to dress, leaving Celena to rouse with an entourage of handmaidens. Then he recalled the moment he and the heroes were gathered in the throne room. Even it had gone by in a quick blur. Celena was the only constant, dressed in a simple white and blue dress with her princess circlet on her forehead. Her mother had a whole speech for the nobles congregated to see the heroes off, but Sol hadn't committed it to memory. All he recalled with distinction was Celena's last touch as she gave each of the heroes a favor so that one day, they may return it to her, safe and healthy.

Sol had to bury the thought telling him it wouldn't matter and instead, cherished how her touch had lingered on his hands as she tied the sheer rose-pink scarf to his wrist.

And then, they were leaving. Sol begged time to stop so he could spend a little more of the morning with Celena. Take their garden walk together among the heathers and daisies and pretend he wasn't leaving. It never happened. Time persisted. Last night felt like it should have been more poignant. They'd spent it asleep, comforted by one another in the dark, and Sol hadn't told her anything he'd wanted to before Alyssa led him away. There hadn't been time, even if he'd had the ability.

So, this was it. A silent farewell. Her last gift tied tight around his wrist, tucked into the leather cuff at the end of his sleeve. He'd also been gifted the use of her mare, Stardust, because, as Alyssa quietly put it, she wouldn't need her soon.

Sol sat upon Stardust now as they headed through the city under the flutter of flower petals. The horse was dark with white spots and had her light hair gently brushed and braided down one side. Celena used to take her riding across the castle fields before she'd caught Sol. Her hands had become too stiff to hold the reins afterward.

Saddled to Stardust were the traveling supplies Queen Celeste had requisitioned for him and Gareth. Material for a tent, furs to stay warm, and food supplies carefully wrapped together. Anything they would need on the journey. Sol rode beside Loren's horse, a brown thing a little bigger than Stardust named Philie, and she was equally fitted for the road, although she didn't seem to have quite as much.

Those were the only horses they were bringing. Sol wasn't sure why there weren't more and he felt awkward atop his while Nebora and Mira walked between, but he couldn't figure out how to ask if they wanted to ride Stardust instead or if it would have been proper for him to do so.

Gareth marched in front as apparent leader, with his white armor gleaming while his crimson cloak fluttered behind him. He was all smiles, waving at those around them, even blowing kisses. It almost looked picturesque. A valiant, handsome knight in white marching beneath a shower of petals from the sky. Sol might have believed it if he didn't recall how tense Celena had been watching Gareth and how the man's blood still buzzed.

Nebora didn't let the knight outshine her any, thankfully. For all the kisses he blew, she must have blown twice as many and garnered as much attention in return. Her labrys was strapped to her back and gleamed as bright as Gareth's armor as though not to be outdone. She waved high and low, the largest grin on her lips. Mira, meanwhile, strummed her lute as she walked. The notes mixed with the good cheer and farewells, and from her lips came the beginnings of one of the bard tales. Her voice was as easy now as the bards had been during the feast. Loren waved like the others from atop his horse, but his smile was subdued and small. Perhaps he didn't like the attention any more than Sol did, yet they were the ones in full view atop their horses.

He drew his gaze upward, searching for how long until they exited the twisting city streets he didn't care to memorize, and in the far distance, amongst the sky like a mirage at daybreak, was the flickering phantasm of the star. A twinkle at most from here, but Sol felt her eyes on him. The thrum of her voice as it worked its way through the city, echoing up to Sol. His name carefully carried with the wind.

It won't be long now, he promised her, mouthing the words. He'd see it done.

Soon, the city was an echo behind them. The drawbridge pulled shut once they were across the moat, and they were alone on the road. Sol was glad for the sudden silence.

The azure sky lasted until they reached the nearest crossroads. The darkness the scourge had wrought ate away the blue in all directions except for back toward the capital, but it was only a matter of time before even that darkened again.

Sol wasn't even sure *what* peeled itself across the sky when scourge had free reign. Likely scourge, but how it covered the very sky was beyond him. Whatever it was, it resembled a black shroud and veiled the sun so it shone a glowing red. In response, the land was hushed in subdued hues like the color had been stolen away. Sol hadn't been sure what to expect, but it wasn't surprising. Enough light to see, make scant crops grow, but miserable all the same. Deep shadows stretched across the land, trees grew scraggly and gray, grass became dry in search of meaningful sunlight, but it all still persisted in the face of its looming death. A wonder of itself.

They followed the road between flat lands of overgrown grass and brush, with only a few old windmills still turning in the breeze. They had likely been abandoned when the scourge arrived. Bits of the large blades were black, creaking in the uneasy silence around them. That it was already so close to the capital was concerning, but if it was this benign, the Queen wouldn't have to worry for some time still.

The capital's walls were still just in sight over the dip in the road when Loren slowed Philie and Sol followed suit with Stardust. Loren easily slipped off, patting Philie on the nose affectionately as he went around her, and Sol waited for a reason, confused. A hum surged up to him, following Gareth as he shouldered past Mira and Nebora redistributing the weight of their bags, and he yanked Sol off Stardust.

Sol would have fallen outright, too shocked to resist, if Nebora hadn't swung her arms wide to catch him. "Fuck!" she snapped.

"Horses are too valuable to ride all the way there," Gareth said and fixed some of his gear to Stardust. She looked ready to bite him, but stopped when he produced an apple from a pouch. She relaxed and happily munched on her snack.

Sol bit back a huff. *Traitor.*

"She shouldn't even be out here. We have so few horses as it is."

"Next time, just ask him to get down." Nebora set Sol on his feet and stepped in front of Gareth, stopping him from returning to the front. Nebora propped her hands on her hips. "Or are you knights too good for simple requests?"

Gareth blew out an angry sigh and a scowl hardened the lines in his face. This was not at all the man who'd swept nobles off their feet nor the one smiling so charismatically throughout the city.

"We're wasting light." He brushed past Nebora and walked. Nebora didn't let him go quietly; she kept up and the silence filled with them bickering back and forth.

Mira rolled her eyes and finished what she'd been doing to the horses. Lamps now hung from their saddles, casting a soft, flickering orange around them. Not enough light to see far, but at least they'd always know where the horses were. Once Mira finished, she happily returned Stardust's reins to Sol and ushered him along to catch up.

By the time they did, Gareth ceased all inane bickering with a loud groan and whipped to face Nebora like he'd considered striking her.

"Will you quit it?!" Gareth shouted, halting Nebora's ramble, and she graced him with a mocking little smile. "This is useless. We are fucking wasting light. Move."

"Stop," Loren snapped from the other side of Philie and headed over to stand before Gareth. "We need to get a few things straight—"

"Like what?" Gareth spat out. When Loren

narrowed his eyes, Gareth rested his hand on the ornate sword hilt hanging on his belt. "I have a single goal: get *it* to the spire alive."

Loren laughed, making Gareth's face flush with anger, and the sound was absent of joy. The man Sol had spoken to last night buried completely. "This isn't about *you*." Loren tilted his head with a mean smirk. "Although, what was it I heard? You didn't even *volunteer* until the Queen ordered it?" He snorted and Nebora chuckled. "Some hero you are."

"And what of you?" Gareth snapped. "A month we waited."

"Safe inside your castle walls while we were protecting our own with no help or supplies from you and yours," Loren shot back. "How much scourge have you actually dealt with? Any of you in there dealt with?" He waited a moment and cut Gareth off as soon as he'd opened his mouth. "*One* beast laden with scourge let loose in the castle only to give you some credibility. You think servants don't talk?"

Celena had told Sol about the morning a beast taken over by scourge had gotten past the castle walls. Curiously, the town had been left alone. She'd been suspicious too, but it was quickly laid low by a knight and he'd been hailed a hero.

"While safe in castle walls, you left us out here to

everyone, but Nebora brushed past him to continue walking. He whipped to face her, face red again, and she flapped her hand dismissively at him.

"All you knights are the same," she said. "Slay one little beastie and you think you're so big and bad. All you want is glory—you couldn't care less about us out here. You just do your job, protect the castle, then drink yourself stupid."

And she kept going, dressing down everything about the Norian Knighthood, about the nobles, and then about the kingdom as a whole. Gareth tried to cut in, but Nebora only spoke louder, drowning out every protest. She named knights and nobles Gareth must have known, giving them the same dressing down, and Sol was honestly impressed with how much she knew. At least until the names sounded made up. Mira caught his gaze a few fake knights in, stifling a laugh.

"You doing all right?" she asked.

Sol cut his gaze away and focused on walking. Mira let the lack of an answer roll off her shoulders and kept in stride as she talked.

"You can tune them out if it makes it easier," she said. "It really won't be interesting until Nebora threatens to chop off body parts. Intimate ones." Loren snorted from in front of them and Mira grinned mischievously.

Sol refrained from smiling at the absurdity. He didn't want friends or comrades. Instead, he did what Mira said: tuned them all out. He burrowed himself into the fur inside his cloak and listened for Celena.

Her hum was so far away now, a distant echo, but if he wanted to, he could have traced it back all the way through the dark. They were linked because of Sol's scourge and that in itself kept them connected so. Sol wondered if the scourge around them was the same; could the previous star could feel all the way out here even from her tomb in the Barrens? Likely and a little disconcerting.

He didn't reach out to Celena; he was supposed to be letting go. It warmed him all the same, however, knowing he could still sense her, at least this far.

✦

THE ROAD WAS LONG. THE LANDS EMPTY. THE WIND had such a biting cold, it almost felt like knives as it pushed into Sol. His fingers ached, holding the reins tight to make sure he didn't lose Stardust, and his legs hurt. Even when they took breaks to eat, it didn't help. Resting made everything worse because it gave his body time to protest. This was nothing like the strolls in the garden.

After a time, Mira peppered the silence with strums of her lute and practiced some ballad she must have had in her head. It wasn't anything Sol had heard in the castle. Better than silence, at least; Nebora and Gareth had long since run out of insults for one another and the air was heavy between them with tension. After his initial words, Loren remained silent. Sol missed the talkative and curious man he'd been at the ball. The way Loren's voice had been warm and the relaxation therein listening to it—but Sol immediately dashed the emotion away. It didn't matter.

Though the sky was dark, the sun still made its daily path, and was sinking toward the horizon as the day grew late. It was all Sol could do to keep one foot in front of the other. Maybe tomorrow would be better. Tomorrow he'd be a little more used to traveling.

As Sol debated about how best to prepare himself for tomorrow's just as arduous trek, something crawled across his connection with Celena. It shivered through him as a garbled hum choking on its voice. Up ahead, Loren, Gareth, and Nebora had slowed, each of them staring out into the dark meadow. Mira ceased plucking her lute, leaving everything silent, and Sol heard it clearly. Scourge. Moving through the long grass. A darkened gaping maw lifted itself from the brush and stared at them from behind the guise of a wolf. Its eyes were hollowed out and its fur was matted with blood from where the scourge had pushed its bones out of its skin to make room for itself inside.

Sol hadn't seen beasts infected with scourge before, he distantly realized, and couldn't take his eyes off how grisly it was. Though it sung like Celena, its voice was uneven and raw. A cry hidden within its warbled song. While the infection took to her with grace because of his own desire not to cause her pain, this was a stark difference. The scourge didn't care about the wolf and pulled it apart regardless of the pain to make sure it had room for itself.

"Mira." Loren's voice was short and sharp and she jumped into action. She slung her lute against her back and sped around Sol to reach both horses. With quick flicks, she unfolded the blinders on the bridles, and then went for the saddlebag on Loren's horse. Out came a crossbow almost as wide as she was and she positioned herself in front of Sol.

Meanwhile, Loren, Nebora, and Gareth had drawn their weapons.

One wolf against three heroes. Until it horrendously split into two. The skin and bones snapped apart, the face bisected itself as scourge spilt forth across the grass, and then it was one half the wolf it had been and the other a mockery of it seeping with blood and scourge. Two wolves now never to be whole again.

Sol had watched knights and guards run drills in the courtyard with Celena countless times. Practiced swings, spars, and the drills were predictable. Easy to follow and sometimes intriguing. This was every-thing but. The wolves leapt, snarling as scourge flung from their mouths as spittle, and the heroes met the challenge, blades singing through the air. Mira dragged Sol closer to the ground and they both ducked low to make themselves the smallest possible targets. Howls echoed into the sky and as weapons connected, scourge flung overhead like blood.

And worst of all, there was pain.

Each slice finding its home in the wolves felt like it went through Sol himself. Pain wasn't quite the word for it, but it felt so similar, Sol bit back cries of his own as the blades sunk into the wolf's skin. As Nebora's axe came down, bisecting one of the heads in two, cutting off what life it had left. Loren and Gareth took care of the other, working in tandem. One blade went through the mouth and the other through its back. Then more tormented beasts came. Drawn in by the scourge spilling across the field and the stench of battle.

His blood heard the same call and without conscious thought, the scourge connected to him. His own body faded away, leaving only what he felt through the beasts being eviscerated by both sword and axe before him. Beasts leapt from the meadow like the wolves and went down the same. Their blood soaked the land as they howled in pain, and it felt like Sol's own. His cry. His blood. The dying gasps of the beasts bled through his ears, bringing with them fleeting memories. Glimpses of humans long since dead paraded across his vision, once alive and healthy, now dead and pulled to pieces by scourge. Visions of poor beasts left abandoned when they were infected and how the scourge twisted inside every fiber of their being until the poor thing was driven mad.

All those memories burned themselves deep into Sol's thoughts, leaving scars he desperately wanted to claw free from his being, until the carnage ended with a final swing of the axe. The scourge let go, cutting Sol off from the dark, and left him hollow inside his own body.

Panicked breaths erupted from his lungs as he remembered to breathe, but it was like there was no air. Sweat stuck to his skin, ghosting a chill across him he couldn't shake. The world wavered and turned, spinning the more he tried to steady it. A deep cry was trying to crawl out of his throat from his own heart.

And he was sick. Very sick.

Mira must have said his name as he jerked himself to the side of the road. She must have gone after him, for she was right there at his side as he vomited into the grass. She wasn't vomiting. She was gently pulling his hair back as he retched everything he had into the grass.

It wasn't long before he was empty, the last few retches coming up with nothing, just an ache pulling itself through his entire body as his eyes struggled to stay focused past the fuzzy darkness encircling his vision.

"Well," Loren said from behind them, his voice distant beyond the dying hum in Sol's ears. "We've all been there."

"Not me," Gareth said and Sol glanced toward him. He was cleaning his sword off on the grass until the black stains were gone. The scourge was dead. Dormant for now without a host or until it pulled the viscera together in a new body.

Nebora shoved Gareth. "You drink so much, your stomach's simply forgotten how to vomit." She ignored the look Gareth gave her and went to the horses. "Aw, good girls. Didn't even get spooked."

Another retch escaped, leaving Sol trembling, and Mira was rubbing his back now. Gentle circles between the shoulder blades. Loren had knelt at his other side, and tucked more of his hair back. His touch sung warmth through Sol, so sudden and stark, making him flinch.

Mira removed herself and stood. "Any wounds we need to flush?"

Right, Sol thought distantly to himself. If scourge managed to break their skin, it could enter their blood and infect them. Only their infection would be harsh and raw, nothing like the softness Celena's had.

"Not me," Nebora said after a cursory check of her arms covered in leather she'd already cleaned.

"I'm fine," Loren said, still rubbing Sol's back.

"As am I." Gareth sheathed his sword. "We should get moving. You know this will attract more if we linger. So, get him to his feet or I will."

"There aren't anymore," Sol snapped so suddenly, he ended it with a sharp breath. Everyone stared at him and he cursed inwardly. He hadn't meant to speak, but his patience had grown too taut to withstand his own silence.

"He speaks." Gareth's boots crunched against the earth as he drew closer. Loren stood up so fast, Sol hardly saw it before Loren was already between him and Gareth. "How do you know?"

Sol swallowed, tasting acid in his throat, and his thoughts grew frantic. "Listen," he whispered, voice raw. "Th-They hum."

Everyone stilled, holding their breath. Sol still *heard* a hum—but it wasn't the animals crying out for mercy. It was something deep inside Gareth, turning in curiosity. It wasn't a *lie*. Not technically. He didn't know if it was known stars could *feel* the scourge and he wasn't about to admit it aloud. Not while his plan lay suspended precariously on the notion they trusted him completely. If they really knew how closely linked the stars and scourge were and what he'd promised during his fall, they wouldn't bring him anywhere near the Onyx Spire.

Nebora huffed. "Never noticed that," she said, but she wasn't arguing. "I usually just immediately start chopping."

The sensation of blades ghosting across his skin made Sol shiver. He swallowed another retch. No more. He had nothing else in his stomach.

Mira had bent beside Sol again, her eyes twinkling like Celena's did whenever she was curious. "Really? Do you know *how* the scourge hums? It's just... liquified darkness, right?"

Honestly, it was a good question. Sol didn't know and bit back from saying so. Because therein was the lie: the hum wasn't audible, at least not in a way humans could parse it. The word was just what Sol found closest to what he felt. He couldn't tell her all that, but she awaited an answer. He struggled to piece one together until Loren spoke.

"They're gone," he said and returned to Sol. "We should leave. Arcridge isn't much farther." He bent down and his hand joined Mira's at Sol's back. "You good to stand?"

No, but Sol nodded anyway. Both hands were taken away and he stood on trembling legs. It was a miracle he didn't fall right back down with how weak they felt. At least he'd live, unlike the piles of viscera and scourge among the grass, darkening the ground. Sol swallowed, dragging his gaze away, and jumped as a water flask was thrust at him.

"Wash out your mouth," Nebora said, handing it over. "You'll feel better."

As he did so, Nebora patted his back so suddenly, he almost choked on the water. She smiled at him as he spat it out. "Arcridge isn't as fancy as the castle, but I'm sure they'll have a feast all the same and you'll forget about what you left there." She winked and slipped her flask away. "Keep it together—we'll be there soon."

They must have been. As Sol turned his gaze to the dark horizon, where the sun bled red as it dipped out of the sky, he saw a shimmer of flickering torches.

Keep it together, he told himself, putting one foot in front of the other.

> *"Fair knights, bawdy adventurers, and soft minstrels*
> *became her trusted friends and company.*
> *Together, we traveled across kingdoms and lands,*
> *searching for the voice in her memory."*

—Fragment of "She, Born of Starlight," Anonymous

ARCRIDGE WAS AS ITS NAMESAKE: UP ON A RIDGE that arced across the flatlands around it. Because of its position and its many watchtowers, Arcridge was also a perfect lookout for incoming dangers. Nebora insisted if they were allowed inside one of the watchtowers, they could have seen all the way to the Barrens. Sol doubted there was much to see at this point; scourge blotted out anything meaningful. Perhaps there would be a few towns and villages lit up like dying embers, but the rest would be dark and gray.

Regardless of the empty world around them, guards patrolled the town like it was the castle itself, as Arcridge was one of the first defenses for the capital in this direction. Thankfully, everyone knew the heroes were coming and greeted them with smiles and open arms.

Once they were inside, the gates were shut tight for the night and light fanfare followed their arrival. Nebora headed the brief explanations for the delay, earning oohs and ahhs when she described the scourge they had vanquished, and once the crowd's curiosity abated, they were taken to the largest tavern and inn the town had to offer.

Like Nebora guessed, the tavern threw them a feast. It must have already been planned given how fast the place filled, how swiftly the food came, and how quickly everyone happily descended into their cups to drink the night away. Unlike the feast in the castle, this one felt *real*. These were the common folk, not preening nobles vying for attention from the Queen. They were those who dealt with the daily threat of the scourge. Clinging to life and celebrating anyway.

The smell of cider and cinnamon baked the air like a far-gone harvest feast once they'd settled in and it made Sol quite warm. They'd eaten together at the same table this time, plates full of a sampling of all what Arcridge had to offer—roast pork seasoned with spices Sol couldn't name but enjoyed, warm bread baked with garlic, and a creamy soup of dumplings and vegetables—but now he sat alone while everyone else mingled. Sol didn't mind; he was happiest right here as an observer of humanity.

His drink this time was spiced, but went down his throat smoothly. Made his stomach warm and the room a little fuzzy the more he drank, but it softened the edges keeping him alert. Helped him ignore the soft whisper in the wind carrying his name.

There was a minstrel playing an instrument Sol didn't recognize—something with keys and a handle he spun—and before long, Mira had grabbed her lute to join in. She hopped around, singing bawdy songs unabashedly with the minstrel and he happily kept it going. Mira was tipsy and energetic, not the shy girl she'd been at the castle feast; it was nice to see. The room sang the verses with her, clapping along, and she had the largest smile on her lips, like the world wasn't on the brink of ending.

Nebora made the rounds throughout the room, eagerly pulling people to dance with her with one hand while she held tight to a tankard in the other. No one avoided her here like the nobles had and happily joined her in dance after dance. Gareth was near the back where there was a knife throwing game. Sol wasn't sure that was such a good idea given how humans acted while drunk, but Gareth—though drunk enough to waver as some of the locals fawned over him—threw the knives quick and true. Never once missing the center. Each time his knife hit its target, the group around him cheered and Gareth had a large grin plastered on his flushed face. At least he wasn't glaring at Sol.

Sol had lost sight of Loren at some point after he'd left a generous pie slice for Sol to enjoy. Though Sol tracked the many bodies across the room in search of him, Loren was nowhere to be found. Sol missed his presence, but the warmth and life in the room helped him ignore it. Tonight was for peace. Not whatever feelings Loren inspired within Sol.

Stories were traded back and forth, each one louder and more over the top than the last. Old tales, histories kept alive on spoken word alone through generations, stories of humanity facing the dark and coming out alive, and then loud proclamations of what everyone wanted to do once the darkness lifted and the skies cleared. Hope thrummed through the room, everyone believing it would happen just like it had before. They'd get the world back and move on with their lives. And Sol was so fuzzy and warm, he actually believed it.

For a time.

He ate his pie—apples and pears smothered in

cinnamon and spice—and some of the fuzziness ebbed with more food in his stomach. He was still warm, at least, forgoing his cloak altogether like everyone else, but despite the warmth, the noise began grating on him. Too much of a good thing. The stories turned very quickly from heartwarming to loud and raucous, lies told to themselves to make living bearable. The voices thundered through him, bubbling up an unease he couldn't swallow, and he took it as his body telling him to rest. The feast wasn't for him anyway and it wasn't like anyone braved coming near to speak with him. They soaked in the heroes as they should. Not the dull and uninspired star no one would remember.

Sol much preferred it, wanting none of their attention, but loathed to admit perhaps loneliness had indeed taken root. Not much to do about it but rest. Quietly, he left the room to its celebrations of a dawn never to come and welcomed the chill of the stairwell leading into the inn.

The stark change jostled him out of his fuzziness; the blazing tavern hearth had made the room bright and orange, lighting up tavern goers and making their shadows dance, but merely a threshold away, blues and purples reigned instead. It brought Sol some clarity of mind at least, and helped him ignore the doubt.

All Sol wanted was the noise out of his head. Sleep and rest would help, he was sure, but then there was a sudden fear. This would be the first time he'd slept so far away from Celena. Ever since he'd fallen, she'd been a vibrant presence at the edge of his mind—soothing him—and now that same presence was too distant to truly parse. He felt alone in ways he hadn't thought possible.

Except he couldn't change it. He had to accept it for what it was and let go. Sol gathered himself up, taking in a deep breath, and as quietly as he could, began ascending the stairs.

The whispers of the faraway scourge bled through the walls, seeping into his ears with honeyed words as though trying to soothe him in lieu of Celena. Sleep would help him ignore it all. Sol repeated it to himself as he reached each step, slow and steady, until he heard footsteps behind him.

He picked his head up and turned. Gareth stood there, wreathed in the golden glow seeping in from the tavern threshold. Alone. Scourge hummed so loud and clear in his arm as some kind of acknowledgement of Sol's own. Gareth wavered, watching him, and alcohol wafted so thick off his breath, Sol couldn't help but scrunch his nose.

"Where you going?" Gareth said, somehow speaking clearly. "Party's not up there." He came up and stood one step below Sol.

It was no use answering. Sol averted his gaze and continued walking. He thought Gareth would take the hint—*leave*—but as Sol reached the upper landing, Gareth followed him, footsteps heavy, and overtook Sol.

"Hey, hey, hey." Gareth placed his arm on the wall, blocking Sol's escape into the hall, and Sol glared up at the man. "Why don't you fucking talk to me?" Sol immediately looked away and attempted to move around him, but Gareth caught his chin with his other hand and jerked Sol to face him. "Won't even look at me half the time. You got no problem with Loren. Why am I so different?"

Because of reasons Sol didn't understand himself. He pushed Gareth's hand away and attempted to pass him on the other side of the hall. Gareth immediately turned and looped his arm around Sol's waist, encircling it, and pulled him back. Sol's back hit the wall hard and he stilled as Gareth pressed him against it. Sol's entire body buzzed from how close they were, overloading his thoughts with the sound of the scourge, and it was only worse when Gareth touched Sol's face again. This time, it was softer. Almost like a caress.

"Or, I mean, if you want," Gareth murmured, "we can have a party up here. Just the two of us." He waited like the statement had been a question, but Sol had no idea what he was asking. Rolling his eyes, Gareth pushed his leg between Sol's and forced them apart. His gaze flickered downward. "What *do* stars have down there, anyway?"

As Sol attempted to push Gareth's leg away—he did *not* like it there one bit—the knight intercepted the hand. Their skin touched and the scourge within Gareth's arm sung against Sol. Nothing like Celena. This was a violent buzz, like thorns sticking into Sol's skin. Gareth pressed in closer, making it worse, and Sol's pulse thundered in his ears. Whatever this was, he wanted no part in it. Except Gareth was much stronger than Sol—pushing him made absolutely no difference.

Panicked, Sol threw his thoughts into the scourge connecting them together. The hum filled his head once invited, bright and loud, and his vision spotted. Sol thought that would be it; he'd just have to accept what was happening, until the scourge within reacted to Sol. A shockwave of pain pierced through Sol and it must have done the same to Gareth; he jerked away with a cry to hold his arm. Before Gareth could respond, Sol twisted the scourge in his mind. The pain intensified, closing in around Sol's head like a vice, and Gareth gasped. He dropped to the floor, holding his arm, and the skin *twisted.*

Human arms weren't meant to do that.

Sol let go as quickly as he could and the scourge's hum silenced, like a thread snapped. The arm fashioned itself as a human arm again, and left Gareth panting and shaking on the floor.

He stared up at Sol with sudden clarity. No matter how drunk he was, he knew what Sol had done. What Sol hadn't even known he *could* do.

Sol ran back down the stairs, composing himself briefly at the bottom, and let his legs carry him through the tavern and out the front doors. He had no idea where he was going—why his heart hammered and his mind raced—and the dark and cold crept in on him. Too absolute. No. He swallowed in air, reminding himself how to breathe, and searched for somewhere Gareth wouldn't follow. Where no one would. Somewhere he could piece his thoughts back together before he was caught and every single promise and plan spilled from his lips in panic.

The stables. Horses were kind. Sol turned and headed for where they'd left Stardust. The closest thing he had to Celena. He rounded the corner, following what the veiled moonlight above lit in a ghostly red, and saw a figure sitting against the stables. Fight or flight jerked Sol still instead of anything useful and he waited until his eyes readjusted.

Loren sat there, back against the stable doors with his cloak wrapped around him like a blanket. Seeing him so made Sol realize just how cold it was outside and he wrapped his arms tight around himself, suppressing a shiver. It only drew Loren's attention and he jumped.

"Oh." Loren laughed and relaxed. "This time you came to find me in the cold?"

"Not by intention." Sol blinked, realizing what Loren had said. "Y-You looked for me before?"

"Yeah—at the castle feast. You looked lonely after the princess left." Loren tilted his head toward Sol and stood. "Where's your cloak? It's cold out here."

"I'm aware."

"Want to go back inside?"

"No."

Loren paused, thinking, but before Sol could insist on the lie that he was fine, Loren had pulled off his cloak and had draped it across Sol's shoulders. "I'm used to the cold," Loren interjected as Sol opened his mouth. "Don't worry."

Sol swallowed his complaint. It was rather warm, after all with the ghost of Loren's own body heat wrapping him up. And there went Sol's face growing warmer for thinking such silly things. "Thank you," he mumbled and hated how his heart sang seeing the small smile on Loren's lips in return.

"Little loud in there, huh? Came to see the horses?"

"Perhaps." Sol drew the cloak tighter across himself. "I enjoyed the pie you left me."

That made Loren smile wider, his eyes crinkling. "I thought you would." He glanced back at the dark stables. "Although, I think the horses are tuckered out and asleep by now."

"I see..."

"You can sit with me if you want. I don't really like how loud it gets either. Out here I can listen to myself think, at least."

Thinking was good. Sol hesitated another moment, trying to piece his wayward thoughts together so he could say more than mundane platitudes, but his head remained empty. He was brought back to Loren as the man sat down, leaving enough space beside him for Sol.

Part of Sol told himself no—to simply find somewhere else and not make an attachment—but he was sitting before he'd even understood the thought. His shoulder bumped against Loren's as he settled down and Sol drew himself tighter. Loren didn't react; he simply returned to staring at the darkness above them. Sol peered up as well. Nothing.

"What are you staring at?" he asked.

Loren shrugged and crossed his ankles. "I thought maybe I'd see some stars, but what you said before was right. Nothing there but the moon." He chuckled and glanced at Sol. "Although, I guess you're here now... Maybe that counts."

Sol's cheeks flushed and he dipped his head to hide it. His lips shifted into a smile, but that only brought Gareth's words back to the forefront of his mind, souring the same smile. Sol didn't mind Loren; Gareth wasn't wrong. Why was this single man so different? Human emotions were *vexing*.

"I'm going to be sad to leave the horses here," Loren murmured as he looked over his shoulder.

Sol startled. "We're what?"

Loren raised his eyebrows and settled against the wall. "You didn't get told? Queen's not gonna let a priceless mare like Stardust go on a trek that might get her killed. Gareth wasn't wrong. There's hardly any horses left."

Sol's heart clenched. "Is she going to be safe here?"

"Arcridge has good people," Loren said. "She'll be with Philie, at least. I'm leaving her here for a proper mule. Queen's probably going to send someone here to pick Stardust up when she deems it safe."

"Where did you get your horse from if there are hardly any left?"

"Farmer who had her was putting down all his animals," Loren said. "Said all of them were infected with scourge. Only did a few at a time since it killed him to do it, but well, if they were infected, better a mercy kill. Mira and I took our chances and stole her since we needed a horse. Didn't have scourge in her as far as we could tell."

"How do you tell?"

"The first sign is eyes going black. Philie's never did."

"I'm glad you saved her."

Loren smiled sadly. "Me too. Kinda wished I could have convinced him to look, though."

They went quiet and Sol tilted his head back to watch the dark above them. It really was absolute. It didn't even glitter like scourge did.

"You..." Loren paused, thinking, and Sol peeked at him. He was staring ahead now at the shuttered streets only aglow from the opened tavern doors. "You really aren't used to life outside the castle, huh? Harvest festivals and whatnot?"

"The only thing I know about feasts is the two we had in the castle and I was absent for one of them," Sol said and drew his knees to his chest. "This is a little different, I suppose."

Loren nodded. "My home had harvest festivals with the same kind of energy before the scourge came. We'd be up all night celebrating we'd grown enough to live through the winter." He chuckled, folding his hands over his stomach. "Then we'd have another festival once spring came for surviving winter and living to another cycle."

Sol frowned. "There are many festivals for simply surviving."

"Humans are just glad to be alive."

Alive. Sol's frown deepened. Alive meant everything hurt. Meant confusion about what everyone wanted from him. Alive was simply suffering as far as Sol was concerned.

"Are..." Loren hesitated until Sol looked at him again. He'd drawn his eyebrows tight with clear concern. "Are you not?"

It wasn't a simple yes or no answer; Sol wasn't going to pretend otherwise. "What do you know about stars?" he asked instead. Question for a question.

"Whatever the bard tales have told me," Loren said. "So, I apologize, but not much."

At least he admitted to it instead of acting like what the bards and legends said were the quintessential truth. "It hurts... making a body, I mean." Sol wrapped his arms around his knees and rested his head on them. "I wasn't glad or thankful to be *alive* until Celena held me. Until I opened my eyes and saw her."

Loren smiled gently. "I think it's understated how close you two were. People whispered that she looked lonely, but then you came along." He turned his gaze back to the sky. "Then they said she was exuberant. Alive in ways everyone thought long forgotten."

"How do you know that?" Sol asked. "You weren't even there."

"People talk," Loren replied. "Servants go home to their families, that family goes to the market, and it's retold, over and over again. Our lives are a little meaningless in the dark, so when our beloved princess is suddenly very, very happy with her new friend, we all kinda hear about it eventually. Brought us hope."

Sol glared at Loren. "We *were* friends."

"Never said you were anything but—I wasn't being cheeky." Loren glanced at him again. "I remember what you told me, don't worry." He chuckled suddenly and tried to hide it behind his hand. "You'd look more like me if you were anything more, wasn't that it?"

Sol's cheeks burned, but he relaxed and buried his frustration. "Are you close to Nebora and Mira?"

"As friends can be." Loren's smile turned sweet. "Mira's like a little sister. Nebora treats her that way too. Actually, she treats me like a little sibling too. Maybe that's just what she does to everyone she likes."

"How did you meet them?"

A wistful look came to Loren's eyes. "Well," he said and chuckled, "you already know about Mira. She and my family had homesteads next to each other. Saved her from the scourge and she's been with me ever since. Not that I'm complaining." He stretched his legs out in front of him and tilted his head back. "Nebora, we met maybe five years ago? Mira and I had been wandering the land, looking for a safe place to lay low. We ended up in the Swallows and Nebora and her people stole Philie and with her, all our stuff. I would have cut my losses—I was not going to do well against a crew of bandits, believe me—but Mira's lute was included in that and she was devastated."

"Why'd they steal everything?" Sol asked.

"Desperation. Five years since the start of the Umbral Cycle and the scourge was choking everything. Nebora's people were hurting all the same. Besides, Philie was a *horse*. Could have sold or traded her for a lot." Loren shrugged. "In any case, we trudged on through the Swallows and confronted

Nebora—the so-called Queen of the Swallows."

Sol raised his eyebrows. "Queen?"

"That's what her people called her. They haven't thought highly of our Queen for years now, so they'd taken to calling Nebora's father King of the Swallows. Naturally, when he died to scourge, she became Queen of the Swallows."

Interesting. He'd already thought Nebora's boldness was refreshing before, but now it was even more so. Sol squeezed his arms around his knees tighter and nodded for Loren to go on.

"When we found her deep in this little hideaway, she thought we were ballsy for coming at all and proposed a deal." A little smirk spread across Loren's lips. "If I won against her in a duel, I'd get our horse and everything back."

"And if you lost?"

Loren winced. "She'd parade me around naked in front of all her people before throwing me into the closest pit to be swallowed up." He waved his hand dismissively as Sol frowned at the idea. "I don't think she was *serious*, but wanted to make me reconsider. I didn't. Mira would have been devastated if I couldn't get her lute back at least.

"Nebora let me choose which weapon to fight with and I chose her axe, which she also found ballsy so she chose my sword. When the fight began, I threw her axe as hard as I could somewhere over everyone's head to get it out of the equation—she would have murdered me with it otherwise—and she was laughing so hard at the audacity, she didn't see me charge her." A laugh bubbled out of Loren's throat and he tried biting it back. It was amusing to imagine, Sol couldn't deny. "Maybe I won by virtue of that alone—she threw my sword too and we grappled, but you've seen her. Muscle. All of it. I was skinnier then and there was no way a malnourished guy was going to win against that. But I did. I managed to pin her down and she acquiesced. Got Mira's lute back and Philie."

There was a pause and Sol tilted his head. "And then?" he found himself asking. Loren's voice was soft and so easy to get lost in; Sol was sure he could have listened to the man all night. It helped the story didn't quite feel as large and embellished as the legends told amongst the castle or within the tavern now.

"And then we never left," Loren said, smiling at Sol. "Mira and I had nowhere to go and I think Nebora realized that, so she took us into her fold. Imagine what the Queen would think if she knew three of her heroes were hardly more than roadside bandits."

Made more sense why she'd forced one of her

knights into the group.

"Do you think you'll go back to that after everything's done?" Sol's thoughts betrayed him when they vocalized and he wished he hadn't asked. After everything's done didn't matter. He didn't want to know.

Loren shrugged and stared skyward. "We'll see."

His voice had turned forlorn, like it was something he thought about often and never found a suitable answer. Sol left it there and followed his gaze. Still dark. Still hushed with only the echoes from the tavern around the corner.

"What about Gareth?" Sol asked softly. "Did you know him beforehand?"

All of the warmth evaporated as Loren's jaw tightened, his unease palpable. "Didn't know him before last night," he admitted. "If it was up to me, we would've already ditched him. Sits high and tall like he knows how it is out here." Loren pushed out a breath and shook his head. "He doesn't. The Queen just wanted one of her fancy asses to be a hero so it was more than just nobodies."

"I see."

Loren faced Sol sharply. "Did something happen with him?"

The touch against Sol's face. The unwanted arm around his waist. How close Gareth had pushed himself against Sol. It shivered its way through his body, but Sol panicked thinking of admitting anything had happened at all. Too much was at stake and if anyone *knew* how the scourge had reacted to his panic, they'd piece together everything else.

"No," he lied. The word burned on his tongue, acid bubbling up his throat.

Then came the trembling. Was he afraid of Gareth, then? Sol couldn't stop it, even as he wrapped Loren's cloak tighter. The air was simply cold and the wind biting, that was it. He wasn't afraid. He couldn't be. He hardly knew the man or his machinations.

Except Sol couldn't get warm, no matter how tightly he held himself. Something must have been wrong with him.

"Sol?" Loren placed a hand on his arm, the touch singing through Sol like a hymn. There wasn't scourge inside Loren—not a drop—and Sol didn't know what made the song in his head. "You're shivering. Might be time to turn in?"

Sol shook his head. "I don't want to leave you out here alone."

Loren took his hand away. "I'm ready to turn in too, honestly. This is the last bed we're gonna have for a while, I bet. Not going to waste it by sleeping on hay." He gently knocked Sol with his elbow. "I know you're used to beds every night in the castle, but a bed when you're traveling is a godsend. Promise."

Sol snorted, biting back the snicker, and Loren stood, grinning. "I knew I could get a smile out of you," he said and Sol let him see it this time, glad it made Loren's grin soften. He bent down and held out a hand. "Come on, let's go get warm inside."

"Thank you for regaling me with the tale of how you bested Nebora in battle."

Loren covered a laugh and glanced away. "Don't tell her I told it so simply. She likes to embellish it—pretty sure Mira is gonna make it sound grander than it was."

"I promise I won't."

The smile they shared was one that lit a quick warmth throughout Sol's entire being. He didn't know what it was about Loren, but he accepted he was strangely drawn to the man. He'd thought it only possible with Celena, although with Loren, it was different. There was something else blossoming through Sol every time Loren smiled at him. As their hands touched. Made the world softer.

Sol buried the feeling as far down as he could. It wouldn't matter. It would all be wiped away. Burned to the ground until only ashes remained.

Or, at least it wouldn't matter because he wouldn't live long enough to enjoy it.

Loren took him inside, gently holding his hand like it might break. The tavern still buzzed, but it had grown quieter. A new minstrel strummed their instrument in one corner, entertaining a group around the table that might have been too drunk to understand the song, while others had retreated to their own groups. Subdued and quiet, but still happy and relaxed. Nebora and Mira were gone and so was Gareth. Loren paid the bartender a quick thank you, smiling at her, and led Sol into the stairwell before anyone thought to stop them.

Sol's heart raced as he retraced his steps from earlier, but then it relaxed as Loren stayed beside him. Whatever Gareth had done before wouldn't happen again because Loren was there and even Sol's body realized it.

Loren thankfully didn't hurry Sol. He moved like he noticed Sol's hesitation, but never asked about it. Sol was glad and led the way forward slowly. They reached their room without incident—no one waited for them in the hallway—and Loren peeked inside.

The room would have been too dark to see if the moonlight wasn't ghosting inside. In the center of the room were three beds in a row. Gareth had taken the one on the far end of the room, away from the doorway, and had passed out fully dressed atop the blankets. The scourge within his arm had quieted, growing dormant. He must have been fast asleep. Certainly didn't stir upon their entrance and Sol breathed easier. Nebora and Mira, meanwhile, were on the other side of the room, leaving the middle bed empty, and were passed out the same. At least they'd managed to crawl underneath the covers.

"You can bunk with Mira," Loren whispered close to Sol's ear, making him jump, and led him over. "She's small." He let go of Sol's hand and bent over Nebora to whisper to her. She groggily pulled her face out of the pillow and tried waving him away, but Loren was insistent.

"Yeah, yeah, *fine*." Nebora pulled herself from the bed—clad only in a short tunic that showed just how long her legs were—and padded over to the middle bed. She promptly fell into it with a flop and pulled the blankets over herself.

Loren shook his head. "Melodramatic," he whispered. He gently nudged Sol toward the space Nebora had vacated. "Get some sleep. I'll see you in the morning."

Sol hastily gave Loren his cloak back before he stepped away. "Thank you."

In the dark, Sol almost missed another smile Loren graced him with. "Any time."

For some reason, even though the room was

almost too dark to see, Sol's face flared as Loren turned away to pull off a few layers. His torso was exposed too quickly for Sol to avert his gaze and the way the moonlight cast itself across the musculature of his back worsened the heat in Sol's cheeks. He felt like he was on fire.

He finally turned sharply, trying not to think about how it would have felt to run his hands along the exposed skin. Gods, what was *wrong* with him? He angrily shed a few layers, frustrated, and folded them neatly on his bag near the door. Only when he heard the middle bed creak with Loren's weight did Sol deem it safe enough to head to his own bed.

Mira stayed curled on her side as Sol gently slipped in and he turned his back to her. The blankets were warm from Nebora at least, and smelled like whatever she used in her hair. Fragrant herbs of some kind—Sol didn't know which ones. Not unpleasant. He pulled the blankets over himself and sunk into the pillow.

All of it—the warmth, the aroma Nebora left behind, Mira murmuring in her sleep as she stayed resolutely on her side—was enough to keep Sol from going too deep into his thoughts. There was a murmured conversation between Loren and Nebora as well, something too quiet to parse real words from, and the soft song from the minstrel down below echoed through the floorboards. It was hushed and soft, soothing Sol as he slowly drifted to sleep. As the dark gently pulled him under, he memorized the way Loren had smiled at him to take it into his dreams.

*"We introduced her to our gods, Lovian below and Faeion above.
Even as she pressed her ear to the earth, listening for life,
and even as she spoke to the sky, whispering her love,
our gods remained silent to her plight."*

—Fragment of "She, Born of Starlight," Anonymous

THERE WAS A TWINKLE IN THE ABSOLUTE DARKNESS of sleep catching Sol's attention. At first, he ignored it, but it only persisted until he could ignore it no longer. He followed it as it took him through its twists and turns on a road too hazy to see until light stole the dark away. His eyes watered, blurring the scene, but when it cleared, he stared into a vanity mirror. It was not his reflection staring back, but Celena's. She caught his gaze in hers and paused. Like she was as unsure as he was, but then she smiled.

Except he wasn't there. He couldn't have been. Even though it felt like she was as close as they had been in the castle. Like he could touch her still. The deal with numbers that continued to spread without once thinking to give us any help," Loren continued. "You are not a hero any more than I am, so you don't get to treat us like dirt."

Gareth was glaring at Loren with such venom, Sol thought for sure he'd lash out. Humans were emotional, after all, but then Gareth eased out a breath and turned toward the road. He squared his shoulders and headed forward.

"We're wasting light. We should not tarry here."

Nebora sighed and quickly caught up to him. "We're only going as far as Arcridge today," she said. "We're wasting *nothing* by getting our shit aired out. We'll be there by midnight even if we crawled so keep the stick out of your ass." She gazed back at Sol and Mira. "You two got a handle on the horses?"

Mira nodded, Philie's reins tight in her hands. Sol hadn't let go of Stardust.

"Arcridge?" Gareth slowed and stared at Nebora. "We can go farther in a single day."

"The bulk of our supplies are there," Loren said. "If you want to keep walking, be my guest, but me and mine"—he paused and glanced back at Sol, raising his eyebrows, and Sol quickly agreed with a nod—"and our star will be stopping for the night."

Gareth looked like he was going to argue; there was a curl to his lips and his eyes darted between connection between them hummed loud and bright, making Sol feel like he was home, and he watched her in return.

"Hello there, Sol," Celena said, just as unsure as his voice would have been, and her voice hummed all the way through his body.

He couldn't reply. He had no mouth in which to do so. No body to even wave at her. Disconcerting, like he was a star again, but he couldn't be.

"I think that's you." Celena picked up her brush and gently took it through her curls. The sensation ghosted across his own hair, reminding him what he had no longer with their soft mornings. Her bare hands glittered as scourge traced lines through her skin and he felt them as his own. "It feels like when we're rooms apart." She drew her gaze downward and her smile was gone.

His heart cracked seeing her sad and he understood deep in his bones why she was. She missed him. The friend she plucked out of the sky and spent an entire month with beneath the sunlight all but gone now. She didn't need to say it. He wanted his own words to tell her he'd come back right then and there—she didn't have to be alone—but he had no voice. She breathed out a shuddering exhale and smiled at herself—at him—in the mirror again.

"Thank you, Sol," she said. "For checking in on

me. You should focus on your journey. I won't go anywhere. I promise."

The scourge inside her hummed such a soft and sweet song as it followed her voice. Sol couldn't stay focused. It traced its fingers through his very soul, akin to Celena's fingers through his hair. The room blurred and bloomed with bright colors until all Sol could do was close his eyes. Darkness greeted him and he listened as intently as he could for Celena's heart. It was there, resounding sure and right against the scourge glittering inside her.

✦

DAPPLED SUNLIGHT STREAMING THROUGH THE window did not wake Sol this time; it simply wasn't there to do so. Rather, once the dream of Celena let go, an aroma was there to rouse him instead. Scrambled eggs and porridge spiced with cinnamon and sugar. He blearily opened his eyes, finding himself buried in the blankets, and caught Mira setting the plate down on the stand between the beds. She jumped seeing him awake and nearly dropped the utensils.

"Good morning!" she said, her chipper voice hiding her fright. "Got you some breakfast! Loren, Nebora, and Gareth are getting our pack mule ready to go, so time to get up!"

Sol considered her, wondering where the

feigned chipper mood was coming from, but when all he received in return was an innocent smile, he let it go. Didn't matter. "Why did no one wake me earlier?" He pushed himself into a sitting position and winced, his body protesting the movement. Not quite as bad as last night during the trek, but he wasn't looking forward to walking.

"Loren figured you could sleep in a bit more since we won't be doing that on the road." Mira gathered her bag and slung it over her shoulder. She was dressed for traveling, her cloak already tight across her shoulders. "Don't complain too much. It's been *boring* waiting. I should have slept in too."

Sol rubbed his eyes, hoping to clear the blurry edges. "Thank you for waking me and bringing me breakfast, then."

Mira smiled again. "Just don't dally. Get that food in your belly and get dressed. As Gareth *loves* to say: we're wasting light."

Sol rolled his eyes, making Mira giggle, and she headed out of the room. Alone, Sol flopped back into the pillows with a sigh. Truthfully, he wasn't hungry, but it certainly smelled nice and she *did* go through the effort of making sure he got a plate. He had to try.

He was only a few bites in, savoring each forkful, before his stomach wanted no more. Last night's nerves hadn't left him completely.

He cleaned up with the small basin in the wash room adjoining their room and caught himself in the mirror. Still him. No reflection of Celena this time. He focused on the link between them, but it was woefully distant once more. Heartbeat too far away to hear and her simple presence a distant speck in his mind.

At least it was there. Soon it wouldn't be at all.

Gently, he brushed the few tangles out of his hair. Ghosts of Celena's fingers slid through the strands like the many mornings before and Sol fondly remembered doing the same for her. Never again. She'd never tie it back for him, braid flowers into it, or even touch it, and neither could he give her the same courtesy.

Dwelling made him despondent; he had to concentrate on something else. The desire led him back to breakfast for a few more bites. Stomach felt better with food in it, at least. Not the twisted knots it'd become thinking of Celena. When he tired of eating again, he concentrated on dressing.

Though his arms and legs hurt—even his lower back, as he quickly found out—he managed. When everything felt snug, he fastened his cloak around his shoulders, glad for its fur lining. Thinking of that, however, drifted his thoughts back to how heavy and warm Loren's cloak had been last night. He quickly ignored the fluttering sensation making him smile that followed. Didn't matter. The rest of breakfast did.

As he finished the last few bites, the door opened.

Loren peeked in and smiled seeing Sol. "Good morning," he said and nodded toward the empty plate. "Glad Mira got you to eat. We're about ready to get a move on, but the town wanted us to pay respects at their chapel first for luck."

"Respects?" Sol picked up his bag and followed Loren out the door. Lights and candles were lit along the hall this morning, sheathing it in warmth that was absent last night.

"Yeah, to the Gods." Loren glanced back. "You never done it?"

Sounded like something the castle had done. Every week, the Queen and Celena had congregated in the small chapel inside the courtyard and paid their respects. Others inside the castle tended to join them, but Sol had never been invited. Celena had wanted him to come, but her mother worried his presence would unnerve the castle parishioners. Sol never argued; he didn't even know what paying respects to the Gods meant.

He chose not to reply, letting it be answer enough, and Loren led him to the stables where their new pack mule was waiting. Loren gave the mule an affectionate pat before he helped Sol affix his bag beside the others.

"His name is Varros," Loren introduced. "Seems friendly. Hasn't bit me yet."

"Hello, Varros," Sol said and the mule eyed him warily. "Thank you for carrying our supplies." Loren smiled and Sol's cheeks flushed as he glanced away. "You said Stardust will be safe here?"

"Did you want to tell her goodbye?"

"Perhaps."

All in all, Stardust was being spoiled with all the comforts a horse could ask for and Sol felt silly thinking otherwise. No one would mistreat a horse they knew the princess owned. Stardust eagerly came up to him as he entered her stall and he gently patted her.

"You'll be back with Celena soon," Sol said, hoping it was true. "Thank you for helping me get here." Stardust nuzzled his hand and he gave her a gentle hug. He'd miss her, perhaps only because she was one of his last connections to Celena, but he would have hated it all the more if she'd been hurt. It was better she was left here.

Once goodbyes were finished—Loren had been giving Philie a last nuzzle as well—Loren took Sol to the small wooden building in the center of town.

Townsfolk already gathered around the opened doors, many the same as the ones from last night. The number of people made Sol's skin prickle, especially when their chatter hushed as he and Loren headed inside.

Nebora, Gareth, and Mira were crammed near the front with a handful of others. The only person standing inside was a man in plain robes and behind him was the altar of the two gods. Both gods had long hair, one as brown as the earth and the other as white as the brightest star. While the locks intertwined the gods together like a constantly flowing wave, the rest of the visage was rather formless and Sol couldn't tell the two apart.

For that reason, among maybe many, Sol felt wrong kneeling with the others. Paying penance to gods he'd hardly acknowledged was a sham. Stars simply *were*, philosophies about gods never once crossing their minds because, in some fashion, they themselves were so similar to gods. As a result, what he knew about the gods was very little and told by Celena herself. In lieu of praying, he tried to recall her words.

Humanity believed in two main gods: the one asleep beyond the cosmos, Faeion, who made the sky to help house the new world and who created the stars to watch over it. The other, Lovian who slept beneath the earth, created the very earth itself and fashioned humanity in their image. Humans believed that upon death, their bodies returned to Lovian to sleep and share all their dreams and aspirations with the god. If Lovian ever awoke, they would take all the gathered souls into the cosmos and rejoin Faeion.

Humanity only prayed to Faeion when they were seeking guidance and prayed to Lovian for bountiful harvests, always thanking them for the earth and life they granted.

Whether they were truly there or not, Sol did not know. As a star, he'd heard whispers beyond the scope of the stars he knew, but it literally could have been anything. Not necessarily a sleeping god no one could reach.

In any case, Sol clasped his hands together like the others in silent prayer as the man in robes pressed a droplet of water and a petal to their foreheads. The water signified what rained down from the skies as a sign Faeion dreamt of them and the flower was a blessing from Lovian's body in the earth.

Sol received no divine answer throughout the whole ceremony. Praying simply was and then they were leaving. He certainly didn't feel any luckier, but perhaps it had been for the town's benefit, knowing they sent the heroes off as prepared as they could.

Leaving Arcridge wasn't like leaving the castle. There was no sunlight shining from parted skies and petals certainly didn't rain down from above. They did, however, receive many well wishes from the townspeople who had gathered outside to see them off.

They headed out alone into the underwhelming dawn where the wilderness was full of dark shapes made large from the veiled sun climbing the sky.

Sol walked alongside Mira like before and she held Varros' reins. She wasn't playing her lute this time; it was fixed to Varros with everything else and Sol missed her little songs. Instead, she had her crossbow slung across her shoulder and a quiver of bolts tied to her waist. In front of them walked Nebora, Gareth, and Loren in a line. No one bickered this time. Gareth hadn't even looked at Sol once today. Small miracle. Not that Sol complained; the less he thought about last night, the better his body fared.

It would have been a silent slog, listening to their footfalls and the very distant scourge trawling the wilderness inside some poor animal, if Mira hadn't begun talking. To Sol. Specifically to Sol. He'd almost tuned her out at first, focusing on the trek, but then realized she patiently awaited answers. When he gave her one hesitatingly, she continued talking. It was one thing to respond to something going on around them, but she was literally trying to engage with him. Sol stumbled on his words, out of place. First Loren and now her and he hardly knew how to respond to either; Celena was the only one in the castle who'd bothered to speak to him at all and even then, it'd taken time to warm up to her.

All Mira's questions were mundane too; mostly about legends and bard songs to which Sol haltingly gave her answers. He liked some of the legends; no, he thought the stanza meant something wildly different; yes, Princess Celena had shown him the basics of swordplay (why she asked this was worrisome, but she left it at that). More and more, Sol found it easier to converse and wondered if it was a ploy so Gareth wouldn't interact instead. With Mira as a buffer, he'd have no chance. Even more, if he'd shown signs of wanting to turn the few times Sol struggled to answer, either Loren or Nebora would say something to gather his attention instead and the three of them would have a hushed conversation just as trivial as what transpired between Sol and Mira.

The lengths everyone went through to keep Sol from Gareth made him wonder if he should have told Loren what happened. Clearly, the three of them already didn't trust Gareth. At the same time, however, Sol still didn't quite understand what it all had meant other than he did not like it. Made his heart race thinking about it again. If he told Loren, however, and Loren confronted Gareth, it would come out that Sol had used the scourge in Gareth's arm—likely something only Gareth was supposed to know about—to cause him harm. He'd never once tried controlling Celena's scourge despite the temptation, but what if he could have saved her?

Except, human bodies were so tightly put together. Trying to extract it would surely cause more harm than good. Like the way Gareth's arm had twisted. It was a wonder the bone hadn't snapped. Gareth was certainly favoring his other arm today. Sol abandoned the idea and took solace in the fact he *could* protect himself if need be.

Sol drew his gaze across the hills sloping to either side of them, filled with sparse pines crystallized with scourge upon their nettles. The shapes and shadows hummed in acknowledgement as his gaze swept past them, but they weren't as stark as Gareth's. No controlling the trees, then. Perhaps it required an initial touch. He couldn't think of an excuse to go and touch a tree, however, and kept it to himself.

It was then he realized Mira had stopped talking. He blinked and peered at her. She looked slightly panicked, like she wasn't supposed to run out of topics. Sol scrambled to bridge the sudden silence himself.

"W-What—" He swallowed, words stumbling, and Mira's eyebrows lifted. "What do you want to do when this is all over?"

Terrible topic. Sol should have asked her what her favorite color was. What she wanted to do when it was all done wasn't something he *wanted* to know because it would never happen. Yet, it was there now like he truly cared, and he hated the way his own heart soared seeing the way Mira's expression brightened.

"I..." She paused and drew her brows tight, stumped. She huffed and put her hands on her hips. "Wow, I haven't really thought of it." She chuckled, shaking her head, and drew Varros away from a weed he'd gone to nibble on. "I've been traveling with Loren for so long, not traveling seems wrong."

"What would you have done if the scourge hadn't come?" Sol's voice worked without his conscious input, part of him wanting her to keep talking. The wind had picked up, coating the silence with whispers from the distance he wanted buried.

"I don't actually know!" Mira laughed. "I was *twelve*. Not very old, mind you." She stretched her arms in front of her and fidgeted with her gloves.

"Maybe I'd still be telling stories or maybe I'd be looking to marry." There was a small, bashful smile on her lips as she lowered her arms. She sidled closer to Sol and dropped her voice. "My ma wanted more grandkids—I had older sisters who'd given her plenty already, but she just liked the little ones—and maybe I would have stayed home to do just that."

"Is that all?"

"I didn't dream big when I was little," Mira continued, shrugging. "Life just was, you know?" She picked up her gaze and stared at Loren's back. "I probably wouldn't have known Loren as well, that's for sure. I knew *of* him since, you know, he was that hunky neighbor."

Loren snorted from in front, but didn't look back.

Mira grinned and leaned closer to Sol, dropping her voice even more. "Maybe my da would've played matchmaker. My family and his were friends and that was all it really took to pair your children. My younger self certainly wouldn't have minded." She nudged Sol, giving him a playful look, and he gave her a weary one in return. "Oh, come on. I've seen you looking."

Sol nudged her back and she covered her laugh, but no one else noticed how flustered Sol must have looked. Good. He burrowed himself into his cloak to further hide evidence he was.

"Is it different now?" he asked out of curiosity.

Mira tilted her head. "Well, I actually know him now." She eyed Loren a moment and leaned back into Sol, whispering so quietly, he hardly heard her over the wind. "As it turns out, he's not attracted to women. He likes other men." She chuckled and elbowed him. "I was disappointed when I was younger, but it is what it is!"

Sol ignored the obvious teasing. "What about Nebora? Do you like her the same?"

Mira's eyes twinkled. "Oh, I have a whole ballad I'm planning around her misadventures!" She grinned wider when Nebora barked a laugh. "Want to hear the beginning? It gets raunchy as per her request."

Without meaning to, Sol made a face, but he was glad it only made Mira giggle.

"Ah, not a ballad person?"

"Not really," Sol admitted. "I heard many waiting and they were all about how heroes saved the world. They became very rote."

Mira considered him, her earlier exuberance replaced with something far more thoughtful. "I can take criticism," she said. "I know I still have a lot to learn."

"No, it's not that—"

"Oh! I know!" The grin came back just as fast. "I

can give you an entire segment! Just tell me what to write and I'll make it pretty!" Out of nowhere came a leatherbound notebook and a small pen filled with ink. She threw open the cover, sped past scribbled pages, and found a blank one. "There are many unknowns concerning stars in ballads. Almost like you're an afterthought. The only one who got anything substantial was the very first star and her journey, but it only made her vague and pretty. Hardly anything compared to the ballads we get of her heroes."

Vague and pretty. What Sol would become should he follow the footsteps of all the other stars. He grew pensive and Mira went quiet, words snuffed out despite her excitement. This time, he didn't bridge the gap. He didn't know how.

Gareth blew out a sigh and glanced back. "Fucking finally," he said and Mira glared at him. "How the fuck are you so talkative? I swear you haven't stopped since we left."

"I like other people." Mira shoved the pen and notebook back into her jerkin.

"He's not wrong." Nebora snickered from beside him. "You *have* been chatting Sol's ear off since we left. Surprised you haven't downed the entire water flask just to keep your throat from drying out."

Mira sighed loudly, hanging her head. "Oh,

come on."

Loren glanced at Gareth. "She's excited with a new ballad to write. You don't get that every day. I'm sure when she writes about *you*, you'll be talking her ear off."

Gareth huffed, but there was a small smile at the edge of his lips.

"Yeah!" Mira leaned toward Sol and whispered the next bit: "I'll write what an *ass* he was."

Sol couldn't help but snort and hunched down into his furs to stifle the sound. It only drew Gareth's attention and he shot them both a wary look.

"What?" he snapped.

Mira raised her head. "I'd sing about what a nice ass you have!"

Nebora threw her head back, laughing, and one of her hands darted out to grab Gareth's cloak like she'd intended to lift it to look for herself. Gareth shoved her hand away and quickened his pace before she could grab it again.

"Real fucking funny," he said and huffed. "Let's shut up and walk. Planar Village is our next stop and I'd like not to be stuck out here if we arrive too late for them to let us in."

Mira rolled her eyes melodramatically and dipped her head toward Sol. "Killjoy," she whispered and went right back to chatting. This time, she pulled

Nebora and Loren into the conversation, ignoring Gareth grinding his teeth at the new noise.

Sol didn't join in this time; he was still hung up on the lack of stars in ballads. Their names were never recorded, even if the heroes' were, and though Sol was sure he'd known each and every star at some point in his life before he fell, even he couldn't parse the syllables of their names now. They remained a noise deep in his head. A drone of who they'd been.

His memory failed him no matter how hard he tried and it chilled him to think if he failed, he'd suffer the same fate.

✦

THE WALK WAS LONG. SOL IGNORED EVERYONE'S conversations after the first break for food, and doing so let him relax. Beyond the inane buzz of their voices, however, he caught whispers of his name. Different than the phantasm. Older and such a soft tenor, like it feared spooking him. The words tugged at him, but every time he looked in the direction it pulled him, he lost the thread of magic. It almost felt like it was leading him somewhere and he might have let it too, if he'd known what it wanted. All he knew was that it was warm, akin to an old friend. Magic so familiar tracing across the land unseen.

He began keeping an eye out for it after the first

instance and found it as footsteps in the field. Safe steps untouched by any scourge lingering between fresh grass blades. Curious.

Planar Village came up as the sun was halfway bowed out of the sky. It lay past the farmlands growing high beyond the fences along the road. The fields were filled with empty husks of what once was, rotten all the way through with scourge clinging to the stalks, and the scarecrows therein seemed to watch them in the dark, their still lit lanterns hung around their necks illuminating their grotesque faces.

Everyone slowed, surveying what was left, and Loren exchanged a worried glance with Nebora. No one needed to say it. Something was wrong. Nebora freed her labrys, holding it steady, and Gareth un-sheathed his sword. Nothing came. Only the breeze as it pushed the stalks together until they cracked, spilling scourge and rot across the field. It was nothing that had power or will to attack them until a poor animal ate the dead harvest.

The soft magic returned, glinting a magic sheen across the air as it passed Sol, and he tried following it this time. Its path took it through the broken fence on the other side of the road and followed a thin trail on the other side. No harvest lay there, just an incline leading to a thicket of trees in the distance. The magic disappeared inside, winking at the edge for just a moment as though beckoning him. It started again in moments, following the same path, almost like an impression repeating itself.

No one else noticed. Perhaps Varros did; his ears twitched and he looked toward it, but he dutifully followed Mira as she headed forward with the others. Sol huddled down into his cloak and kept up. Planar Village's walls were in sight.

They arrived to wide open gates, no militia guarding it, and empty streets. The buildings were dark all the way through, none of the wall torches had been lit, and with the sun dipping out of the sky, dark shadows drew across them.

Gareth's jaw tightened. "Didn't we send a messenger from Arcridge?"

"First thing I did," Loren whispered. "We didn't see him on the road."

"I'm not going in there. Too dark." Nebora turned. "Let's find another place to camp. Arcridge gave us enough—we'll be warm."

Gareth's face pinched. "With scourge literally everywhere?"

"We've done it before." Mira cast her gaze across the fields, right past the magic tugging Sol's hand for his attention. "Just need a decent patch..."

Gareth waved his hand toward the gates. "If the

town's empty, I'm sure we can take any building."

Nebora shook her head and faced him. "No. Something's *not* right and I'm not going to be stupid enough to waltz in. Being a knight hasn't taught you any sense, has it?"

"I agree," Loren said. "If its people taken over by scourge, we don't have the means to completely protect ourselves. You've never seen it, but it's not a pretty sight."

Though Gareth glared at them both, like he considered continuing the argument, the fight left him with a sigh. "Fine. You're right: I haven't," he said. "Where do we camp then? Road might get us overrun—no shelter."

"And everything's dark now." Mira frowned and fretted, adjusting the light atop Varros. "I can't tell shadow from scourge."

There was the tug again and this time, Sol faced it. The magic tittered down the path, cutting into the grass, and toward the same trees. He watched it, listening, and heard a soft hum this time. It resonated with him, but unlike scourge, it was welcoming. An image bloomed to mind of a small circle of land surrounded by tall trees. Fuzzy travelers, details too smudged to see, sat around a glittering fire and he smiled lovingly at them. Then the vision receded. He raised his eyebrows.

He knew what this was.

"I know where we can stay," he said softly and everyone stared at him. "It's safe. Not far." He turned and hesitated when they regarded him with confusion.

"How do you know?" Nebora asked.

Sol turned back, tracing the magic with his hand. "There's old magic here," he said. "Maybe from the first star's pilgrimage where the old bard tales sang of havens she left across the land." Mira brightened, nodding enthusiastically; he figured she would have heard of them at least. "They're said to be the places *she* slept under the stars, safe and sound." He pointed at the trees. "Her magic is leading me there."

Gareth scoffed, coming closer. "I feel nothing. How can you be sure?"

Sol narrowed his eyes. "Of course, you feel nothing. You are not a star."

Gareth glared at Sol. "The Queen gave me a gift so I could track your kind. Nothing is there but possibly danger."

"No," Sol said. "It was no gift. She made you feel scourge *with* scourge by carving it into your arm." He was undaunted as Gareth's jaw dropped and everyone's eyes flitted from Sol to Gareth. No one else had realized it. "And scourge is dead. This magic yet lives." Sol spread an arm toward the road. "Should you think the road is safer, be my guest. But as you say, we're exposed there."

Mira hastily stepped beside Sol, bringing Varros with her. "Varros and I vote we camp with Sol," she said. "If Gareth wants to camp elsewhere—he can have it all to himself."

"Aye," Nebora said. "Lead the way, Star Eyes."

"I'm not staying here," Gareth growled.

"Then shut up and follow," Loren said.

Sol was uneasy taking the lead, but at least he wasn't alone. Aside from Mira in step beside him, the star's magic caressed his hand and body as he headed after her long gone footsteps through the meadow. Warmth bloomed through him, like he walked into the embrace of an old friend. Even though she was countless years older than Sol, her magic must have recognized his. Perhaps this was how she'd touched him—with hands soft and warm—when Sol was in his infancy.

The treaded path led into the trees and past the tall birches, there was the clearing he saw. In the center was a raised piece of land, the grass new and alive compared to its brethren everywhere else, and in the dirt, old sigils had been drawn. Not any symbol he knew, but it must have been what kept her magic cycling here as it did. Sol wondered if he could weave magic the same, but quickly reminded himself it was no use. He was not here to protect anyone.

As Sol stepped past the drawn sigils, magic lifted his gaze upward. Whispers spilled down from above from the patch of stars glittered between the reaches of the branches. Sol's heart ached. He'd missed the stars and their soft whispers so much.

Mira stood beside him, eager, and she smiled. "Oh," she said. "This feels *safe*."

It did. So safe, like the rest of the world's dangers never mattered. Nebora came up next, nodding, and set her axe down. "Good," she said. "Hopefully we'll get some sleep then." She patted their shoulders. "You two help Loren pitch the tents. Knight Boy and I will gather some firewood."

"*Knight Boy?*" Gareth sputtered. "I have a name."

"Yeah." Nebora propped a hand on her hip. "Knight Boy." She grinned as he bristled. "Come on. Firewood."

They bickered loudly as they went, but it soon became an echo past the trees. Almost intentional, like the haven itself was protecting everything within even from sound. Sol felt at home. He didn't mind the bundle Loren graced him with and didn't mind listening as Loren and Mira showed him how to pitch a tent. Even let himself believe perhaps his journey wouldn't be the end.

Until another voice slithered into his ear. "*Oh, my*

little star. Do not forget."

He glanced up and though he couldn't see the phantasm of the star held high in the sky beyond the trees, he felt her. Even as the haven lulled safety and security into him, he could not escape her sadness that had orchestrated his fall.

"You promised me."

"She taught us how to bless lands once lost to drought
with symbols carved into the earth, shaped to ward her fears
to make even the darkest nights safe
as the days wore into months and then into years."

—Fragment of "She, Born of Starlight," Anonymous

THE WHISPERS OF SCOURGE BECAME A LONG-GONE memory beneath the crackling of the campfire. The stars softly looked down upon them and Sol could *hear* them; so unlike the buzz in the scourge, this was a tender song only for him. Yet, he couldn't understand the words. Even in a haven touched by the first star, he was cut off so completely from what he'd been. The thought tried to sober him, but he ignored it, and instead, focused on the cozy camp.

Three tents were huddled around the fire in the middle. Sol had learned very quickly he was *bad* at pitching a tent, but between Loren and Mira, the tents were serviceable. Varros had hunkered himself down between two of them, at ease enough to lie down entirely once he'd finished grazing and eating. The fire was bright, pushing back the darkness so everything shimmered gold and orange. Mira had cooked some of the provisions with a pan over the fire, humming all the while. It was mostly dried meats and grains mixed with vegetables and they ate the honeyed bread Arcridge had given them with it. Simple, but tasted nice. Each of them even had a mug of something bitter and warm, chasing away any lingering chill. Sol ate and drank slowly, hoping his stomach would accept the offering.

The soft silence would have been nice, if Sol hadn't noticed Gareth staring at him over the flames shortly after the provisions were doled out. Sol tried to avoid his gaze, but the knight stared so intently, Sol caught it too many times to pretend he hadn't. Gareth wanted *something* and Sol was afraid of what it was.

Nebora spotted it first, eyebrows high as she glanced between them. She nudged Loren—nearly making him drop his plate—and once he noticed, his face went hard. It was another few careful bites before Loren put his plate down and spoke.

"You done memorizing our star?" he asked and Gareth gave him a withering glare. "Or do you have something to say?"

Gareth nodded at Sol. "How did you know?" he asked. "It's out in the open now what's in my arm—but *how* did you know what the Queen did?"

Sol hesitated. No. Gareth clearly didn't know about the connection between stars and scourge, or else he wouldn't be asking. There was no reason to admit to it. He swallowed. "The princess told me."

Gareth's eyes narrowed. He didn't buy the lie and Sol internally cursed himself. Of course, he didn't. Celena was never in on her mother's plans. She was simply the pretty princess kept oblivious and safe. Nothing more.

"Hold on." Mira pointed her fork at Gareth. "What *did* the Queen do to you?"

Sighing, Gareth took off his gauntlet to roll up his sleeve. Against the pale, scarred skin on his wrist was a dark, shimmering mark not unlike the way Celena's skin had looked. While Celena's had been something Sol recognized as part of himself, this was anything but. A stranger. It didn't quite feel like the previous star either. One far older.

Studying it soured Sol's stomach. The Queen went looking for a piece of scourge that had lingered between cycles to utilize it as a tool and infected her own knight with it. All she'd done was condemn him to a slow, painful death when all was said and done if Sol wasn't able to fulfill his promise.

"She injected me with what she called the end of a star," Gareth said and watched Sol. For his part, Sol remained impassive. Queen Celeste must have known more than he'd given her credit for naming it thusly, but Gareth still clearly hadn't pieced it together. "It was so I could sense nearby scourge and to keep an eye on our star. I'm still getting used to it."

Nebora held out her hand, expectant, and Gareth let her look. She practically dragged him off his stump despite his protests and studied the mark in better light. It shivered beneath his skin in what Sol could only describe as confusion. Nebora let go and Gareth covered his arm again.

"She *really* thought you'd lose him?" Nebora waved an arm over Sol. "His hair not bright enough for you?"

Gareth rubbed his wrist through the sleeve. "She thought *something*."

Something. Sol tensed, but Gareth didn't elaborate. There could have been many reasons, but Sol thought back to the morning in the garden with the Queen. Dull and uninspired, she'd called him, suspicion lacing her voice. Sol tightened his jaw. He wondered if she'd ever trusted him.

Too late for all the what ifs; he had a knight now specifically watching for anything suspicious. Not to mention last night. The memory crawled through

Sol's head uninvited and surely it was next. Surely Gareth would ask him what he'd done to his arm, but minutes rolled by and he didn't.

Sol wasn't sure if that was better.

"Well." Mira broke Sol's thought spiral. "Want me to mention it in your tale of the nice ass?"

Gareth glared at her and clasped his gauntlet back on with a click. "Why are you so flippant about this whole venture?"

Mira glared right back. "I'm not. I know it's important, but what good is it to growl and mope?" She turned away from Gareth, ignoring whatever muted reply he'd begun, and with a scowl, he stood.

Nebora and Loren immediately tensed and Sol's heart leapt into his throat, expecting an altercation of some kind. The knight, however, simply turned away from camp and headed toward the nearest trees. Both Loren and Nebora watched him go, taut and ready themselves, but Gareth only began throwing his knife at the trees. No one spoke right away and the rattle of the trees being struck punctured the silence each time the knife found its home.

Mira hadn't looked worried one bit; she had her eyes on Sol and smiled when he acknowledged her.

"Since he's too grumpy for his tale, how about you? Tell me something I can put in my ballad about stars." Once more, the journal and pen came out of a pocket Sol hadn't noticed. "We hardly have stories for them and I want to change that. Once the venture's over, they disappear from history. I don't want that this time. Tell me: what is it like up in the cosmos?"

There were too many sensations Sol couldn't put words to. Nothing humans would find comparable. As he searched for the words, he caught Loren watching him softly. If he wasn't having trouble then, he was now. The tips of his ears grew warm.

"I hear it's pretty when a star falls," Loren said. "I don't think we saw it all the way in the Swallows."

Somewhere to start. "Celena said the same," Sol whispered and dropped his gaze to his plate. He hadn't finished eating, but his stomach wasn't going to tolerate any more. Nebora watched him set the plate aside and made a motion, like asking if he was done. When he nodded, she took the rest for herself.

"She saw glittering streaks of colors across the night sky. It lit up the castle gardens all up until she caught me. For me, it hadn't felt like anything but a burning light and pain." Sol twisted his fingers around his wrist, following the pale line that once bisected his skin. "U-Up there in the cosmos? I'm... I'm not *there*. But I'm also there and see everything. I could see everything below me, all the colors humanity made and the hymn of your voices reaching into the cosmos, but it was also nothing at the same time because days became seconds, years mere moments slipping by. I just... watched."

It was hard to put to words how it felt. He hated he tried; instead of how sublime it'd felt, how alive and right, it sounded like simple rambling. Mira wrote it down all the same, nodding, and he resisted the urge to take her journal to see how she'd understood what he'd said. It wasn't like he *could* read well had he taken it and he twisted his fingers into his cloak instead.

"I'm sorry. It's hard to describe." Before Mira looked up at him, he stared into the fire, letting himself relax. To ignore how Mira listened so intently to everything he said. How his body flinched each time Gareth moved to retrieve his knife. "It's not like it is here. Where I'm tired and exhausted all the time. W-Where I can tangibly feel things." He tested his fingers, remembering the first day they were his own and how unlike himself he'd felt simply trying to pick up a teacup. "Up there, we *exist*, but I can describe it no clearer than that."

Mira was still nodding like she understood everything. At least one of them did. Her pen scratched across the page in loops and paragraphs Sol wished he could read.

Nebora finished her plate and settled it beside

her. She was watching him thoughtfully. "Did you know the star before you?"

"Likely in some fashion," Sol said. "But vaguely. When we fall, we're cut off. I don't remember her name, but she was at least a century before me."

"Two," Gareth said and his knife struck the tree. "Two centuries, actually. We'd actually begun to think it wouldn't happen again, but even after we'd picked ourselves up in those intervening years, we were thrust right back to darkness like we'd never left it." He retrieved his knife and looked over the blade. "Shit if you ask me."

Sol drew himself tighter. "It's a cycle."

Nebora waved her hand dismissively. "Yeah, but he's right. It's shit," she said. "For some unforeseen reason, humanity gets culled to the edge of existence from darkness made solid unless a star comes down to save us." She rested her elbows on her knees. "One day, we're not coming back."

Mira picked her head up from writing. "I studied the last bard's telling of his adventure. He gave a really good picture of the world back then because he'd been a traveler before the star fell. It hasn't changed much since then." She sadly looked at her notes, flipping back a few pages. "We've advanced, sure, but every time the world goes dark, we lose so much history and progress. Darkness wipes so much out. Whole lineages." She frowned, her voice growing quiet. "Whole towns."

Like her home. Her family. Sol felt a pang in his chest.

"Just wish people made peace in the intervening years," Nebora said and sloshed what was left in her mug. "Nations close off when the scourge comes and then when it's light again, they go right back to petty politics and conquests. Cycles. All of it bullshit."

Mira glanced at Sol. "Were you the only star that fell?"

Sol drew his cloak tighter around himself. "As far as I know. We drop one at a time, so I'm likely the only one at present."

"How did you decide *where* to fall? How does it feel?"

"We don't decide anything. I..." Sol considered her question. How had he felt right before the fall? It was a complete haze now, like a faraway dream he forgot as each day went by. "I felt the sky give way beneath me and then there was this light."

And a great deal of pain. Like a body he didn't have was being ripped apart and sewed back together.

Mira was nodding and hunched over her journal again. "The previous star was from the northern kingdom... uh..."

"Kentlim," Gareth supplied and came back to camp, knife safely tucked into his belt again. He didn't sound angry anymore, at least.

"Yeah, that place. Wish we could have gone to check their libraries." She capped off the sentence with a flourish and peered at Loren. He shrugged. "All borders are locked up. We tried to go across once, but no one was at any of the outposts and we're not silly enough to sneak around. You get shot full of arrows that way."

Nebora winced. "Saw that once," she said. "Decided it wasn't worth hopping over."

The conversation slowly petered out as Mira returned to her journal. It wasn't long afterward before Sol found Gareth staring at him again with the same intensity. Loren must have noticed it too; he glanced between them quickly, but before he could intervene, Gareth was speaking.

"Where does the scourge come from?" He tapped his wrist as he spoke and Sol felt his own heart thump in time with it. "It's called an Umbral Cycle because of the darkness it brings, but further research into scourge has taught us nothing."

"I don't know."

Gareth narrowed his eyes. "I think you do."

Maybe Sol lied too fast. Everyone stilled, but Sol remained impassive. Gareth knew *nothing*.

"Where do *you* think it comes from?" Sol asked as innocently as he could. "Research must have found something."

Mira piped up immediately, putting Sol at ease despite the annoyance flashing across Gareth's face. "Theocratic scholars posit it's some collective sin against our fellow people," she said. "Do enough bad and *something* in the Onyx Spire overflows and mutates into scourge. Then there's the initial waves of scourge of the Barrens which is formed enough like it has a mind of its own, but then it slows and grows dormant until it's ingested. Still just as deadly."

Gareth eyed her warily. "You sure know a lot."

Though he'd sounded suspicious, Mira met it with a grin. "I have to make sure I have all my facts straight! Loren snuck us into many a library."

Loren sighed. "Don't tell that to a *knight* of all people."

"Why would I care?" Gareth snorted. "Surprised you found any left standing."

"As for what scourge actually is..." Mira tapped the end of the pen to her lip in thought. "I honestly haven't found any texts that supply a solid answer. It's a dark mass that can flood whole towns like water, can crystallize and glimmer, and even appear as goop in the grass. When wildlife eats vegetation that's been infected, it warps even the most docile into the most violent. They never attack each other though—all the ire is aimed at humans." She frowned deeply and eyed Gareth. "When humans are infected..."

"They die," Sol said, refusing to look away from Gareth. "A slow, painful death. Or, they become hosts for the scourge. Neither an ideal outcome."

Finally, Gareth broke eye contact and rubbed his wrist. Sol had to stop himself from shivering as it made his own blood hum. Like Celena, Gareth would die. Only his would be a much more gruesome affair.

Some way to treat a supposed hero.

"What's in the Onyx Spire?" Nebora asked.

Sol shrugged. "I wouldn't know."

Nebora leaned back and sighed. "Should have figured. We don't even know," she said softly. "No one guarding the Barrens' gates let anyone through and those walls are nigh unclimbable. When the heroes *do* come back, they only talk about their adventure. Not what's out there or what really happens."

"I'll write all about the Barrens!" Mira said, smiling. "I'm not going to miss a single detail, I promise!"

Endearing words, but in the end when Mira was dead and gone, she'd have no way to protect her tale—if it even got far enough to be told.

"What took you so long to fall?" Gareth asked.

Sol stiffened.

"It was ten years," Gareth continued. "Ten years since the scourge swallowed all the immediate towns. Other stars didn't take that long—not according to the stories."

No answer Sol gave would be satisfying enough. The truth would invite more scrutiny. He stayed silent and stared at the fire instead, wishing it would swallow him whole so all the questions would end.

"Oh." Gareth's voice dripped with ire. "Did you run out of words again?"

"Drop it," Loren said and Gareth glared at him. "I think it's time to retire. It's late and we want to leave at first light."

Nebora groaned like it was the last thing she wanted to do. After she'd gotten it out of her system, she collected the plates and mugs. "I'd really hoped we'd get into Planar Village for more supplies at least or another feast," she said. "The closer we get to the Barrens, the less there will be."

"I'll take first watch," Gareth said. "Can't be too careful even here."

"Not a bad idea. I'll take second," Nebora said. "Gives me time for a beauty nap."

"Then I'll take the last watch," Loren volunteered. He nodded at Mira and Sol. "You two rest up for now, all right? We'll work you into a watch rotation later."

Sol opened his mouth to protest—how hard could watch be?—but Mira touched his arm. "Shush," she said. "Watch is dead boring. Sleep through it until we can't."

Nebora snickered from their supplies as she packed up the plates and mugs. Her laugh only evolved as Mira collected her lute from beside her and danced over to Nebora's tent. She rolled her way inside before Nebora could stop her.

"Your lute's too big!" Nebora complained. "No—you're near the edge with that thing. Shoo!" Mira's giggles echoed out as she was rolled around inside like it was a game.

How warm and loving they were to one another made Sol smile, but he immediately wiped it off his lips as panic shot through him. He had no idea which tent he'd be in. He glanced at Loren's—small—and then at Gareth's—larger. It was the one Queen Celeste had requisitioned and she must have intended for them to share it. Sol went cold.

"You can sleep in mine," Gareth said, noticing the panic, and got up to stretch. "I won't mind."

Sol's throat tightened. He felt the arm around his waist, making his blood sing. The way Gareth had pressed close until all Sol could feel was him.

"Mine has more room," Loren said.

Gareth raised his eyebrows and glanced between the tents. He scoffed. "It does not."

"Do you want him to sleep on your armor?" Loren tilted his head almost mockingly when Gareth snapped his jaw shut. "Or do you sleep in it yourself? Can't be too comfortable."

Of the heroes, Gareth wore the most armor. It still gleamed like it had when they left the castle and Sol honestly thought it had been for show, but then he'd kept wearing it. All a silverish white with Queen Celeste's heraldry of a sunburst engraved on the breastplate.

Loren glanced at Sol. "Unless you wanted to sleep in his tent. Your choice."

Sol shook his head. "Yours is fine."

Loren's tent was rather small, barely enough room for Sol's small bag and for them both to sprawl out in, but Sol was not about to complain. Thankfully, he never did sprawl out much; according to Celena, he tended to curl up tight when he slept. Loren had a bundle of furs layered on one side, but he didn't take them. Instead, he took the other side where his bag was. He slipped off a few pieces of his leather armor, leaving him in his tunic and pants, and laid with only his cloak and sword.

Sol hesitated and attempted to give some of the pelts to Loren, but Loren pushed them back, shaking his head. "I'm fine," he said. "Mira always hogs it all, so I'm used to it. I won't need any until we get closer to the Barrens."

Maybe the warmth from furs and blanket would help Sol sleep. They smelled like Loren. Leather and some kind of flower. Maybe a yarrow. Sol wouldn't know, but he liked it. He afforded himself one deep breath to memorize it and then curled up within it to will himself to sleep.

It didn't quite happen.

The firelight danced against the tent fabric, but the heat remained outside. The cold sunk deep into his skin, making him tremble, and part of him wished he'd just slept beside the fire. Maybe then he'd stay warm. Even if it meant being alone with Gareth.

He must have dozed off briefly at some point watching the light. One moment, he listened to the whispers of the stars against the crackling of the fire, and then the clink of Gareth's armor jolted him fully awake. His shadow passed Loren's tent and went to Nebora's. His voice was soft when he spoke to her and then Nebora was replying with a mighty yawn. She padded out, letting her shadow stretch across the camp, and Gareth's shadow disappeared into his own tent. His armor clinked again as he settled in to strip it off and then it ceased. The fire became brighter and the aroma of coffee floated through camp.

Loren rolled over to his back with a quick glance in Sol's direction and he flinched. Sol watched him, curious about the reaction, and a quiet chuckle bubbled out of Loren's throat. "Can't sleep?"

Ah, he'd been checking to see if Sol was asleep. "I have a question, actually."

Loren raised his eyebrows. "Hm?"

"Why'd you offer your tent so readily?"

That caught Loren off guard. He studied Sol, his mouth trying to work, but no words came.

"Gareth's tent is the one Queen Celeste had given us to use. It *is* bigger," Sol amended. "Even with his armor... so, I'm curious."

Loren inclined his head to gaze out of the crack in the tent flap. Nebora was humming to herself, a low husky song not unlike the one Mira had been strumming on the road. There was no sound from Gareth.

"There are rumors about Gareth," Loren said it so quietly, Sol had to lean closer to listen. "He gets... handsy. Nebora's already keeping an eye on Mira."

Handsy. Sol rolled the word over in his mind. "What does that mean?"

Loren's face tightened. "He enjoys touching

people, whether they want it or not."

Touching people. Yes, Gareth had done that. Sol replayed the motions in his mind, trying to understand why someone would enjoy doing so. Humans and stars were fundamentally different, but here and now, he had a human body to touch. If he wished, he supposed sex also wasn't out of the cards. Realization shot through Sol. *That* was what Gareth had wanted. That was why he hadn't mentioned what Sol had done in response because then he'd have to admit *why* Sol had done it at all.

"Oh." The word vocalized without his intention.

Loren faced him faster than Sol could pretend nothing was wrong. "*Did* he do something?" It was the same question as before, asked so earnestly and concerned.

"He..." Sol struggled to order the words in his head. "He pressed me against the wall and... tried touching me before I came to find you in Arcridge. He—I didn't realize it was like that—I just... I don't..."

"It's all right. You did nothing wrong." Loren looked like he'd intended to reach out, but kept his arm against his side. "He's the one who doesn't keep his hands to himself." Loren propped himself up on his elbows, raising his eyebrows like an idea struck him. "We can ditch him. Nebora and I already have a plan for it."

"No," Sol said quickly, shaking his head. "He'll find us. That scourge will find me. I don't want you or anyone else hurt."

"You don't think we can take him?" Loren asked, but he was amused, not angry.

"I don't think Mira can," Sol said quietly. "I just... it's easier this way, yes? He won't give chase. He won't attack us."

Logic and reason were sound, but Sol wished he'd just said yes. Especially since Loren watched him so sadly; it felt like he'd said something wrong.

Loren settled back down and nodded. "As you wish," he whispered. "But if he does anything else... please, tell me. I won't let him hurt you or touch you especially if that's not what you want."

"I will." Sol burrowed himself back into the furs. "Thank you."

"Try sleeping again," Loren said, closing his eyes. "Long walk tomorrow."

Sol watched him, wondering if he simply wanted Sol asleep so he could slip out and speak to Nebora. If only it was that easy. Another question plagued Sol, one he wished answered before he attempted sleep. For a moment, he hesitated— wondering if he really needed the answer, and then decided yes, he did—and reached out to touch Loren's arm.

"Did that happen before?" Sol asked as Loren glanced at him. "The touching, I mean—to the other stars?"

The pause wasn't reassuring. "I don't know," Loren admitted. "All we know is what's in the ballads and stories. I don't think they'd admit to it if it had."

More concerning than Sol wanted to admit. No one cared about the stars, even when they brought light back to the world. Names and who they were lost, not even bothered to be remembered. All their joy, their pain, everything that made the stars who they were gone to the folds of time. Thinking about it made Sol's blood buzz and made the whispers past the trees even more stark.

Until Loren patted his hand, the touch feather-light as though he was afraid to spook Sol. "You're safe with me, Nebora, and Mira," Loren whispered, his green eyes bright in the dim light. "We won't let that happen to you. I promise." He smiled softly and it melted the ice caging Sol in. "Rest. All right?"

"I'll try."

He let Loren pull the blanket over him and huddled deeper into it. Exhaustion ate away at his desire to remain alert and he hated his body for it. As a star, he'd never had to sleep. He simply *was*. But the longer he was human, the more exhausted he was. Perhaps, when stars fell, it kickstarted their process of dying.

Thinking so chilled him more than he wished, but it was what let his thoughts slow and empty. What helped him the rest of the way was when Loren sat up for his watch and reached over to tuck him in. From his lips hummed the same tune Mira and Nebora had sung before. It left Sol smiling.

Loren was... safe. That was what Sol decided before he fell asleep entirely.

"Through all the days and years, we followed her.
Into the darkest caverns where light never touched;
to the highest peaks to hear the stars whispering above.
But we heard no voice, like it had been hushed."

—Fragment of "She, Born of Starlight," Anonymous

EARLY IN THE MORNING, BEFORE THE SUN HAD EVEN attempted to rise, Sol couldn't pretend to sleep any longer. It invited too many maligned thoughts and he wanted peace. He crawled out of the tent and stilled seeing Loren by the dwindling fire. There was no reason to hesitate aside from the flutter in his stomach when Loren glanced at him. Sol couldn't go back inside to hide now and instead, ignored it and sat beside Loren. He couldn't deny, however, how the small smile at the edge of Loren's lips made his heart sing.

They sat together as the veiled morning sun crawled into the sky, sending meager sunrays through the trees, until Loren stood. He latched his sword to his belt and went over to peek into Gareth's tent. Curious. Sol watched him with raised eyebrows.

"Hey, you have an extra sword, don't you?" Loren asked.

Gareth's mumbled reply was too garbled to understand, but Loren came back with a short sword.

"Come on." Loren beckoned him up. "Let me teach you how to use one so you can protect yourself."

Surely using the scourge in Gareth was enough protection, but since Sol intended to keep that power to himself, he took the offered sword. It was heavier than the one Celena had taught him with, but swords couldn't be *that* different from one another. Loren considered him a moment before he turned toward the trees nearby and beckoned him in. Sol was nervous leaving the fire, but his feet happily trailed after Loren without conscious thought.

Alone in the trees in the predawn light, Loren appraised him up and down before he finally spoke. "Give me your best stance."

Sol thought back to Celena's lessons. She'd stood with grace and poise; shoulders straight, slightly turned to make herself a smaller target, and she'd kept one hand behind her as the other held the sword aloft. Sol mimicked her stance, remembering her gentle touches when she'd corrected him, and watched Loren expectantly. Loren's eyebrows lifted and he tapped his chin with his fingers.

Loren smirked. "I see our princess taught you something."

"She did," Sol replied.

"This is a different kind of sword."

So it was; her sword had been long and thin while this blade was flatter and thicker, not to mention much shorter. Sol frowned.

"I bet hers was a dueling sword. Just for thrusting. That one can slice," Loren explained as he drew his own. The blade gleamed in the early morning light, clearly taken care of despite its plain simplicity. "Let me see what she taught you."

Not enough to win by any scope of the imagination, but Sol enjoyed surprising Loren. Celena had always told him it was best to use his stature as a weapon. Sure, he didn't quite have the reach of knights across the castle or Loren himself, but he made up for it in swiftness. He'd managed to touch Loren once with the blade near the beginning, but every other attempt was easily thwarted because his stance grew sloppy or because the grin on Loren's face made him forget he was practicing. Sol didn't even mind the physical exertion, especially when they both slipped off their cloaks so Loren could properly see and adjust Sol's stance. The ghost of his touch mimicked Celena's and Sol had to stop himself from shivering, feeling the touch anew. Gently on his shoulders, on his arm, even on his hips as Loren turned them. Sol wouldn't have minded doing this all morning had a twig not broken near them, jolting him back to reality wherein they were never really alone.

"You're teaching him how to use a sword?" Gareth was leaning on one of the trees, a mocking eyebrow raised. "I thought it was for Mira."

Loren's jaw tightened. "Mira has her crossbow. She doesn't like swords." He dropped his stance and Sol did too, realizing their dance was over. "Figure it'd be useful he knows how to protect himself."

Gareth rolled his eyes and pushed off the tree. "You're swordplay's sloppy."

An obvious bait. Loren held Gareth's gaze, like he dared the knight closer, but nothing happened. Eventually, Loren eased a sigh through his nose and smiled.

"Not all of us have the esteemed training of the Norian Knights." The words dripped with sarcasm and Gareth huffed. Loren sheathed his sword and glanced at Sol. "I think we worked up an appetite, don't you think?" He waited, hopeful eyes cast in Sol's direction, and Sol hastened to nod. "I bet Mira cooked us up something yummy."

Enthusiasm and good cheer all but evaporated with the new audience. Sol gathered their cloaks and handed Loren his. Gareth watched them move, but Sol pointedly ignored the knight. He didn't matter. Right now, breakfast did.

Mira had made oatmeal and spiced it with copious amounts of cinnamon from Arcridge. The smell was magnificent, especially since Sol had definitely worked up an appetite. Even better, it was warm in Sol's empty stomach.

Breakfast, unfortunately, was quick. Varros was packed just as quickly and they didn't linger in the haven any longer than that. A dreary road awaited them.

Sol bid the now hidden stars goodbye and followed everyone out of the trees to continue their journey.

Finding the haven at all was the high point of the trek. The following nights weren't so lucky. Darkness pressed in at every camp, the scourge murmuring so loud in Sol's ears he couldn't sleep, but morning always came and with it another soft sword lesson from Loren. Soon, however, all the soft mornings juxtaposed themselves to the death lining the road on both sides. If not travelers laid open for birds feasting on the infested carrion within, it was animals slaughtered because their owners had found evidence of scourge. While the carcasses lay still now, the scourge continued living in the wounds, waiting for its next host or reason to rise. Each time they came across either, the darkness glittered within like a dozen stars and it whispered his name, reminding Sol of everything he'd promised.

There was no end to the whispers. The scourge had burrowed into the ground, making the grass black and brittle, and even whole trees lay barren as the scourge hung itself from branch to branch, like a mockery of ribbons.

After the first camp in the haven, they had no choice but to set up close to the roadside with their tents huddled so close to the campfire. Sol and Mira took watches together and Sol did not like them one bit. Time crawled by in silence as they listened to the shifting scourge around them in the distance for a potential attack. Her crossbow always sat in her lap and Sol had his short sword in his. Dawn came so slowly some nights, its rays of light sallow across the dark, and no matter which watch he and Mira took—always the first or the last—he greeted the morning exhausted. Still, he never said no when Loren suggested swordplay practice.

Sol wasn't sure how much he retained from their lessons, but he supposed it didn't matter. Loren's skills may have been sloppy (although Sol couldn't tell and nor did he care) and Sol may have been slow to pick up the nuances of their dance, but he was happy during these stolen moments as fleeting as they were.

Every time they finished, Sol's body buzzed in peculiar ways. Loren always had a soft touch Sol refrained from leaning into, and his voice was soothing every time he corrected Sol or even praised him. More smiles than Sol could count graced his lips and the lessons let Sol forget about the world and what he'd planned to do. He only wished Gareth hadn't interrupted them every single morning. Loren's mood always sharply changed, locking up the kind man he was, and Sol hated it.

No one had asked about stars again, thankfully, and Sol largely kept to himself as they ate food around their campfires. The rest traded stories when they trusted the distraction, but it was always superficial. Always a happy ending while their eyes tracked the darkness.

This far out, towns and villages were distrustful of travelers. The few left standing who let them stay probably only did so because Gareth still wore the Queen's heraldry, but they still checked everyone's eyes and balked seeing Sol's. Proof he was indeed their dull, uninspired savior. No feasts awaited them here. Steady indifference disbelieving Sol brought hope of any kind despite his nature. He didn't blame them given how long it'd been since the scourge took over the lands this far out. Whatever semblance of hope the world had closer to the castle was absent.

There were just as many towns starkly empty or were burned husks of their former selves in an attempt to destroy the scourge. Wells in such places were filled with scourge—it was too deep in the ground to burn away completely. Once, as everyone else searched for survivors or supplies, Sol had taken a handful of the scourge from the well and concentrated on separating it from the water. Idle curiosity, really, but he was astonished when it *worked*. Scourge bled away like ribbons with his concentration and all that was left was clear water.

He didn't quite trust himself to share what he'd found—he was hesitant to accidentally infect anyone else while there was still a journey to be had. He supposed it didn't matter; water was easy and human bodies were not. Besides, he wasn't here to cure the scourge. He was here to end everything.

But perhaps he needn't bother given the state of the world. Maybe it was as Nebora had said: one day, humanity wouldn't come back. Maybe this *was* it, no matter what Sol did. The other lands couldn't be faring any better.

Sol didn't bother counting the days they walked;

he only took solace in the fact each day brought them closer to the Onyx Spire. Closer to the phantasm whispering his name. He eventually tuned everything else out, letting the voice fill his body with how it hummed. It made walking easier. Dulled the pain. Let him ignore the travelers with their chests carved open along the side of the road. The ones where everything had been pulled apart, letting scourge thrive within hollow skin where the only mercy was a swift strike to ensure the person they'd been was already dead.

He only fully tuned back in when they passed swathes of farmland curiously kept alive. Crops flourished, ready for a late harvest. Animals grazed nearby in the pasture without a care in the world. The hum had quieted to a distant murmur and Sol picked his head up. No trace of scourge as far as he could feel.

The others noticed the shift too; Mira immediately approached the pasture fence and cooed at the nearby cow looking her way. It didn't come any closer and continued chewing on grass like the world wasn't ending. Just as well. Even Varros seemed more at ease.

The farmstead past the fields had smoke billowing out of its chimney, further lifting the spirits of everyone. Evidence of life surviving and for some reason, even Sol's heart was glad to see it.

Merely because it was growing late, Sol was sure. Good place to stay out of the elements.

Nebora and Loren headed over with renewed vigor, Gareth hanging back to watch the road, and Mira dragged Sol after them.

"Hello?" Nebora called out as they approached. Loren knocked, loud and heavy, and the sound reverberated through the home. No one answered. Nebora turned the handle and pushed it open. "Sorry for intruding—but—"

Mira and Sol were pushed away too late to save them from seeing what was inside the doorway. Blood was smeared across everything, glimmering from the smoldering flames the in the hearth. The floor, the ceiling, and the walls were covered and it haloed the two bodies lying there. Decapitated and gutted. Human blood was so vibrant without scourge. The sudden fascination made Sol's stomach churn and he didn't resist as Mira yanked him backwards. She vomited into the grass first and Sol's body joined her, even if his thoughts had scattered, leaving him too numb to understand.

Gareth rushed past them only to stop just inside. "Shit," he hissed.

"Not even from the scourge," Nebora whispered. Though Sol's stomach had finished emptying,

Mira was still retching. Sol gently rubbed her back like she'd done for him.

"What were they even after?" Loren asked.

"Maybe people were fleeing from somewhere else wanted help and got told no." Nebora came out and gazed across the farmland. "Altercation got heated and these two were killed. It must have been recent if the animals are still alive..." She tightened her jaw. "Maybe it was those we saw with scourge on the roadside."

There had been so many of those; Sol wasn't sure how Nebora could tell them apart.

"None of them had anything on them," Loren said. "Just their clothes."

"Must have been desperate and then ashamed at what they did." Nebora sighed.

Gareth swallowed and looked away. "Damn it all."

"We should burn their bodies," Loren said. "Before scourge gets them too."

Least they could do. Those on the roadside had been too far gone to save beyond a few mercy kills to make sure. These two, even without the heads, could be filled and controlled according to the darker stories Sol had heard in the castle. As though to make noise, Mira shakily told Sol about the time she, Loren, and Nebora had come across a small village where everyone had been infected with scourge. Their bodies had been broken and their minds too far gone to expect Nebora's axe or Loren's sword.

Nebora and Gareth wrapped the bodies in fabric found inside the house while Sol and Mira were in charge of searching the place for anything useful. Avoiding the mess in the foyer, they started in the attic, where the couple's bed had been. There was hardly enough room between the two of them up there, especially with the sloped ceiling, so Mira took one side with the dresser while Sol stripped the blankets off the bed.

"We used to bury the dead," Mira said, gently rummaging through the drawers. "You know, so we could sleep with Lovian until they were ready to wake. Then, we found out scourge can retake a body, no matter how bloated as long as there was a way to make it move. We burn them now and bury the ashes."

She suddenly stopped, taking in a sharp breath, and sat on the stripped bed. She was shaking her head and had squeezed her eyes shut. "I can't do this. Sol, I can't do this."

Sol peered over; inside the top drawer were children's clothes, sized for a newborn. He hesitated, realization dawning on him, and then gently shut it. Even in the darkest days, human life attempted to continue. Not knowing what to say or do, he sat beside Mira, letting her have a moment, and managed to hold still as she leaned against him for support.

There was nothing useful up here beyond the blankets. When Mira collected herself, wiping her cheeks and blinking back whatever was left, they climbed back down and checked the kitchen pantry. Not a lot of food, but they took what would hold up. By the time they'd finished, Nebora had the bodies outside and laid upon the logs Gareth had dragged from the side of the house. The pyre was complete.

Loren was returning from the animals, shaking his head.

"They've all got scourge," he said.

Sol looked over and felt the buzz so suddenly, he was shocked he hadn't noticed it before. "What should we do?"

No one answered, but they didn't have to. Nothing deserved what the scourge would put them through. Not even the animals. There was one option and Loren went back alone.

The fire burned bright and stark against the dark skies and gray lands. The animals had gone down swiftly by Loren's blade. Sol hadn't been able to watch or help for that matter. Nor had Mira. She'd dragged him to the other side of the house and bent low to cover her ears so she didn't have to listen. It shouldn't have mattered, but seeing Mira react so twisted Sol's stomach so tightly, all he could do was bend down with her and wait until it was over. Then the animals went up in flames right by their owners.

Without anywhere else to go when the sun finally set, they resolved to stay in the farmhouse. Nebora cooked up what meat she found free of scourge inside and they ate in silence, doing their best to ignore the mess of blood still stark in the foyer despite Loren and Nebora's attempt to cover it. Sol and Mira got the bed upstairs while Loren, Nebora, and Gareth made something to sleep on in the kitchen. Even though they had shelter, they still took their watches. This time, Sol and Mira went first and Sol didn't like it. They sat together in the home's doorway, sword and crossbow at the ready, and watched the omnipresent dark.

It felt long, it was cold, and Sol was too nauseous to find much solace in silence this time. He wanted the bubbly Mira back. Just to get out of his head.

It never happened.

When their watch ended, she remained a ghost of her usual self as they curled up in the lone bed. Sol never found sleep. All he saw were the bodies. The way they lit up in the bonfire. How sad Loren had looked dragging animal after animal back with

Gareth.

At this point, whatever Sol did would be a mercy for humanity.

"Grass glittered in her wake, growing flowers aplenty,
    like the world itself bent toward her magnificence
and hoped to be touched by her divine grace.
    Even the wildest of animals bowed their heads in reverence.
And yet still, she found no voice,
    never once."

—Fragment of "She, Born of Starlight," Anonymous

DAWN CAME TOO SOON, BUT SOL WASN'T SURE IF HE wanted it any later. As it was, he was *still* exhausted, pieces of him pulled so taut and thin he thought he'd break soon enough. No one spoke over a meager breakfast and then they were on the road again.

Past the desolate farm, the land had gone flat, too flat, and Sol could clearly see the glittering spire along the horizon, past the treetops. The star shined there out of the dark, almost suspended in place. His bones sung with her as she whispered to him in such sweet honeyed words, wishing for a resolution.

Every step toward her renewed his promise of an ending for her.

The trail they followed led them to a riverside town the farm must have provided for. The walls around it were wooden posts tied together, still whole, but inside, the buildings were rundown. Scourge lay across everything and so did blood. Nebora freed her axe, swords were drawn, all before Sol's body hummed with the mass of scourge hidden inside the looming shadows.

It was fixed to an elk rising from its crouch in the middle of town. Blood was caked into its matted fur where sharp, white bones stuck out at odd angles. Its jaw was missing entirely and the lack of it transformed its mouth into a gaping maw where blood cascaded out to stain the ground below. The eyes were gone, replaced with scourge and within the inky darkness, glitters bloomed like stardust. The elk roared, the sound a gurgle from deep within its torn throat, but it was loud enough to make the nearby buildings shake. It charged, heavy hooves pounding the ground, and Nebora, Loren, and Gareth met the challenge just as fast.

Mira immediately hid Sol and Varros behind an overturned food cart nearby where food lay scattered with rot and bits of scourge. Sol yanked Varros away from what he immediately went to nibble on and Mira hugged the mule's head close. While she kept him still and calm, even as swords swung and the elk screeched, Sol peered around to watch.

The beast was fast and easily shucked off all paltry strikes. Even when Nebora swung a leg off, the scourge righted itself with a new leg made of dripping darkness and she narrowly dodged its attempt to trample her. Gareth's attacks were precise, lodging his sword again and again into the poor beast's flank where it should have had an effect, but each time the blade was taken back, the scourge wrapped the wound up. Loren moved swiftly, striking his sword across its skin and with each strike, Sol somehow felt closer to Loren. Like a piece of him was carried through when the blade came away. Intoxicating, despite the pain.

As though upon the acknowledgement, the connection came. It wormed itself into Sol before he could stop it and rooted itself deep inside his head. Each slice the heroes took carved him through the same, like ghost blades plunging themselves in again and again. Each strike made him flinch, made his vision spot with pain, and he wished for an end as he barely kept himself together.

The battle wore on, becoming more about endurance than brawn, and strikes finally made an impact. Wounds festered as scourge became too slow to sew its diseased skin back together. Blood spilled across the street as reds and blacks ribboned together. The less that healed, the more open and raw the wounds felt on Sol's own person, even as his skin remained unpierced.

Finally, as though answering his prayers to finish it already, Nebora launched Loren at the elk's head and he pierced his sword right through the poor beast's skull.

The hold the scourge had on the elk snapped like it had been the thinnest thread. The sensation shot through Sol too, letting pain cascade through his body like a wave, and he fell to his knees as the elk did. He slumped behind the food stall, barely able to help himself, and turned to vomit. All the pain, all the nausea—everything his body had to give came out his mouth and spilled across the grass.

And in the vomit was glittering scourge. It oozed through his fingers as he tried to catch the next retch. No. That shouldn't be happening. It gleamed in his hands like tiny stars against the night sky. His heart sped with the whys and it was in that moment he let Mira get close.

Mira's eyes widened and as she began to rise, Sol yanked her back down more forcefully than he'd meant to. She clattered against him with a grunt.

"No." His throat was almost too raw to speak.

"Please. Do not tell them."

Mira hunkered as close as she could and she drew her flask free. She popped it open, even as Sol watched her in confusion, and yanked the scourge ridden hand over. "Loren can help," she whispered as she poured the ice-cold water on his hand.

She was helping him hide it. The realization took the air from Sol's lungs.

"He can't." Sol wiped his trembling hands clean. Mira's face pinched and he shook his head again. "Please. Th-This is what I am—what all stars are. We *are* scourge." Mira's eyes grew wider. "All of this scourge you see everywhere? It's the previous star."

Mira touched his hand. "No," she whispered. "No. This—this has to be wrong. We have to tell Loren. We can change this—we can—" She suddenly dropped her voice as Nebora and Gareth bickering over the elk petered off. "Let me tell him."

And then what? he wanted to ask. If they refused to take him to the Onyx Spire to reset the cycle as they should, he didn't know what he'd do. He *needed* the spire to keep his promise. Before he could answer, or consider if Loren would listen, Loren was calling their names. Varros picked his head up, ears flicking.

Mira hopped up and brought Sol with her. "Here! Safe. Varros is good too." She jerked the mule away from the same scourge laden food and dug into her bag for a distraction. "Varros keeps trying to eat the damned scourge, though."

Gareth eyed them as he wiped the scourge from his face, suspicious. Loren at least looked relieved, his face already cleaned. Nebora took the stained cloth from Gareth and wiped her axe clean before discarding it all the same. It'd never be clean again.

"Well," she said, her voice a little winded. "Town's saved."

Loren's expression changed so sharply, Sol's blood went cold. "We didn't even have to come in," he snapped and Nebora glared at him. "There was nothing in here to save and yet you fucking ran in."

Nebora huffed and straightened her back. "Like you didn't want to take it down. You've been itching to do something substantial. And besides!" She threw out her arm in frustration. "It would have noticed us—you know that. We were already too close to get away without a fight."

"And what if one of us had *died*?" Loren yelled, making Sol and Mira jump. She tugged Sol closer and shook her head at him. She didn't want him to get involved. Not that he wanted to. Gareth looked between Nebora and Loren, silent with his eyebrows high in amusement. For once, he wasn't the one being yelled at.

"Nebora," Loren lowered his voice, begging her to listen, "we saved *nothing*."

He wasn't wrong. The town was long gone. Dead. Cold. Bodies likely eaten away by scavengers or the scourge itself perhaps. Buildings barely held on as it was while scourge hung from broken windows and masses spilled out from doorways. Any supplies they found here would likely be infected. If Sol had noticed the elk sooner—and he surely could have if he'd bothered to try and pay attention—he could have helped them avoid this.

Nebora's glare darkened, but it just as soon lost its edge when Loren breathed out and looked away. "Mira," she said, tired, and Mira glanced up from giving Varros an apple. "Just say we saved someone when you write about the fight."

Gareth perked up. "Oh, and don't say it bowled me over." He held his side and winced. "Gods, that's going to bruise."

"Give them hope," Loren whispered, not looking at anyone. "Don't tell them everyone and everything was already dead this far out."

Hope. Even if it was a lie. Mira nodded, but didn't reach for her journal. She glanced at Sol, squeezing his hand, but Sol shook his head. No one had made a connection between stars and scourge this long and he wasn't going to let them. There was too much at risk.

Mira led Varros around the cart, letting go of Sol's hand, and he dutifully followed her, never once looking back at the scourge he'd left in the grass. No one would know. It hummed at him as he left it, the softest sound, but he didn't know what it meant or what was happening to him. Maybe this was what happened to stars desperate to cling to life. Those who believed in soft smiles humans gave.

Gareth gazed across the town and his expression tightened. "Guess we should see if there's anything we can take," he said. "Our supplies are running thinner every day."

So thin, Gareth had stopped buffing his armor to a sparkle. It still shimmered under the sun at certain angles, but it was dirtier than it had been.

"I agree." Nebora wiped her hair back and pointed at Sol and Mira. "You two watch the road. If anything shows up or you just feel something wrong, have Mira whistle. I'll hear it no matter where I'm at."

Mira nodded. "Got it."

Loren, Nebora, and Gareth fanned out, each taking a section to search, and Mira and Sol were left at the lone well in the center of town. No scourge was bubbling in the water, thankfully, and Mira brought up the bucket to refill all their flasks. As Sol was concentrating on his, he found Mira watching him too steadily. He raised his eyebrows.

"How do you know?" she whispered. "Th-That this is all the previous star? What does it mean? N-No one ever said what happened to her. Or even the others."

Too many questions. Sol's thoughts itched and he had to keep it simple. "I don't truly know," he said. "After this many cycles, people still haven't made the connection between stars and scourge. I'd rather keep it that way."

Mira gave him a hard look. "Why? If you don't want to let us change something, then what are you planning?" She asked it so directly, Sol froze. "You poisoned—"

"I did not," Sol snapped, anger flushing his face, and Mira flinched. "When Celena caught me, I wasn't even me. I was literally scourge from the stars. That's why whoever catches us dies. It is no fault of mine humans refuse to understand and write it off as them being delicate and weak. Refuse to do anything to stop the cycle on their own to stop us from falling."

"Is the previous star alive then?" Mira asked meekly. "The heroes all came back. Did they leave her in the spire all alone?"

Sol's heart ached from her sincerity. She wasn't angry; she was aghast at her fellow humans. The ones who claimed themselves heroes over and over in legends and songs. Each time, they returned without the star and told their tales full of life and heart. The same stories she took as truth were lies, leaving out the end that would change everything. He didn't have to answer her; realization worked across her face on its own. The reality of what all the heroes before them had done.

Mira covered her mouth and shook her head.

The itching in his thoughts hadn't subsided. Sol winced as he turned, trying to clear them. It felt like something literally crawled beneath his scalp. Somehow between himself—the real sensation of his body—and his thoughts.

Then there was a hum. His eyes grew wide, his whole body stiffening, and Mira looked past his shoulder.

Everything happened too fast to meaningfully react. She screamed, lurching forward, but hands as black as the sky gripped Sol from behind and hurtled him backwards. The hum of scourge vibrated through him as a screech when he hit the ground. Its voice overrode all other sound until Mira let loose a crossbow bolt. It hit nothing but a blackened wall growing behind Sol. The scourge cut off from the elk had pieced itself back together with bits of bone and flesh keeping it whole.

He tried moving, heart hammering too fast in

his chest, but hands shot out of the black. One hooked his hair, yanking him close, and the others grabbed him all over until a million eyeballs opened along the wave. They stared at him, each a brilliant white, and the wall swallowed him, consuming all he was.

Mira's whistle, loud and piercing, became an echo lost to a discordant hum. The scourge tried wrenching his body apart, but it was too whole. Then it filled him from the inside out instead, crawling out a cry from his throat, and connected him to everything. Like he was a star again.

Except this felt wrong. Like needles across his skin as he brushed up against whatever the scourge touched all around him. Blotches of thoughts and feelings of those infected flew through him, overriding his own. He pushed against it. Once. Twice. So many times, he lost count until he managed to tear himself out of the scourge, gasping for breath somewhere dark and wrong. It didn't last long before the scourge surged again and drowned him.

He couldn't feel his body. He had to find it. It was his and scourge couldn't change that.

Find his thoughts. His mind. His physical body—the one Celena had given him. The scourge he'd left behind—the piece of himself left dead and glittering in the grass—called out first. Unhelpful as it was, but it led him to another piece of himself. The one he'd left in another singing so softly. The dark streaked with colors as he reached out to touch it. The heartbeat he knew so well was slow against his. The fingertips dipped in glitter as his star scourge had worked its way through her entire arm.

Celena.

He felt her there, inside him. Outside of him. One and the same. She opened her eyes and exhaled. She lay in her bed, her brown curls haloing her head against her pillows. Her lips were a pale violet now as scourge made them glitter. She'd turned pale and gaunt, the veins so bold against her skin. And yet still, she smiled when she noticed Sol. She stared at him so clearly, he really believed he was at her bedside. Trembling, she touched a hand to her chest.

"There you are again," she whispered. "I love you, Sol."

Before he could whisper the same, her heart stopped.

Sol ceased fighting the scourge. He let go, leaving her and everything else in the room— someone yelling her name, Alyssa rushing to her bedside, and another handmaiden leaving to tell the Queen—to fade into the ripples in the dark. His body lurched, pain dragging across his skin like even it knew he shouldn't have been there, and it spat him out, body and all. Reality returned in a rush, leaving him severed from the scourge completely.

He gasped again, drawing in a real breath for his starved lungs, and opened his eyes. He was in a room he didn't know. Too dark to make out anything substantial, but at the same time, he didn't care. Even when scourge hands ripped his arms painfully back, securing him to the chair, he did not care.

Because tears blurred his vision and sparkled down his cheeks.

Celena was dead.

A door scraped open and Sol lifted his head. He could barely see until a woman came in with a flickering lamp. Scourge writhed across her form, the lamplight making it glitter like a star, and her mouth parted with a smile. Scourge spilled forth from between her blackened lips, coating her exposed jawbone, and dripped into the hole in her chest.

"There you are," she said, her voice gurgling out of her throat. "Sol of the Cosmos."

"Winds sung her arrival into lands unknown.
Lands ravaged from humanity's aggression.
She helped those displaced and inquired if they'd heard the voice.
And still, no one had an answer to her obsession."

—Fragment of "She, Born of Starlight," Anonymous

THE SCOURGE SUNG WITH A SONG INUNDATED WITH so many distinct hums, they played deftly one another like they'd always been connected. Like Sol was among the stars once more, except his song was fractured now. The pieces too jagged to fit together. The more Sol listened, however, the more the scourge warbled, fraying. No. Not together. Made to feel that way as they were forced together by another hand.

This was wrong. He snapped himself back to the room and studied the woman who sang like the stars. Her body was dead and the skin would have sloughed off the bones and muscle if not for scourge piecing her back together. What was worse, *she* controlled the scourge. With one flick of her hand, the scourge on the walls leapt to close the door for her.

She shouldn't have been alive, much less able to command the scourge.

Her milky white eyes were absent of all color as she watched Sol. Scourge slid down again from blackened lips and she gently wiped it with a soiled sleeve. She wore a rag of a dress once bold with blues and blacks and a blouse once a pristine white now stuck to her skin like wet paper, soiled with blood and scourge. Bones stuck out of her ribcage, piercing through the dress because the scourge didn't understand the human body as it threaded her together any more than she understood the dead stars when she'd threaded *them* together. Her hair was gently braided over one shoulder, starkly blonde and clean despite all the dirt and grime.

As she drew her skirts around herself, the scourge shuddered beneath her. Even pieces of Sol wanted to move to the woman's silent command, humming under his skin, but he pushed the desire back and bit down his anger. She was using his dead brethren—many of them, it seemed, from throughout the cycles—as a thing to sit on. A *chair*. She happily lowered herself down and crossed one leg over the other.

"Hello, little star twinkling vibrant in the dark," the woman cooed, if it could be called such with how her throat tried and failed to vocalize her words with clarity. She sounded more like she was drowning on air. "So very, *very* bright."

"Untie me," Sol said.

She raised her eyebrows and leaned languidly back. "No. I think not, my dear."

It'd been worth a shot. "You know my name," Sol said and tried to even the trembling in his voice. From anger and not fear, he insisted to himself. "What should I call you?"

She blinked, revealing a hazel color behind the foggy white before it washed back out. She rested her jaw on her hand. "Meredith," she said. "Meredith of the Cypress Moor."

Not that Sol knew *where* that was, but he nodded. "Why am I here?"

The scourge writhed at an unheard command and the song within turned violent and bright as it brought Meredith closer. It stopped her short of pressing her knees to Sol's and the rags of her skirt ghosted around him. With a hand still mostly skin—scourge having only eaten away the nails, leaving wells of purple glitter behind—she drew her fingertips along the faint line bisecting Sol's cheek.

"A star like all the others come to cleanse the world of the dark," she said. "Ten years ago, the dark came. It flooded over the Barren walls, taking without a care faster than it had cycles before. And yet, all is silent now and you walk amongst a dead world. It waits for you." She tilted Sol's head to follow hers. Sol tensed, gaze flicking downward, and found the gaping hole in her collarbone where scourge kept her heart beating. "Curious."

Meredith traced her fingers down the other side as Sol refused to reply. The tip of her finger dipped under his jaw and followed the line down the middle of his neck.

"W-What are you?" Sol asked.

She withdrew her hand and tapped her jaw. "A scholar, of sorts. Years before the dark came, I and a team of others sought to research scourge found in the darkest caverns. In the highest mountains. We learned as much as we could, keeping our samples close, and then the Sixth Umbral Cycle began and we had so many more pieces to work with." She leaned back and crossed her legs. "We built our theories upon scholars of old who tried the same but died before they mattered. Before transcendence." The scourge pulled her back and settled her comfortably away from Sol.

"And you've learned to control it," Sol whispered.

Meredith smiled, scourge coating her lips again. "It's quite malleable once you stop fearing it." She raised her arm and the scourge around them strained to follow it, their song breaking.

"It's eating your flesh," Sol said. "Humans are not meant to touch us like this. It *will* kill you before long."

"Oh, what a liar you are." She clicked her tongue and the motion sent another cascade of scourge bubbling out of her lips. "Stars were never meant to fall, and yet here you are with a stolen human body. We are both anomalies existing when we shouldn't. One day, I suppose, the lies may kill us both. But why fear the dark?"

Talking to her was useless. Whatever twisted reason she had for all this didn't matter; Sol had to get out. And he knew a way. She wasn't the only one who could control scourge. It coated the walls, the window, everywhere in the room at her behest, but its voice reached Sol with curiosity. A mix of honeyed whispers and dying gasps of those before still clinging to a life stolen from them. Recognizing him as one of them. The binds holding him still softened into friendly touches exploring his skin.

Meredith didn't notice.

"I can continue this path." Meredith's voice cleared into the one she must have had before all the scourge. "With you, I can control it *all*. Wipe everything and build the stars as they were."

"These stars are dead," Sol said.

"Are they now?"

"When we fall, we begin dying," he argued. "Whatever is left behind is corrosive—our deaths made manifest as something tangible. Whatever you do with us—whatever pieces you've forced out of slumber for this—it's not building us as we were. It's parading around our dead husks. This is sick."

As much as he wanted it to be true, these were not those he'd once been nestled beside in the cosmos. They were echoes of who they'd been, hardened into scourge and then left behind when the light returned. They would never again be who they once were.

Meredith's face twisted into a sneer and she spread her arm toward the darkness dripping off the walls. "We could cleanse the world on a fundamental level. Bring down the barriers and truly be free of all this pain."

"Why?" Sol asked in a desperate bid to keep her talking and distracted. The scourge still held his arm too tight despite how soft it was. He needed more time so he could convince it he was truly a friend. That he'd let them rest whereas she would not.

Her smile returned and she eyed him up and

down. "The world has done us no favors. The stars and I are practically the same."

Sol bit back from wasting his breath explaining to her the differences between a human infected with scourge and stars. She was too delusional. Helpfully, the scourge binding his arms finally let go and Sol forced himself still lest he give it away. His brethren gently kissed his skin, leaving behind sensations of who they'd been. Fragments of different lives threaded together all on the will of one supposed scholar hoping for transcendence.

"Again and again," Meredith continued, shaking her head, "we follow these cycles of light and dark. I've tracked it and through everything I could get my hands on, it has never changed once." The scourge fixed to the wall hummed with her, their song turning hopeful. It was too far out of reach for Sol to convince it otherwise. "Except for now." She sat back and the scourge shifted her chair, their muffled cries beneath her. "We can end it, don't you see? Humanity is at its tipping point."

It couldn't be this way. Whatever plan she'd tricked herself into believing wasn't freedom from the cycle. She was forcing the scourge to act on her whims. Another kind of prison. A lack of understanding of what humanity already did to stars. It would simply cause another star to fall and the cycle would begin anew.

Meredith giggled, the sound reverberating through her chest. "Aw, my little star, don't look so scared. I will not end you. I've been waiting for you since you left the castle."

"Since I left the castle?" Sol repeated softly.

"The scourge told me you'd left and I knew you'd come by here because it's the safest road to the Barrens. All I had to do was wait and welcome you when you arrived."

Sol swallowed. "You killed the whole town."

Meredith rolled her eyes with a huff. "Well, I *had* to. They would have attacked my elk otherwise." A trickle of scourge escaped behind one eye and made a line down her face. She wiped it away and flicked it into the ground. "I merely helped them along to their eventual demise."

Eyes opened along the scourge nearest her. Grotesque shapes and sizes, each one blood shot with white sclera. Not the black of stars; a mockery matching Meredith's own. Sol refused to look at them, maintaining his eye contact with her to show no fear, but his body betrayed him and had begun trembling. He was no closer to escaping.

"Star scourge from something alive is truly remarkable. Have you noticed? It's the piece we're missing. With it, I can remake this whole world."

Sol's thoughts went right to Loren and Mira. How much they didn't deserve the darkness she wished. The darkness he himself wished for. He slowly exhaled, trying to even his voice. "You'll kill everyone, then."

"Everyone left me to die when I manipulated the scourge to help us," Meredith said, the good candor in her voice gone to ice. "Left me bleeding out on the road after striking me through. It was our noble purpose and they abandoned it when they deemed *me* the monster."

"And you think this makes your plan just?" Sol's anger made him raise his voice and Meredith narrowed her eyes. "To use me and mine like tools to unmake the world? You are no better than the rest of humanity!"

The scourge shoved Meredith to her feet and before Sol knew it, her hand had struck his face. It came so fast and hard, the scourge lax against his arms tightened anew to keep him from falling. His vision spotted and the room spun as he snapped back to look at her.

"You understand nothing!" Scourge flew from her lips as it augmented her voice, pushing it into a screech. She hit Sol again and again as she repeated herself. Each strike shot white hot pain throughout his entire face, spiderwebbing from his cheek up into his head. Only when he couldn't help but flinch at the oncoming strike did Meredith see fit to cease. She gazed at him, eyes clear and wide as though daring him to speak again.

He didn't. His vision had gone blurry with pained tears and blood trickled down his chin from a cut lip. His breathing had grown shallow and he took a few deep breaths to even it. When Meredith remained where she was, he peered at her from behind the hair had had fallen across his eyes. She watched him another moment and finally sat back down.

Then there were footsteps.

They went across the scourge and echoed into the room. Meredith flicked a glance upward and a smug smile warped her face.

"Oh, I think I understand it now," she whispered. "You've grown soft for them. Like that little princess who stole you from the sky?" Her smile only widened, cracking the stain on her lips. "But you know she's gone, right? You felt it. I did as well. I listened to her heart give when I chased you there. You've no reason to deny me. She's dead."

Everything else—the pain, the broken stars pieced together, how close everyone was to finding them—became so small and distant as Sol stared at Meredith. There was so much glee in her voice.

"She did not steal me," Sol said, his voice breaking.

"She plucked you out of the sky," Meredith said and stretched the words. "Stopped your catastrophic fall and caused your body to rip itself apart to mold into her desires. Barbaric." She leaned back and laughed. "Why else would a star's scourge affix to those who catch them? It's simply revenge from your primordial state." She leaned forward and rested her chin on her palm. "Did you love her? Do you think she loved the real you?"

Sol's voice was too heavy in his throat to answer.

"Did you think she'd see the light again?" Meredith's face twisted as her smile only grew. "If she survived much longer, I daresay her eyes would have been next."

"Stop," Sol forced out. "You know nothing about her."

Meredith pouted. "So, you *do* care about her then? All those humans who will care not for you when they rip your body in two? Fold you into the Onyx Spire until all you can do is vomit scourge years from now?"

Sol took in a sharp breath. "You know what happens."

"Sometimes buried legends can be unearthed— not that anyone wants the truth when it's hard to swallow." Meredith tilted her head. "And yet, you still deny me. I wish to change your sorry ending while everyone else believes the lies heroes tell. Why can't you understand?"

"It's not up to you," Sol said.

"And why should it be up to you?" she screamed. "This world isn't yours. It should be up to us. *Me.* It should be my decision how the world ends, not a star who has hardly walked the earth!" Pressing a hand to her chest, the scourge buzzed beneath her bones as a dissident chorus to her anger. "*I've* walked the earth. I know what the world needs. What we *all* deserve."

"No!" Sol shouted back despite himself. "You are holding my brethren hostage for this madness and I am tired of humans using us as tools." He flung an arm free and the scourge sung across his arm with the warmth of a fire. Her eyes went wide. "I won't let you hurt me."

All of Loren's lessons flew through Sol's head as he freed his short sword, but Meredith was just as quick; scourge fashioned itself into a blade around her hand and she swung. The scourge had to tear him out the way. He caught the next strike on his short sword, but his blade shattered upon impact. Once again, his dead brethren tore him out of the path. He slipped backwards, dodging a wide slice, and touched the chair he'd been tied to. With a mere request, the scourge propelled it at Meredith, but it became splinters as her blade cleaved it in two. Sol let the scourge lead his legs, dodging her strikes singing through the air as a cry.

What he needed was a weapon. Something solid. As though hearing the plea, scourge latched around his arm. A smaller blade formed, the only thing his concentration could fashion, and it met the end of Meredith's. Each strike made the scourge on both ends cry, but he had to keep going. His movements caught up to all the lessons in the soft mornings and became fluid. She was still quicker. Had a more practiced hand, but the scourge was beginning to resist her.

And the longer he held the scourge, the more it peeled off the walls to aid *him* in glittering bursts that became shields from her strikes. Breathed lives he never knew into his lungs for a second wind. Flashes of hope and belief—of stars who sought to do good. Those who wanted to save the world and help their dead sibling at the same time, only to cry out when their end came so abruptly.

He'd be the same. A single cry snuffed and gone once the adventure was over. His will faltered, but his dead brethren yanked him to one side. Meredith's blade singed his cheek and he hit the far wall as the scourge overcorrected him. Eyes bright with fury, Meredith approached him, but Sol was faster. The darkness surged by his hand as a wave and blew her back. She hit the door she'd come in at and the force erupted a cough from her lungs. More scourge spilled across her as she heaved herself back to her feet.

Sol gripped the scourge around him with all he had until the hymn it made together burned through his head. He would not be the same as the stars before him and it certainly wouldn't be by *her* hand. The darkness flaked off the scourge around his arm, revealing a glittering brightness below not unlike the stars hidden from view. Meredith gasped, her ghastly face lit up, and Sol hesitated.

The door opened. An axe took Meredith's head clean off—no time for a scream or a prayer—and Sol dropped the scourge as fast as he could, leaving it as blackened ash at his feet. Gareth shoved himself inside, sword drawn, but there was no more threat. Even still, he stared at Sol so intently, not even looking away as Loren came in next.

Gareth had seen it. He must have the way his face steeled in the light of the tipped lamp. Sol looked away to avoid him, but that only drew his attention to the scourge flaking off literally every-thing. Sol gasped and held his hands out to stop them.

"D-Don't breathe it in," Sol said, choking the words out as his heart pounded hard against his chest. He hadn't realized how dizzy he was or how weak his lungs were.

"Holy shit." Nebora lifted her gaze and covered her mouth. One more yank and her axe was free, scourge and blood marring the blade. Sol couldn't bring himself to look at the body sprawled on the floor. Not where her head had landed. He fixed his gaze on Loren alone, desperate.

"It's all scourge." Loren pulled a cloth from his tunic and held it up to his mouth.

Gareth glared at Sol. "What did *you* do?"

Sol shook his head, trembling. "N-Not me. Her." His eyes darted downward. One second and it was all he needed to see she was very, very dead. Crimson blood ribboned with black. "S-She was controlling the scourge." Nebora's eyes went wide and Loren grew still. "S-She killed the town. She was waiting for us."

Gareth finally gazed at the body. The scourge writhed under his stare, screeching unheeded, but then he kicked it. Her body fell apart beneath his boot, silencing everything, and Sol couldn't help it when he flinched. "How long has she been doing this?"

Gods, this man and his questions. Sol seethed as he swallowed air. He was only comforted when Loren edged between him and Gareth. "S-Since before the cycle began anew."

"Did she say why?" Loren whispered.

"She wanted an end," Sol cried. "Everything to end so the cycles would stop." He felt out for any lingering scourge. The hum in the walls had grown so soft and quiet, dying as their will inside Meredith was spent. Hopefully no one would disturb them this time. "So everyone ended but the stars she unearthed."

Nebora narrowed her eyes. "Stars she unearthed? What *is* the scourge? You know, don't you?"

The answer was right there in front of her if she bothered to *look*. Within her grasp if she just thought for one moment. And yet still, Sol clammed up, shaking his head. He couldn't trust them. Heroes who lived and breathed the old stories. Where stars didn't matter. Their cries below the earth ignored until they spilled out all they had.

Gareth advanced on Sol and Loren tensed. "What were you doing with her?"

"I was not here of my own volition—she forced me!" Sol's voice broke. "*You* must have seen it! I—"

"All I saw was you disappear into the *scourge*," Gareth yelled over him and Sol snapped his mouth shut. "How did you do that?" He took one step closer, bones softened with scourge crunching beneath his heel, and Sol pushed himself back to the wall to maintain his distance. Loren never moved. He stayed steadfast between them like a shield.

"Loren," Gareth growled. "Move."

"No," Loren said, his voice calm.

Gareth glared at Loren so darkly, Sol thought for sure he'd strike. "He's *lying*." Gareth sheathed his sword. "You know he is." He emphasized each word with a finger jab into Loren's chest. Still, Loren did not move. Gareth glared at him for what felt like an eternity before he turned. He kicked the body again and Sol flinched despite himself, pain igniting throughout his torso. He was only glad when Gareth left to head back up the stairs.

Nebora watched Sol too, suspicious, but then she breathed out. She hoisted her axe over her shoulder and went after Gareth. "Mira!" she yelled. "We're coming up! Don't shoot me!"

"Or me!" Gareth bellowed, his voice making the room shake.

Sol meant to hold his head high, follow them up, but he couldn't breathe. It came out in spurts, mangled gasps, hardly able to draw in air. Everything hurt so absolutely. He wanted to curl up and cry. Bury himself in scourge and end it here.

It wasn't until Loren came closer did Sol realize he'd been speaking. Only when he touched Sol's shoulder did reality slot back into place through the buzz in Sol's head.

"Sol?" Loren whispered. "Are you all right?" He looked at Sol's face and frowned. Taking the cloth covering his mouth, he risked breathing everything in as he gently pressed it to the cut on Sol's cheek before putting it to Sol's lips. "Didn't know stars bled white."

Nor had Sol. Loren let him have the cloth and Sol stared at it. Glistening white even. Like a star. His gaze darted to the embroidery around the edges. Celena's careful stitching.

Without meaning to, tears streaked down Sol's cheeks anew even as he tried to rationalize them away. It didn't work. He began sobbing. Quiet and choked until his whole body rattled with them. It wasn't helped when Loren pulled him in so suddenly, arms tight around him. Not the hugs Celena had given him—chaste, delicate things—but all-encompassing and safe. Warm.

"It's all right," Loren whispered into his hair. "You're safe."

That wasn't it. Sol shook his head. "No," he choked. "N-No. It's..." He swallowed, the act making his throat burn. "She's dead. Celena's dead."

Loren froze.

"I felt her die." The words slipped out.

Loren pulled away and held Sol steady. When Sol didn't look up, frozen instead with the words out in the open, Loren gently turned his chin upward. Loren wasn't angry or suspicious. He was worried. "How do you know?"

Mira trusted Loren absolutely. Sol trusted her and Loren with his life as much as he could. He had to tell him. He swallowed and pressed the cloth to one eye to dry it. "Stars *are* scourge. It was how I could go *through* it. When Meredith was dragging me here, I felt myself in Celena. I felt her heart give out because it was my star scourge that killed her." More tears came, his face crumpling, and he shook his head. "It's why those who catch us die. I knew it was coming, so why am I crying so hard? I-I don't understand."

It wasn't a shock. He and Celena had both known she'd die before he reached the Onyx Spire. Yet, his heart was torn in two. The tears wouldn't stop. He wouldn't see her again. Her smile. Her warmth. The way her eyes twinkled in curiosity. How soft her hands were when she guided him through the gardens. *Her.*

Loren pulled Sol in again, his arms stronger this time, and they stayed together in the blackened

basement of a house full of scourge until Sol managed to pull himself together. Nebora and Gareth
were upstairs, digging through the place, and yelled
back and forth at each other while Mira shouted
from somewhere outside.

"How'd you know I was here?" Sol asked to
ignore everything else.

Loren parted and nodded upward. "Gareth could
feel you like you said. Just took us longer than it
should have because there was so much scourge." He
turned his gaze around the room. "Might be best to
burn the place."

Sol gripped Loren so suddenly, the man jolted.
"Don't tell him. Her. Don't mention anything about
what I can do with the scourge. Mira already knows.
Just not them."

Loren paused as his eyes grew wide. "You mean
Gareth and Nebora."

"Yes," Sol said. "Please. I-I don't know what
they'll do. Please. Just... don't."

Confliction wrapped Loren's face up tight as he
started and stopped perhaps a dozen sentences. It
was unfair, given the history between Loren and
Nebora, Sol knew that, but he held fast. Loren
exhaled through his nose. "I won't," he whispered.
"Listen, Sol—"

His name—how Loren said his name just like

that with all the softness in the world—made Sol's entire body shiver on the inside, but whatever he'd meant to say cut off when Nebora's voice boomed from above.

"Come on out you two!" she shouted. "Let's burn this place down and *go*. I think I know where we can camp!"

The small house lit up in bright flames within its hideaway past the scraggly trees. Everyone watched it burn golden in the growing dark. All Meredith was and her secrets gone with her. The scourge turned to ash with everything else, silent as though it had never sung, and all Sol heard was the murmurs in Gareth's arm crying out for its dead brethren.

"Months and years hence,
with tears in her sparkling eyes, she had to know
if she'd been mistaken.
Her companions could not bear to see her so
and helped her float beneath the stars
to seek guidance from them once more."

—Fragment of "She, Born of Starlight," Anonymous

THE HOUSE HADN'T BEEN FAR FROM THE EMPTY town and the elk. No one talked on the way back and no one spoke still as Nebora led them to the riverbank past town. They followed it upstream and Sol's pain ebbed the farther they went. Old magic traced his skin gently as they went, afraid to spook him, and he gazed into the water. Pure. Protected from the scourge with magic sunk deep into it, or rather... Sol looked forward. Magic floated downstream from somewhere ahead of them. Perhaps it was why the well had been clean. The place would have been blessed if Meredith hadn't let her elk loose.

The more they walked, the less scourge clung to the trees. Foliage thickened around them and flowers sprouted in bundles for any sunlight they could find. They passed a sign Sol didn't bother trying to read before Nebora hollered happily and sped forward.

"A hot spring!" She extended her arms wide as they followed her past the sign. "My father took us here when I was a kid. I knew I recognized the land! And look: no scourge!"

Trees bent protectively over the spring, each willowy branch suffused with magic as it touched the surface of the water. The largest tree in the far back practically twinkled as the magic within ghosted through its roots and branches. Scourge would never touch it—not for years yet—and Sol smiled at it.

Another haven.

"Before we set up permanently in the Swallows, my dad would bring us all here after a hard day's work. We'd laze around all night and no one bothered us," Nebora explained.

Gareth scoffed, eyeing the water suspiciously. "Hard day of *looting*. I know who your father was. That was not work."

Nebora quirked an eyebrow. "And you know he'd wipe the floor with you if he still lived. I'm sure even I could." She waved a dismissive hand at Gareth, cutting off his next remark. "Missing the point, Knight Boy!" She faced everyone as he bit down and glared at her. "Look, I know for a fact that after this, we'll be lucky if we find a town not covered by scourge. We should take this moment after all that shit to get a nice soak. Barrens aren't far now."

Mira perked up and Sol was glad to see it. She'd been so quiet since Loren led him out of the scourge house. "Yes," she said and patted Varros beside her. He'd already started to chew on the grass. "Varros likes it too. Maybe we could give him a good wash."

Nebora snickered. "Why thank you for volunteering, Mira."

Her eyes went wide. "Wait—hold on!"

"It's your idea! You get to do it!"

As Mira and Nebora bickered—Loren announcing he was staying out of it—Gareth turned away from the spring. Everyone's good cheer paused as they watched him.

"I'll keep watch then," he said. "Someone has to. Give me Varros before you send him into the water with all our stuff." He held out his hand for the reins.

Nebora snorted and put her hands on her hips. "Didn't take you for a prude."

"I'll set up camp down over there," Gareth said, pointedly ignoring Nebora, and led Varros down the path until they were past the brush surrounding the spring.

Nebora rolled her eyes. "Fucking men."

Loren chuckled. "I'll help him set up." Nebora made a confused motion at him and he shook his head. "I'm coming back—I promise! I'd like to find us something to dry off with—gods know we grabbed enough from the farm; we might have something." Nebora rolled her eyes. "I know you're made of harder stuff, but I think Mira and Sol would appreciate being dry afterward."

"Definitely," Mira cut in.

"*Fine*! Be sensible!" Nebora set her axe down with a thunk and rolled her shoulders. As the creaks and cracks worked its way out of her, she turned a mischievous grin on Sol. "Well, Star Eyes? You look like you could use a soak. You in?"

✦

THE CASTLE BATHS HAD BEEN QUAINT LITTLE rooms housing porcelain tubs filled with hot water. The heat steamed the whole room, making it fuzzy, and Sol had liked spending time soaking there all by himself. The privacy had been nice. Now, while the heat wafting up from the hot spring rivaled that of the baths, it wasn't as enclosed and privacy certainly did not exist.

As Mira dug into her bag, mumbling about using

something for cover, Nebora held no such qualms about modesty. She stripped off her clothes, leaving them in a small heap, and jumped right in with a big splash. Mira dragged blankets free from her bag—ones liberated from some poor town they'd passed—and gave one to Sol.

"In case you're shy like me," she said. Before Sol could insist otherwise, she'd undressed as quickly as Nebora and had herself wrapped in the cloth. She hurried into the water like so and waded in until she was covered from the shoulders down, all the while ignoring Nebora teasing her about how red her face was.

Though Sol had wanted to insist he was not shy, embarrassment wormed its way quickly through him as he began to undress. It didn't used to be this way. Human bodies were more or less similar, after all, but as he undressed, he thought of Loren doing the same. His entire body warmed too fast for his liking at the mere image. He quickly wrapped what Mira had given him around his midsection and decided it would be enough.

He was tempted to go in as deep as Mira for more privacy—water was now up to her neck—but he hesitated. She had short hair. It would dry very quickly. His would not. The air was too cold away from the spring and he didn't want to risk his hair freezing overnight. Not that Nebora seemed to care the way she swam under the water, but perhaps what Loren had said was right—she was made of harder stuff.

Instead, he perched on his rock, where water sloshed up past his stomach, and kept his hair out of harm's way. Sol was content here. He tried to empty his mind of all sorts of worries and focused on the magic lingering across the water's surface. It whispered soothing words he didn't understand. Maybe someone had comforted the first star here and the action coupled with her magic to make a lasting impression. She'd likely bathed in the same place long ago with her heroes. A welcome connection across time, it calmed him and bled the pain from his body. It might have even lulled him into a nap if he hadn't heard movement at the shore.

Loren had slipped into the spring. Ripples carrying magic brushed against his naked skin and Sol's traitorous gaze peered downward. Loren had covered himself too. Probably for the better, given how warm Sol's face felt that he'd gone to look at all. He tracked his view upward anyway, never once straying from Loren as he gave in to the desire to memorize the man.

Faded scars from fights long gone marred Loren's skin, but then there was the splash of freckles across most of his shoulders and chest. A small tattoo of a yarrow was at the base of his neck, only noticeable when he turned to Nebora to say something. Selfishly, Sol wanted to trace it with his fingers to memorize it.

The thought of doing so left Sol flustered and he immediately forced himself to look up at the darkness above. He only caught Mira's gaze doing that. She'd lifted her head from the water, eyebrows high, and shot him a smug smirk. He resisted the temptation to go over and splash her.

"Hm?" Loren noticed him and smiled; Sol's ears grew warm. "Don't want to swim? I won't let you sink if you're worried."

"No—I just..." Sol gently touched a strand of hair already wet. The rest was over one shoulder, helpfully out of the water.

"Oh, your hair." Loren waded closer and somehow, Sol grew even warmer. He waved at Sol to come over and continued smiling. "Here, let me tie it up for you. I had a lot of sisters who showed me how to do their hair—bet I can do something high enough."

"Tie it with what?" Sol asked.

Loren brought up a hand, showing the faded string bracelet on his wrist that Sol hadn't noticed before. Loren glanced over at Mira who was watching them like it was the most entertaining thing in the world. "You mind if I use it, Mira?"

"Go right ahead! I can always make you a new one when this is all over. I'll make you one too, Sol."

Sol hesitated, even as Mira was nodding toward Loren, eye contact solely on Sol like she would have pushed them together if she could. His heart buzzed in his chest, making his mind race, as Loren gently peeled the string off his wrist. Loren beckoned him again and Sol's limbs felt detached as he forced himself closer. It was better when Nebora resurfaced and turned Mira's teasing look away. Sol lowered himself into the water, dragging his hair up before it touched the surface, and turned around.

Loren was gentle as he drew all of Sol's hair back. The touch of his fingers along Sol's scalp, the nape of his neck, and all the areas between sent a soft pleasure coursing through his body. Curious sensation; Celena's fingers had been pleasurable, but not quite like this. Loren gathered the hair into one hand and lifted it off the nape of Sol's neck. The warm air of the spring kissed his skin, giving him goosebumps, but Loren didn't comment as he diligently worked.

He twisted the hair, pulling it taut, and threaded it through the string a few times until it became a small bundle above Sol's neck. A few wisps here and there still tickled Sol's neck when Loren let go, but the rest of it remained out of water's reach. Part of Sol wished Loren hadn't let go, but he immediately dashed the thought. Not the time for that. He gently touched what Loren had done and found Loren smiling at him still.

"Better?" Loren asked.

The smile melted through Sol and he nodded, unable to do much else but let his lips follow the motion. Loren headed deeper into the spring and settled into a spot against the rocks forming the sides of the spring and Sol followed him over. The water went up to his shoulders and on Loren, a little lower. Mira gave Sol another sly look as she passed them and this time, he gave in and splashed her. She cackled, dodging into Loren's other side, and Loren snickered.

"She'll splash back," Loren said.

Mira was all grins as she lowered herself in the water and Sol resisted another splash. "It's really nice here," she said. "I wonder what else the first star enchanted. I wish I knew her name."

So did Sol.

"Was it only her that made havens?" Mira asked. "Or can you do so too?"

It was a good question, but Sol had no answer and shook his head. Mira grew deep in thought, face scrunched, and Sol settled softly against the rocks behind them. Could he? He thought of the way the blackened scourge had flaked away before in Meredith's house, turning into something bright and warm. Almost as warm as the magic here, but it wasn't the *same*. Then again, the first star was also quintessentially different.

In the end, however, it didn't matter what Sol could do with it.

The three of them were quiet, thinking too hard on such little information, and a dark shape swam up to them. Nebora emerged from the water and threw her hair back in an arc. Mira clapped for the display and mystified, Sol followed suit. It only made Nebora smile as she wrung out her hair with both hands. Water trickled off her muscles and curves, outlining them vividly. She had more scars than Loren, but across many of them were geometric black tattoos matching the circles and flowers on her shoulders. A careful patchwork of art borne of battles long past.

"Is Gareth really going to be a stick in the mud?" She gazed past them, toward the flickering fire just past the brush. "Didn't even bring us Varros."

"Varros decided a nap was better than a bath," Loren said and Mira made a relieved sound. "I asked Gareth if he was sure, but he didn't really answer me.

Maybe he's hiding how far the scourge has moved up his arm."

Mira frowned. "It's not like we'd care."

"Evidently, he does."

Sol preferred him as far away as possible, but kept it to himself.

Nebora sighed and waded to the shore, unconcerned with modesty. "Avert your eyes. I'm coming out!"

Mira laughed so loud, it echoed. "We can see everything already!"

"Then enjoy the view!"

Sol didn't have a chance to decide if he wanted to or not. She was out of the water, swooping up one of the designated towels, and Mira swam around to Sol's other side to settle in, distracting him. She was close enough their shoulders bumped and Sol appreciated the touch. It felt like friendship.

"Hmm." Mira kicked her feet in the water, making ripples, and cast her gaze on the tree shimmering with magic. The long branches swayed, sending its leaves dancing across the surface. "Why do you think the first star had this spring enchanted in particular?"

"I'm unsure," Sol said. Nebora finished behind them and her shadow became long as she picked her way back to camp. Sol slid a smile at Mira. "Although,

I'm sure *you* have an idea."

Loren chuckled and Mira splashed Sol.

"I bet it was a special someone," Mira said. "Seen as how romantic all this is, maybe she wanted to share her love and warmth with them."

A touching sentiment and Sol found himself nodding as he peered toward Loren beside him. Loren was watching the ripples in the water thoughtfully, his face soft in the dark, and Sol once more resisted the urge to trace it like he'd done so many times with Celena.

Thinking of her at all stole some of the warmth away. He'd tried so hard not to, but there she was. He swallowed and groped for words to continue the conversation.

"Is—" He hesitated as both Mira and Loren looked at him. "Is there anything written about her? The first star?"

Mira pondered a moment, drumming her fingers against her chin. "I always hear snippets of what people call her quintessential ballad, but it's fragmented. Like someone cobbled it together from retellings. Maybe the other lands have more—like wherever she fell—but it's not like we can travel past the borders right now."

Loren hadn't taken his eyes off Sol. "Do you know why she fell? It wasn't dark then, right?"

Stories about her fall were whispered through the cosmos from star to star, but they were as vague as the ballads down here. "She heard a voice," Sol said slowly. "She was curious and wanted to help whatever it was. So, she threw herself from the cosmos. Anything more tangible, even the stars don't know."

Mira considered him for a moment. "Why did *you* fall?"

The question sent Sol's heart racing and he stared at Mira. "Pardon?"

"Hear me out." Mira put her hands in front of her. "We are told stars fall because they hear *our* suffering in the darkest night. Whoever listens— whoever truly feels our plight—falls to aid us. But I want to hear your reasons from *you*."

From the perspective of humanity, her reason for the fall was a warm tale to tell in the dark when nothing came. It made sense. "There is crying, yes," Sol said, honesty bubbling into his throat. "But I don't think it's humanity's cry."

That made Mira pause and Sol didn't have to look to know Loren had the same concerned expression. Admitting it to humans made Sol un-comfortable; he should have kept up the pretense. As he tried to decide how to backtrack—change what he'd just said—Mira began to nod.

"Not a perspective I've heard, but it's not like anyone has truly asked the stars. We just assume." She smiled, but it was an attempt to bury the unease settling across them from a simple honest answer. "I think I want to jot that down. I'll even go make sure they're making dinner while I'm over there, so feel free to soak some more. I'll come get you when it's ready." She flicked a glance so quickly to Loren then held Sol's gaze, eyebrows high.

Sol had no idea what the motion meant.

Mira wiggled her fingers at them and as she waded toward shore, Loren gently turned Sol away from her. He understood that motion, at least; not everyone was as bold as Nebora, and Sol looked away to give her privacy.

"We're first watch, Sol!" Mira called out. "Don't let Loren keep you forever!"

Loren snorted and gave Sol a look. "If you want to get out, I won't mind."

Sol shook his head. "I like it here." He tucked himself lower in the water. "It's warm."

They went quiet, relaxing against the rocks, and only when Mira announced her departure did Loren's gaze travel back to Sol. Not at him entirely like the way Sol had been trying not to and failing to do to Loren, but rather at his face.

"I'm curious," Loren said, "what are the lines

for?"

"Lines?"

Though Loren looked like he was about to reach out to touch Sol—and part of Sol wished he had—he pulled his hand back and instead, traced his fingers along his own face. From the bottom of his eye, curving around the cheek, and then outward toward his ears.

Sol felt his own face and a chill touched his fingers. "Oh," he said. "I'm sorry—I forget they're there."

"They go farther than I thought," Loren said.

Sol's entire body warmed thinking of how Loren must have noticed them much more starkly when he'd held his hair up. How the line went down his back, traced his hipbones. No. Sol shook the thought free and focused instead on the question.

"They're the seams left behind when my body finished forming." He lifted an arm out of the water and showed Loren the line on the inside of his wrist. It went up through the crook of his elbow and followed his arm up to his shoulder. Loren didn't touch it, merely watched Sol's own fingers. Sol tipped his chin upward to show Loren the line from the bottom of his lip, through the underside of his chin, and how it went down his throat and toward his heart. All lines led there. "They're supposed to be thinner and less noticeable, but Celena's mother took her away from me too soon."

"You said forming was painful before," Loren whispered as his eyes traced each line.

"Immensely, until Celena returned and held me." Sol's voice broke saying her name yet again. He blinked back sudden tears, unsure what to do about them or the lump forming in his throat.

"You two really were close," Loren said.

"Closer than we ought to have been." Sol pressed a palm to each eye to stem any tear attempting to fall. "Sh-She didn't think to step away."

"Would it have saved her?"

Sol closed his eyes and released a shuddering breath. "No. It wouldn't have."

Had that simply been why? Had she used knowing she was going to die regardless as a reason to not hide her affections? Sol tried to shake the thoughts away; he didn't want to think about how he'd never see her again. He wanted to focus on sitting in the spring with Loren.

"I heard a bard ballad once about a star a few cycles ago," Loren said, stretching his legs out underneath the water. Sol looked up and found Loren was watching the rustling leaves. "I don't remember from which cycle. The bard sung it like the star was in love with the prince that had caught him and the prince returned his feelings. The prince went with the star on his journey and died on the way." Loren tilted his head. "I think we all sort of know whoever catches the star dies, but hearing it in a heroic ballad of all things shocked people. Made us think too hard. The crowd booed the bard for it, so he amended the tale."

Sol wondered how many stories suffered the same fate. Amended every time they were told, burying details thought too sad or distressing. To make it more heroic than it truly was. Like what they wanted Mira to do if she retold the tale of the elk.

"How did he end the story?" Sol whispered.

Loren shrugged. "He didn't, actually. He wove an entirely different ballad into it before he reached the end. I don't think he could have made a better ending on the spot since there's been nothing written about stars after the journey. So, if the prince lived, but the star didn't exist after the end, then it would have been sad again and he'd be booed all over again. All he knew—all we all know—is stars disappear."

He said it so sadly, Sol wanted to tell him what really happened in the Onyx Spire so he knew. So he could prepare himself, but Sol hesitated. The violent truth was stuck inside out of fear what they'd do if they knew. If Sol blurted it out now, Loren might not take him. The journey *had* to happen. It had to end.

He swallowed the words and cast his gaze downward. Sparkles danced across the water's surface, almost like stars.

"Do you think Celena wanted to come with you?" Loren asked.

"Her mother would have stopped her if she'd tried."

"Do you miss her?"

"Immeasurably." Sol drew his shoulders inward and sighed. "It's not fair. Why did Celena have to die, yet her mother continues to live?"

Loren laughed suddenly, making Sol jump. His cheeks flushed, not understanding what had been funny.

"Sorry," Loren said. "That was just a very brazen thing to say and I don't want you saying it around anyone else but us. A lot of people *like* our Queen despite everything."

"She's a warmonger," Sol argued. "When the world is saved, she'll go back conquering and killing anyone who doesn't agree. No one learns. This happens every time the cycle ends. The world ignores the horrors they endured and becomes the horrors they once were. Everyone good has long since died."

Too close to the truth. To admitting the world needed to not come back. Sol's blood buzzed with anger shooting through him and he clamped his mouth shut, trying to calm down. Loren didn't deserve the burst of anger.

What made it worse, however, was Loren didn't respond right away. Of course not, Sol realized distantly. One of the good people long since dead had been his father. Yet, Loren simply watched Sol with resignment. Understanding. Sol tore his gaze away, breathing in, and Loren reached out to push a lock of escaped hair behind Sol's ear.

"Maybe when this is all over, Mira and I can steal you away before the warmongers eat us alive. You don't have to disappear." Loren stared earnestly at Sol, his green eyes warm. "Nebora wants to go back to her people—maybe Mira will too—but I want to travel. I'd be happy if you joined me." He smiled softly and gently touched Sol's chin. "Think about it. You don't have to answer me now." He pushed off the wall and dunked his head into the water. When he resurfaced, he wiped his hair back with both hands. "I'm going to swim a little. You can join me if you'd like, but I won't be long."

Sol stayed where he was, too stunned to answer, and Loren drifted away as he swam beneath the surface. There was a gentle smile stretched across his lips every time he resurfaced and Sol couldn't help but return it. He liked the way Loren's shape moved beneath the water, and more and more, Sol wanted to join him. Even if the thought of doing so frightened Sol. Blurred a line he'd drawn between them so Sol wouldn't grow attached. So he wouldn't begin to believe in humanity, lest it make his conviction waver.

But what did that matter right now? In a haven hidden from the omnipresent gaze of the previous star?

Sol ignored everything and went after Loren, and was overjoyed when Loren swam back to take his hands to lead him along.

Swimming with Loren made him forget about the world in the dark. The promise whispering to him. The cries left in the burning house. All of it became distant, buried underneath Loren's soft voice as he taught Sol how to swim.

"As though in answer to her prayer,
*   the voice suddenly became a cacophony for all to hear.*
A deep, dark whisper once nothing, now a fevered hymn
*   making the strongest of humanity quake in fear."*

—Fragment of "She, Born of Starlight," Anonymous

THE NIGHT WAS HUSHED UNDERNEATH DARK SKIES glimmering with stars peeking in on Sol. Their whispers slid through his thoughts with ease and he found comfort in them as they mixed with Mira chatting on and on about her epic. He'd missed hearing about her ballad. It was different from the others he'd heard dragged through the castle. Personal. Truer. But perhaps, those ballads had once been the same, only to be fractured each time they were retold until a new version had taken its place.

Mira hummed verses, strumming together sound and pitch until it seemed intentional, and then she'd pause to jot down the notes. Then came stringing the words to it and then to the plucks of her lute. The vibration of her voice as they rested their backs against each other was calming. She watched one way, lute in her lap, and he watched the other, sword in his. The fire blazed at their side, the crackle joining her voice, and Sol was glad it was warm.

Not as warm as the spring, or how warm Sol had felt when Mira was teasing him at the beginning of their watch, but it was comfortable. Everyone else was curled up in their tents, fast asleep. All felt right with the world, like he could once again forget the dark.

Sol began to drift off, eyelids closing too long between blinks, until Mira's strumming ceased and she pushed her back against his.

"You're falling asleep!" she said.

"Lies." Sol pushed back and sipped the coffee she'd brewed earlier. He'd been letting it warm his hands through the mug instead of drinking it. The bitterness soured his face and he regretted not leaving it where it was.

"Uh huh." Mira tipped her head back and rested it on Sol's shoulder. "Need to get you talking!" She grinned teasingly at him before he shrugged her off. "Now, you're absolutely *sure* there wasn't anything more than swimming? I can make room for something steamy."

"Please," Sol said. "I already told you what happened. We *swam*. He made sure I didn't sink. That's it." He left out the little touches, the way his body sang against them, and how he *wished* it'd been more. Gods, what was wrong with him?

"I wanted to write something romantic!"

Sol gave her a withering look and she giggled.

"Fine—fine!" Mira shook her head. "How about this then: tell me more about your life as a star. I want to understand it, you know? Preserve *your* history."

Sol hadn't meant to sigh, but it pushed through his lips. He tilted his head back and rested it against her shoulder. "I don't know how to explain it," he said and there she went, scribbling away in her journal like he'd said something profound. "We have no bodies up there. Nothing tangible like humans. We're just *there*."

"Yet, you're still distinct?" Mira asked.

He could say now with surety yes—they were distinct. He had a body, a mind, emotions never once felt suspended in the cosmos. But it was only through the act of falling that made him real. Something quantified. He shook his head. "I can't answer that because I am fundamentally different now than I was up there. I don't want to misspeak."

Mira went quiet, her pen scratching the paper

for a time. He wished he could read, just to be sure of what she wrote. The sound came to a stop and she straightened her shoulders. "How much of the world did you watch before you fell?"

"Countless years," Sol whispered slowly and brought his knees to his chest. "They blend together, so even I can't say how long. And then, I lost many of those memories when I fell. They bled off me."

"Do you ever get to go home?"

She must have been building to that question given how quickly she asked it next. Sol wanted to tell her the truth that no, fallen stars never return to the cosmos, but he found the answer stuck in his throat. His blood hummed thinking about it, equal parts fear and desperation. Returning was never an option, but he missed it so much. Staying wasn't an option either, but his body yearned for it the same. To travel with Loren and continue existing as he was, dying human body and all.

Mira leaned her head back again. "I don't want you to turn into scourge," she whispered with a sad smile on her lips. "I'm sorry for all the questions. I just don't think a bard has tried quite so hard to connect to a star and I don't want to mess it up. I'm fascinated with what you've shared with me and I want to write something true."

Sol returned her smile. "Thank you for being

curious."

"What do you miss the most?" Mira asked.

"The absolute vastness of everything connected together," Sol whispered and turned his eyes skyward. "Here, we're so small and inconsequential. Although, I suppose I was just as inconsequential up there, but I never thought about it or humanity for that matter."

Humanity never truly crossed his mind until he'd begun his fall. Until he'd been nestled in Celena's hands. Or until Loren smiled at him. Surely, humans weren't meant to invoke these sorts of feelings in a star of all things, but again and again they did. How many other stars fell for the same folly, he wondered. He freed the scarf Celena had tied around his wrist what felt like so long ago back at the castle. The pink was still bright, protected in his sleeve cuff. He'd never be able to return it now.

"But you think about us now," Mira said.

"Too much, maybe," Sol whispered, ghosting his fingers across the fabric.

"Do you miss Celena?"

Sol sighed and hid the scarf again. "Too much."

"What was she like? I didn't get a chance to dance with her." Mira leaned against Sol again. "Was she as nice as everyone says?"

His lips tugged into a smile. "I thought so. She'd

take me for walks in the gardens. Sneak me into the kitchens so we could share treats and spoil our dinner. Tell me legends and stories she grew up on when we couldn't sleep. Never let me feel lonely."

And never would she again. He swallowed, trying to enjoy her memories and not linger on the fact there would be no more of them, but tears stung his eyes anyway.

"When the sun returns, I'll find a garden and walk you through it," Mira said. "I'll read you all the legends and stories you want, too!" She was grinning when he glanced at her and she nudged him. "I'm sure Loren would *love* to go swimming with you again."

"Oh, stop it," Sol said, but a laugh bubbled up his throat. It petered off shortly thereafter as he lingered on Mira's words. *When the sun returns.* Repeating it to himself brought on a shiver and he held himself tighter. "Mira?"

"Hm?"

"What... What happens when the sun does return?" The words sounded heavy on his tongue. Thinking of it at all was blasphemous and he wasn't supposed to care. "I mean... everyone and everything seems to be dead out here. What happens?"

Mira paused and flipped through her notebook. "History says kingdoms tend to offer great incentives to fill out towns left abandoned—especially the farms—and there are always rebuilding efforts. You probably didn't see it, but the capital was rather full. To the point of tents in the streets if they didn't bother to hide them during our march through. People escaping scourge filling the place until the Queen closed the gates indefinitely."

And in time, people made new homes and prospered. "I suppose that makes sense," Sol whispered. "I was curious. Thank you."

Mira watched him, expecting more, but when he offered none, she stretched her arms in front of her. It must have been near the end of their watch and thinking of it let him realize just how tired he was despite the coffee.

Slipping away her journal and pen, Mira stood. "I gotta pee—that coffee's gone right through me! I'll be right over there."

Sol hardly had a chance to glance at where she pointed before she was off. He faced the fire instead and tossed in a twig. It lit up gold as it burned to ash. Talking about himself and everything related wasn't what he'd ever intended to do. Mira had a way of helping him string it together by presence alone. Endearing, if dangerous when he had so much he didn't want to say still.

So much he wondered if he wanted the

inevitable to happen any longer. Loren's smile came to mind, how kind he'd been, and the way it lit Sol up from the inside out. Peculiar, but never entirely unwanted even if Sol found himself vexed more times than he'd like to admit. He squeezed his arms around his knees and rested his chin on them.

Yet, Loren was one human in the face of countless who had left his brethren to suffer. Time and time again—the sorrow, the anger, the complete anguish couldn't be forgotten. One human couldn't fix it.

Sol wanted his thoughts to end on that note, but they didn't. Faith in his promise wavered. *Could* one human make it so it didn't matter? Undo the years his brethren suffered only because he made Sol happy? Something akin to fear coiled in his stomach as the torrent of blasphemous thoughts tumbled through him and he turned his gaze to the dark sky.

"Tell me," he whispered, a prayer to the stars who listened and watched. So inconsequential in human lives. "Tell me, *please*. Just tell me what I should want."

Movement from a tent dragged his attention out of the stars above. Nebora was next watch, but her tent remained shut. Sol turned his head, searching, and a hand gripped his hair tight to wrench him backwards. It was so sudden and sharp, Sol's vision flashed white with pain. He flung his limbs out in an attempt to stop his assailant, but they did nothing and he hit the ground hard. Everything swam as he opened his eyes and by the time he'd recovered enough to react, Gareth had crawled on top of him, pinning him in place. Both hands at Sol's throat.

Squeezing, Sol distantly realized. He thrashed, clawing at Gareth's hands, but the knight's grip was too strong. Gareth lifted Sol's head and slammed it back down.

"What the fuck did you do to that woman?!" Gareth screamed. The scourge in his arm screeched so loud, bleeding into his voice, and Sol tried to grab it—desperate. Every time he felt the connection, however, Gareth slammed his head back down and Sol lost it. "Why is it whispering to me?! What are you doing to *me*?!"

Gareth's eyes were black, scourge leaking through the irises so only black pools remained. Sol shook his head. The whispering wasn't his fault. Any attempt to insist it was cut off. Mira screamed somewhere in the fuzzy distance, but even as she threw herself at Gareth, he shucked her off with one hand. Sol's vision grew darker; he couldn't breathe. More screams joined Gareth's. Words too fuzzy to understand. Distant sounds mixing with the crying of the scourge within.

Then the hands ripped away. Sol erupted into coughs, trying to breathe in evenly despite the pain, and scrambled to get out from underneath Gareth. With a growl, Gareth threw Loren off in one direction and did the same to Nebora on the other side, scourge augmenting his strength, but Sol was out of his reach. Gareth fell back himself, legs folding beneath him, and by then, his eyes were very human. Loren drew his sword and Nebora looked ready to charge him with just her fists, but after a panicked look in both directions, Gareth laughed.

The sound was chilling, completely absent of mirth. Mira dragged Sol backwards and Nebora quickly positioned herself in front of them.

"The fuck is your problem?!" Nebora shouted.

"You can't kill me," Gareth said between breaths.

"No one would find you," Nebora growled. "Give me one reason why I shouldn't."

Again, he laughed and slapped his leg. "Y-You think if you come back without me, everything's going to be all flower petals raining from the damned skies?" He looked between everyone, eyebrows high. "If I disappear—what do you think she'll fucking do?"

Loren and Nebora grew still and Mira gasped, tightening her arms around Sol.

"If you finish this and go back to Queen Celeste

without me, you'll have fucking no one." Gareth's voice leveled out. "No home. No people." He spat the word at Nebora and she gritted her teeth. "*Nothing*. Put the fucking sword down, Loren! I'm not even armed!"

Loren narrowed his eyes and did not put the sword down. "You attacked Sol unprovoked," he said slowly. "What the fuck was that?"

Gareth wiped his nose. Blood had trickled down and stained his lips a bright scarlet. "Something is wrong with this..." He waved his hand at Sol, but wouldn't look at him straight. "This *thing*. He hasn't told us everything and you're fucking falling for that pretty little face." His words slurred and Sol finally smelled the alcohol in the air.

"He's drunk," Mira whispered.

"I'm trying to save humanity," Gareth continued, "not *fuck* the thing that'll ruin it."

Loren's posture faltered. "I am not—"

"Oh, yeah?" Gareth sneered. "All those little private sword lessons? You think I'm stupid? I used that one all the time. Then that swim? Come on. I think we all can read between the lines." He held up a hand as Loren opened his mouth. "Hey, you know what, maybe we can take turns, hm? Get it all out of our system? He's nothing. No one. Who cares what we fucking do to it so long as we get it to the spire, right?"

Nebora shifted and Gareth glared at her. "If you even touch him—"

"Nothing happens to me, remember?" Gareth said and he gave her an unhinged grin. "Or you have *nothing* to return to! All you are is convenient fodder!"

He waited, watching them all, and when no one reacted beyond staring at him in shock, he stood and dusted off his tunic. Another glance was thrown at everyone and after thinking better of whatever had been right there to say, he staggered away. Loren watched him pass, tense, but Gareth kept going until he was on the road for the spring. Mira only let Sol go when Gareth's shambling steps couldn't be heard over the crackling fire.

Nebora eased out a hiss from her lips. "What the *fuck* was that?"

"I just went to pee," Mira said and Sol realized she had tears going down her cheeks. "I-I—" She hiccupped with a sob and Nebora immediately gathered her up in a tight hug.

"No, sweetie, this isn't your fault."

"It was scourge," Sol whispered, his throat protesting the noise. Loren had knelt beside him, sword back in its sheathe, and gently turned Sol's chin up. No longer the friendly touch it had been before, but one more urgent. Sol dropped his hands to his lap so Loren could look. "It's in his head. Warping his thoughts. H-He must have wanted to drown it with alcohol, but it only made things worse."

"Great," Nebora snapped. "Drunk and scrouge driving him mad." She exhaled and released Mira, gently wiping the girl's tears. "Still time to leave him in a ditch."

"We can't," Loren said and all eyes went to him. "You heard him: he can ruin our lives even if we succeed. If we leave him—alive—all he has to do is make it back to Arcridge and send a message."

Nebora faced Loren. "Then we kill him."

"And then what?" Loren snapped. "The Queen probably knows where you hid your people—she knows how to ruin mine and Mira's tiny life. Our livelihoods hinge on him returning *alive*. He's right. We were fucked from the very moment the Queen put scourge in him."

The chance of Gareth making it to the Barrens and then back to Queen Celeste was already thin. If the scourge had truly touched his mind, it was only a matter of time before it became too much for Gareth. She'd spin a different tale than what happened, prop Gareth up as the actual tragic hero, and bury everyone else at best, call them traitors at worst.

Maybe it had been her intent all along to control the story.

Nebora hissed out another sigh and looked out into the dark. "Shit. So if that fucker goes and drowns, we're on the hook for that too?"

Everyone paused and listened. Sol couldn't hear anything in the water.

"Maybe he's not *that* drunk," Loren whispered. "Nebora—"

She held up a hand and stopped him, watching Sol instead. He swallowed and immediately winced as the motion made his throat ache.

"Spill," she said. "What the fuck was he talking about? What aren't you telling us?"

Sol watched her, eyes wide, and before he could spit it out, Loren and Mira glanced at each other. Nebora noticed the gesture and glared at them. "The fuck? You two know what's going on?" she asked. "Did no one here trust me?"

"I can control the scourge," Sol whispered. "He's afraid of it. Has been since Arcridge."

Nebora raised her eyebrows. "He knew back then?"

"I..." Sol glanced away. "I used it on him then to defend myself." He exhaled, even as Nebora's expression fell, likely piecing it together. "He's afraid. It's... it's that simple."

Because if Meredith could do all that with her house full of scourge, what all could Sol do being a star? It must have whispered into his head, warping whatever thoughts he'd had since the house burned, and moved him to act. Warped his already paranoid thoughts. It would only grow worse when they crossed into the Barrens, Sol was sure of it.

Nebora eased out a breath and looked between Sol and then Mira. Her shoulders fell. "No one—and I mean no one—is left alone with him if he comes back, got it?"

Mira nodded, sniffling, and this time, Loren headed over and wrapped her up gently. Sol hated that part of him was jealous. Nebora helped him to his feet, at least. She checked his neck the same, gently touching the skin.

"Might bruise," she said. "I'm sorry. I should have been out faster."

Loren released Mira and she went to Loren's tent without another word at Loren's urging. Nebora left Sol and made a circuit around the camp, eyes trained on the dark. Before Sol could decide what to do on his own, Loren had come over and checked him over again. This time, he gently felt the back of Sol's head. It smarted as Loren touched it, but Loren's hand came away clean. No bleeding, at least.

"I'm sorry," Sol whispered. "I didn't do anything

to him. I swear."

"It's not your fault." Loren gently touched Sol's shoulders and squeezed them. Not quite a hug, but the touch was welcoming all the same. Loren didn't let go and Sol glanced up at him. "Sol, what he said... about me—"

"I liked our sword lessons," Sol whispered. "I liked swimming with you." His voice wanted to continue—describe how much he liked Loren more than he'd ever thought possible—but he swallowed the rest of it down. Whether he liked Loren or not wouldn't matter in the end. He had to redraw the line between them and maintain it this time.

"Thank you for always being kind," Sol said instead.

Loren gently smiled and nodded. "We're almost there, all right? Sleep with Mira. Nebora and I will finish the watch tonight."

Nebora returned by the time Loren had made himself comfortable by the fire and Sol finally followed Mira into Loren's tent.

Gareth's words replayed in his thoughts as he went. The way the scourge had leaked into his eyes one moment, and let go the next. The way his arm pulsed with strength. Why of all times did it react then and what was it reacting to?

No answer immediately came. Sol didn't know

what was going on with the man and stewing on it wasn't helping. He crawled in beside Mira and just as he collapsed on the blankets and furs, Mira rolled to face him, eyes sparkling with tears.

"Gods, Sol—I'm so sorry," she whispered. "I didn't know he'd do that."

"I know," Sol said, sudden tears welling up to match hers. "I'm—I'm sorry too, Mira."

She drew him in so fast, so completely, his emotions let go a second time. Tears slid silently down his cheeks as his entire body shook with silent sobs. He was scared. He hadn't been before; everything had made sense at the castle. His path had been set in stone, unwavering. Now it fell, cracked, and bored a great fear into his heart where he had no idea what to do and no one to pray to.

Except, hadn't his prayer been answered? The scourge in Gareth's arm had forced the knight to act and Sol distantly wondered if it had been because of his soft prayer. His betrayal whispered into the sky.

Humans weren't to be trusted and scourge wanted to show him exactly why.

"The voice now flitted through the land,
heard by all, feared by all,
and no matter how much humanity begged,
it would not be stalled."

—Fragment of "She, Born of Starlight," Anonymous

IT DID NO GOOD TO OPEN UP TO ANYONE. IT WAS ALL Sol could concentrate on while Mira slumbered beside him, but he could do no such thing. He remained too alert. Perhaps a little ragged from lack of sleep, from the way his head throbbed, and how his throat ached. Maybe the declaration was because of that. Or everything else. It didn't matter in the end because deep down, Sol knew it to be true.

The fire dwindled as the night grew long, the ghost of its light pressed against the tent all the while. Eventually, humming scourge wept as it drew closer, but it was only Gareth's shambling form. A hushed and angry conversation ensued between Loren,

Nebora, and Gareth, but no weapons were drawn. An uneasy truce was made by the end. Gareth went into his tent and the scourge quieted with him.

Sol had hoped—prayed—Gareth wouldn't return, but then he wondered when hope or prayer had ever done him any good.

It certainly did nothing for humanity. Not now.

Morning came, sallow dawn light hidden behind snowflakes blowing out from the Barrens. It didn't stick to the grass, thankfully, and melted as soon as it hit the ground. Varros refused any attempt to suit him up and after a few tries, they resolved to leave him at the spring. Even Varros knew the Barrens wasn't for him. If he crossed the walls, he'd die and he knew it. At least here near the spring, he'd be protected. Content.

For a time.

Mira gave Varros the biggest hug she had in her and Sol gave him a gentle one because it wasn't Varros' fault what humanity did. He'd simply be caught up in whatever happened.

They redistributed their belongings between themselves, leaving anything not essential for the last leg of the venture with Varros, and set off. Sol didn't like the newfound weight—it felt too meaningful all at once—but he refrained from complaints and walked beside Mira. Hardly anyone spoke or even looked at each other for that matter. Probably for the best.

For his part, Gareth had become the man he'd been before they found the spring. *Before Meredith*, Sol corrected. No mention of what transpired last night. No mention of the whispers Gareth had heard, pushing him to act. The scourge inside him had grown almost too quiet to hear over their footfalls. As usual, he took point, and led them down the trail with scourge on either side. Never once daunted.

Leaving the spring was like stepping into a different world. Evidence of scourge multiplied, staining the fields and meadows a glimmering black like the star had dragged a paintbrush through the land. Unlike before, this scourge refused to speak to Sol. He wasn't sure if it was dormant or if it'd simply heard his betrayal on the wind and now stayed silent.

They found less and less people and those they did find were dead. Corpses torn open by the scourge, white bones piercing through their skin, and their eyes were gaping holes left to stare at the sky. There were empty camps with spoiled food, towns husks of their former selves with nothing left to salvage, and so much of the world was dead, replaced by scourge. Between fights of beasts and reanimated bodies of poor travelers already long gone forced to rise out of forgone vengeance, Sol felt more and more haggard. Each time blades found their homes, the bodies cried out for him. Pain shot through him, mirroring the festering wounds left behind by sword and axe alike. It buzzed with his blood until the scourge let go of life, leaving him empty and cold.

The scourge wanted him to see exactly what humans did to stars like him so he stayed despondent. What humans continued to do to them and likely what they'd do to each other when the cycle ended. It was numbing in an encompassing way. At least, until Loren paused to make sure he was steady. Then something else bloomed in the emptiness. Sol had tried to keep his distance, but the soft smiles checking up on him closed the distance between them each time.

Sol didn't know what it meant. He also still didn't know what it meant either when Mira continued whittling away their night watches with conversations despite his new reluctance to reply. Even the little murmurs she whispered to help him sleep overrode the phantasm in the distance. Almost like a lullaby between friends.

How did they both care about him the way they did? When he wanted to end their lives? Wasn't it obvious by now what he wanted to do, legends be damned?

The answer never came. But what did was the star's voice from the Onyx Spire as they drew ever closer to the Barren walls. No longer were they content to be the soft honeyed words he'd come to know. Each syllable lined themselves like blades, dragging through his thoughts until he was softened enough to control. This was her in truth. A star pulled to pieces who wanted vengeance, any means necessary. And yet, even if it would be easy to let her in and let her control the outcome, he resisted. All because of a smile in his direction.

Mornings came as dull and empty as all the others and after every night, they were quickly on the road again. The weight of promises, his own memories, and the blasted pack on his back moored him to a reality he didn't want to acknowledge. Brought him back to the ache in his throat every time he swallowed. He wanted to block it all out, block everything out, so some of his conviction stayed resolute. The pain should have done that on its own, but here it was: wavering with each step.

It helped no one spoke. Ears trained for the breathing silence in the darkened world around them for signs of scourge on the prowl. It was there, even if unseen. Unheard. Sol felt its presence skitter across the fields. Below them. Watching. Waiting. Sometimes, their whispers returned, but they were so garbled and broken as they tried to convince Sol their intentions were pure and for him to bring everyone into the fields. A trap. The star wanted to deal with his heroes because he wouldn't. Sol ignored the invitation all because of the smiles he wanted to remember.

He was snapped out of listening too intently when everyone stopped. He finally gazed up, squinting against the biting wind coming down from the Barrens, and the bridge they'd been heading toward lay before them. Broken. Wooden splinters replaced the planks that once were and scourge glittered on both ends like it had eaten the structure away. Wasn't much of a threat unless they walked too near, Sol was sure.

The scourge in Gareth's arm tilted, twisting, and he glared back at the group. No, just at Sol, actually. Somehow, he blamed Sol despite sense telling everyone otherwise the bridge was not his fault in the least. Sol glanced away and burrowed himself deeper in his furs.

"Broken," Nebora said the obvious, drawing eyes to her as she approached the edge. "River's dried up too..." She gazed further down and tightened her jaw. The reason being the mass of scourge threaded together as a dam. Evidence scourge could reason and use tactics on humanity at large. Sol wondered if the bard tales sung of that or if this was a new phenomenon.

The empty river wasn't deep. Ground was covered in dead brush and leaves. Likely dried out some time ago. Pieces of humanity lay there too as bones and items left behind. Nothing alarming, at least.

"Feel anything?" Nebora asked.

It was a moment before Sol realized she'd been asking him. He jolted to attention and felt around them. "The dam," he said, "but I can't other than that. Everything's rather loud here altogether so close to the Barrens." He swallowed, aware of Gareth's gaze scrutinizing him as he spoke, but none of what he said were lies.

"And you?" Nebora nodded at Gareth.

"The same," Gareth said, turning away. "Not much good either of us are."

"It's enough." Nebora faced the riverbank and pointed. "Here's the plan: the riverbank's dried up, so we'll just climb down and head across as pairs." She glared at Gareth as soon as he opened his mouth to protest. He promptly shut it and returned the glare. "Sorry, Knight Boy—you've enough weight and clatter for two." She beckoned Sol closer and he raised his eyebrows. "Sol and I will go first and then he'll keep an eye on everyone from across to make sure no scourge can sneak up on us." She clapped him on the shoulder and he tensed. "Loren and Mira will come next. We hold our squishies tight, you hear?"

Loren gave her a weak smile. "Understood," he said and Mira latched her arm around Loren's. Sol awkwardly did the same with Nebora, burying the disappointment he was not paired with Loren.

"Gareth, you bring up the rear and watch the same. Everyone: keep your eyes peeled."

"Why as pairs?" Sol asked.

"So if something happens, we aren't all down there at once." Nebora eyed the dam. It glittered faintly, but it had no reason to disengage itself. It was doing its purpose, after all; it would stay like that until it was given orders otherwise. Or, at least until a foolish human drew near. Better not to chance it.

Carefully, Nebora climbed down, her shoulders tense, and Sol only followed when she was steady, ready to catch him should he slip. It was deep enough he couldn't climb his way to immediate safety and he doubted Nebora could either. She eyed the side all the same, however, as though gauging how fast she could haul herself upward. Once she had her answer—or accepted the lack thereof—she took Sol's arm and they walked forward. Their speed was a crawl, Nebora gently testing the ground beneath them with each step. It was curiously soft, shifting here and there as their weight pushed on it, but stayed solid.

Step after step, Sol concentrated on the end goal of the other side, until he felt something stir beneath them. It sent a shiver through his body, flushing it with goosebumps. Like a hand fluttered across him in his entirety. The sensation unnerved him so much, he flinched, and that was when his foot found a hole beneath the dead brush. Before he could right himself, the ground around the hole caved in with his weight. His heart leapt into his throat, smothering a cry for help, and the ground swallowed him up.

His back hit the ground, then his head, and as his vision swam, he heard cries of his name. Mildew ladened air chilled him as he breathed and as he was getting his bearings in the dark, Nebora came sliding down beside him. She hit the ground more gracefully than he had—a decided jump after him instead of a flailing fall, and she cringed.

"For fuck's sake." Nebora wiped some dirt from her face and gazed skyward. Scant light found its way inside. "We're alive!" she shouted. "Ground's weak—don't come near it!"

"Can you climb back up?" Loren called.

Nebora and Sol looked. The wall was soft, clearly slick with water, and Nebora's mouth twisted into a scowl. "Probably not. Too soft. Think you can attach a rope to the bridge and throw it down?"

"Got it!" Mira answered.

Sol sat up and felt the back of his head. No blood. There was a twinge in his back from the fall and he winced trying to move. Nebora sat down cross-legged beside him and brought a lamp from her pack. She lit it with a match and lifted it higher.

Not much to be seen. Dark ground. Rocks. Dirt.

"Didn't break anything?" Nebora asked.

"No."

"Figures we had a nice clean dip and now we're caked in mud." Nebora snickered and gazed upward. Gareth's armor clattered across the riverbed and his shadow momentarily blocked out the light coming in as he went to the other side. He barked in annoyance at Mira until Loren told him off. Nebora sighed, loudly, and shook her head.

"What a fucking brute." She eyed Sol and dropped her voice. "Your neck feeling better?"

Sol eased his fingers over it. "Talking doesn't hurt as much," he admitted.

The arguing above grew louder and Nebora scowled again. "Dumbass!" she shouted and left the lamp to stand below the hole. "Focus on helping us! Not whatever the fuck it is you're bitchin' about!"

The arguments ceased, at least. Gareth growled

in response and that was it. His scourge made the same motion, clearly annoyed doing grunt work as much as he was. Sol kept it to himself, even as a smile played across his lips in amusement.

It lasted until his skin crawled with the telltale hum of the scourge nearby. There was a small opening behind them, on the far side of the cave they'd fallen into. Covered in dead roots, Sol couldn't see anything beyond, but soft words akin to prayer trickled forth. Before Sol knew it, he was standing with the lantern gathered in his hand, and heading toward it.

The dead roots gave way with a push of his hand. Not a large room—smaller than the one they'd fallen into—but curiously, it had a structure made out of wood and mud. It resembled an offering shrine of some kind with dead candles scattered about and a crudely carved idol in the center. It reminded Sol of the one he'd seen in Arcridge, but it had only one god. Sol cautiously stepped closer for a better look.

Around the idol was a depression filled with a pool of glittering scourge. He retreated quickly, its soft whispers ghosting across him, and Nebora kept him from falling backwards.

"What is it?" she asked.

The scourge sang a mockery of her voice. The previous star urged him back inside, barbs stuck to her voice as it trailed across him, and Sol raised the lantern a second time.

Around the shrine of mud and sticks lay bodies. Blackened and torn with scourge keeping the muscles whole and bones together. Nebora gasped, drawing Sol another step backward as she slid in front of him, and that was when Sol noticed the body looming over the shrine like it had been draped there on purpose. Its eyes opened wide, blackened pools sunk against skin bleached of its color, and it dropped its maw open in a rumbling growl as it lunged.

Nebora's axe took its head clean off, splattering the scourge bubbling through it on the far wall over the shrine. More and more bodies rose from the piles on the floor in response, each one as misshaped as the last. Chests caved open where scourge forced their hearts to continue beating, ribs poking through skin as the scourge pushed it out to make room, and so many more barely recognizable as once human bodies.

"Shit!" Nebora threw her arm into Sol, knocking him off his feet as he clattered back into the first cave, and the lantern went rolling to the far side. Nebora retreated with another swing, taking down the first wave, but another pile had risen and charged her. The dead and gore splattered the walls, but the scourge forced them back together to keep fighting each time.

Memories flickered in Sol's thoughts. Of scourge following people down here as they sought Lovian for guidance and help once the river dried up. They thought they'd be protected within their shrine in the dark and never noticed it was the scourge which began whispering to them. Tempted those hiding to eat the blackened gore to strengthen their resolves, never knowing it was their undoing until it was too late. The star's voice laughed as scourge turned them into this.

Hands flailed outward at Nebora, fingers sharpened with bone and scourge, and she swiped them back. She was going to be overrun. Sol saw it even now—they kept pushing her back and before long, the doorway would be wide open for them all to spill through. Shouts came from above, asking what was happening, but Nebora couldn't get words out fast enough before another attack came.

Sol couldn't leave her to her fate.

Even as the axe swings felt as though they slid across his own skin, even as the pain reverberated from the empty bodies to his, he forced his shaking legs to stand and concentrated.

The scourge made a connection almost immediately, caressing his touch at one turn, but then assaulted his mind at the other, filling him with the sensation of each body being forced to relive its death over and over again at the hands of Nebora's axe. It could end here. He convinced the body in front to freeze. The arm froze mid-swing, its eyes glittering white, until the labrys cleaved its head in two. Sol let go, a blinding pain threatening to bisect his own head, and the other bodies faced Sol.

Traitor, they sang. At once, they charged him and his attention frayed trying to halt them all at once. The closest body came apart with a sickening rip from the attempt, Sol's unseen hand tearing it from the head down. Scourge and viscera went everywhere. The body thumped to the ground, dead, and bile rose up Sol's throat from the pain and disgust he felt in turn.

The flash of a sword came in, halting the next one attempting to strike Sol. Loren's cloak fluttered behind him, the yarrow flower on the back becoming a fixation in the dim light so Sol could ignore the rest of the room. He blacked out the pain, curling himself tight, while Nebora and Loren worked in tandem through the horde of scourge ridden bodies.

"*Let them die here*," came the star's voice. She felt so near as her voice raked its barbs through his skin.

It would be so easy too. The bodies were getting

back up already, like puppets on a string. It was then Sol noticed a humming thread connecting all the bodies together. No one would die here; he could stop it. He forced himself to concentrate on the thread, even as pain burrowed deep in his head from the star attempting to push him out, and he snapped it as hard as he could. "*Rest,*" he begged. "Please. Do not do this any longer."

The whisper ceased, withdrawing, and the bodies all crumpled at once. Axe and sword took them apart to make sure until all was silent and dead, save for them. Sol let go and promptly vomited into the ground. The pain was too much.

A warm hand gently drew his hair back, gathering it up, and Sol knew it was Loren. He wanted so badly to lean into the man so he didn't have to hold himself up, but he resisted.

"Gareth! Let me go! I don't hear anything anymore!" Mira yelled from above.

"You fucking stay up there!" The clinking of Gareth's armor drew closer. "You three better be alive down there!"

"Scourge is dead," Nebora said and wiped her sleeve across her forehead. "We're coming up. Give us some space, all right?"

"Rope is secure," Gareth growled before his shadow departed the hole. "It's growing dark so you guys better get up here soon so you can clean off and we can find somewhere to camp."

Nebora exhaled and glanced at Sol. "Loren, help him up. I'm gonna go up first." She hesitated and glanced at all the dead and blood splattered through the cave. "I'm not gonna mention the shrine and I don't think you guys should either."

She went up without another word.

"Shrine?" Loren asked.

Sol shook his head. "I don't know what else it could be," he whispered. "I think people came here to be closer to their god, but scourge was already here." The room was shrouded in shadow now. He resisted the urge to peer inside again, lest it invite the star to reinvigorate the scourge. There was nothing in there but the dark now.

Loren gently rubbed Sol's back and offered a flask for him which Sol happily accepted. He washed out his mouth and spat out the contents. Glittering scourge greeted him and he gritted his teeth. The anguish lasted but a moment before Loren softly ran his fingers down Sol's hair. The sensation had no right to feel as good as it did.

"We can go up when you're ready," he said.

"I'm ready," Sol insisted. "I don't want to be down here any longer."

Any more and it would begin to feel like a tomb,

especially with how dark the sky grew. All at once, he was disturbed, realizing he *could* have let it be a tomb. He could have left everyone down here, trapped them, and headed for the Barrens by himself at this point. No one would have known. The star, the one who needed him wouldn't let him die on the way, would she have? The bodies certainly tried to hurt him, but only because he'd turned against them first. Would she have killed him if he hadn't reacted?

The question was impossibly chilling. They'd called him a traitor. Maybe she could have used his body like the others, as a puppet, because she no longer had her own. Perhaps it was her intent all along.

No. He wanted to stop thinking so hard on it. What the future held would come once they reached the Onyx Spire. Then all would know what would happen. Questioning everything now would simply undo him and he couldn't let that happen. Not while they were so close.

His arms were too weak to climb. His head too full of dark thoughts to concentrate. Loren helped him onto his back and climbed for the two of them without complaint.

Sol rested his head against Loren's shoulder and held tight to the warm man he was. Sol made the right decision—he was sure of it. Loren, Nebora, and

Mira all didn't deserve to die here. Not now.

As sure as he was of that, it only let another little voice bloom in his head, asking him if they'd ever deserve their coming fate.

He made no attempt to answer it as Loren pulled them out of the river. The Barrens were so close now, Sol could taste the star on the air even though he couldn't see her. The acrid salt soured his tongue as it coasted along the breeze.

The star had grown silent, but Sol would find all his answers in the Onyx Spire. Even if he feared them all the same.

"She followed the voice across an unending shore,
shimmering waves pushing and pulling the world between.
Around and around, she went until answers burned her skin.
Until the waves parted, revealing a chapel unseen."

—Fragment of "She, Born of Starlight," Anonymous

IT TOOK TWO NIGHTS AND THREE DAYS TO REACH THE walls from the broken bridge. Each night closer grew colder and scourge slept hidden beneath frost. The star's voice was clearer, bolder, speaking over any hushed conversation. Watching and waiting for signs of further betrayal. Likewise, as though he felt it too, the closer they came, the stiffer Gareth grew. The scourge beneath his skin writhed. It was finally home with a body of its own. A body he and everyone knew that would one day be carved open like all the others they'd seen on the roadside.

The Onyx Spire lay beyond the walls blocking travel to the Barrens. The walls had been built only after the Second Umbral Cycle ended, when it was obvious the first one wasn't just a one-off occurrence. Scourge came from the spire and thus, walls were erected. Each year it was said they grew taller. Sovereign lands with a border to the Barrens maintained their walls and it was the only place there was ever real peace. What did war inland matter when those living along the walls watched for signs of scourge which would kill indiscriminately?

Each gate in the wall had a watchtower built beside it to keep an eye on the spire and for a time, that was it. Years came and went and small towns began to cluster around the gates to house who guarded it. The walls, the tower, and the towns became the first noble defense against the scourge. According to Nebora, people came here when they had nothing else but something to prove. Maybe there were families back home they wanted to protect and this was the only way they knew how. Families were seldom made here; if the Umbral Cycle began anew, everyone knew it was only a matter of time before the scourge made it through.

Because it always did.

There was a wooden wall protecting the settlement clustered at the gates, but it was in splinters with scourge crystallized across it. The buildings, once passable as houses, had been broken in by the same scourge. The watchtower wasn't spared. A glittering black eyesore hung down from the windows, crystallized in place. None of that surprised Sol. It was what they'd been seeing in each and every passing town. What stopped him dead, however, was at the gates blocking passage into the Barrens.

Bodies were pushed up against it as though they could have kept the gate shut with just themselves and each one was frozen, like they were encased in ice. It was more than a few men and women. Hundreds maybe. All those that had once lived within trapped in a ghostly sheen. Yet, their attempt hadn't seemingly been for naught. Though the gate had opened enough, allowing a cold wind to blow through, no scourge had. Sol blinked and lifted his gaze higher. It hadn't needed the gate opened at all; the scourge had come *over* the wall.

Scourge sat there even now as a wave frozen in time like the bodies, but unlike the bodies who were surely dead, the scourge lay dormant. The gate and their sacrifice had never mattered. No matter how tall humanity built their walls, scourge would still come. The wall was useless; they should have run.

The longer Sol stared—the longer everyone did since no one moved once their eyes fell on it—the more the scourge reached out to him. It eagerly showed him its memories like a friend. First came the pounding against the gate. Strong enough to make everyone *think* scourge would bust through. Once they clambered over one another to stop the gates from pushing open, the scourge took what Sol could only describe as a single breath, and sucked the air into the Barrens. Everything grew cold, but people held steadfast thinking they could win. Once the scourge had them all right there, it surged over the walls as a wave. No time for a prayer. No time to whisper a goodbye. Everyone had died the instant it crashed down, freezing them there in their ghostly sheen. Faces and bodies contorted in horror with silent screams. The scourge remained merely because its job was done. It had been a bridge for everything else and would remain so until it was recalled.

"It really did come over the wall," Gareth whispered, bringing Sol back to reality. "I didn't think the stories were true."

Nebora nodded, shoulders tense. "No matter how tall we build, it always comes." She breathed out. "Gods damn it. What was the point of even having this here if it's always going to be this way?" She glared hard at Gareth. "Your Queen ignored the first signs, you know."

Gareth didn't rise to the bait. He glanced at Sol. "Is it safe to enter?" He nodded at the frozen wave arcing over the wall. "With that hanging over us?"

"It's dormant." Sol pulled his cloak tighter around himself. "We can cross underneath or overtop. Nothing will wake."

Only because he was there, but he left that part unsaid. If they'd been without him, the scourge may have awakened to devour them. Add them to the menagerie of bodies frozen against the gates in horror. All to protect the Onyx Spire.

"How do we go through?" Mira asked. "T-They're in the way."

"We walk," Gareth said.

"On the bodies?"

"They're dead."

"It's late," Loren interrupted and pointed at the dark sky above. The sun had already set, hidden away for the night. Only the moon was seen, a soft red like the sun before it. "I think we should rest. See what we can gather here before we head into the unknown."

Though Gareth's jaw tightened, Nebora was nodding. "I agree," she said. "Let's find a good place to set up camp and go digging. They had storage in the basements, right? Maybe something's left after all this time."

While Nebora, Loren, and Gareth went off in separate directions, Mira and Sol were left in charge of making camp. They headed away from the horror of the frozen bodies and found a small space in the courtyard where stables once must have been. Hay lay scattered across the dead grass and there was shelter still whole without any scourge clinging to it. Mira busied herself making the firepit and Sol set up the tents all by himself. Would have been quaint if there wasn't scourge looming across the wall out of the corner of his eye, or the pile of dead bodies.

Mira was bent over her newly made baby fire, coaxing it into something more substantial, when Sol's blood buzzed. He straightened his back, immediately gazing at the looming wall, but it was silent. No scourge shuddered there and all he heard from beyond was the haunting wail of the wind. He turned slowly, listening, and felt a subtle pull egging him in one direction. Eyes watched him from the foot of the crumbling watchtower and as soon as he caught them, they darted out of sight. Sol felt out, searching for scourge, and heard a soft hum vibrating through a tiny body. It must have been a child.

What struck him as more surprising was that the child was alive.

He reached down and touched Mira's shoulder, never looking away from the watchtower, and Mira glanced up. She opened her mouth until Sol put a finger to his lips. She shot up, eyes wide, and he leaned closer to her.

"There's a child," he whispered.

"Where?"

"Around the tower—should—" He couldn't finish the question before Mira was moving, her footsteps light and quick, and he went after her. Not quite his plan—he'd meant they should find Nebora or Loren, just in case it was a trap—but Mira's face was set. She could handle a child, he supposed. It wasn't like he felt much else around them. Gareth and his scourge were farther off, grown quiet and still, and everything else entirely dormant.

Mira reached the tower, pressing her back against the stone walls, and waited until Sol was beside her. She eased them slowly around the corner until they'd come all the way around. There was a soft hum of scourge, like a lullaby in the night.

"Mama!" a little voice whispered, soft and weak below the howling wind. "Papa! I found someone. Please wake up."

Sol and Mira peered around the final bend. A small tent had been propped against the corner of the watchtower and the wall with a blanket laid out at the bottom to soften the ground. Two adults lay within, another blanket spread across them. They held hands, their foreheads touching, but Sol knew they were dead. Scourge wound inside of them, crystallizing their blood, their muscles—everything it could—before it'd grown silent. No sign of it raising for now, but Sol didn't know enough to say how long they'd remain like this.

Sitting in front of them, shaking them with little hands, was a girl with raven black hair tied in two braids down her back. There was food in front of the bodies, like the little girl had tried to help her parents. Except it was too late.

"Hey there," Mira said softly.

The girl jumped and spun to face them, eyes wide.

Mira knelt down to be level with her "My name's Mira," she said. "Were you looking for someone?"

The girl swallowed, mouthing Mira's name to herself, and eyed her parents. When they didn't respond, she faced Mira fully and pulled a braid over her shoulder. "Mama and Papa said if-if someone could help, th-they might be here. It's why we came a-after our home was taken." She fiddled with her braid, eyes darting from Mira to Sol and then back again. "They went to sleep. Really, really asleep. Walking was so tiring. They—they—" Her face screwed up, thick tears bubbling in her eyes as she lost her words.

"Walking *is* tiring," Mira said, nodding. "Let

them rest for a little while longer. Are you hungry? My friends are gathering some food." She extended a hand toward the girl. "We can make something together and bring it back for them, all right?"

The lie was enough. The girl faced her parents once, worrying over her braid, and then came closer to take Mira's hand. She was thin and short, barely standing past Mira's waist. Her wide blue eyes once more considered Sol curiously before they fixed on Mira.

"My name is Trudy," she said.

"It's nice to meet you, Trudy." Mira nodded at Sol. "This is one of my friends, Sol. Let's see if I can find Nebora for you. She's like a big sister to me. Did you have any siblings?"

Trudy shook her head. "It was just me and Mama and Papa."

Mira kept Trudy close and Sol watched them as they headed back. Yes, there was scourge beneath her skin. Her little fingernails were ghosted with purple and glitter like Celena's had been. Though she had sleeves covering her arm, Sol felt the scourge dance up it. The ghostly murmur of it reached out, making Sol shiver, and he followed it up her arm, down her back, through even to her legs, and then back up. Sol's steps faltered unseen as his breathing hitched. Mira obliviously continued toward camp, asking Trudy if she'd ever seen a lute before. Not understanding what Sol could see within.

The scourge was wound around her heart.

Sol opened his mouth to say something—anything—but Mira stopped on her own and picked up her head.

"There you are!" boomed Nebora's voice from across the courtyard. There was a neat pile of provisions in front of the fire they'd abandoned and Nebora was coming over. Trudy hid behind Mira's legs and then switched to hide behind Sol's cloak when he caught up.

Nebora paused, eyebrows high, and Mira made a few hand gestures at her Sol didn't quite catch. Nebora did; her face softened and she smiled. "And who's that you got there?" she asked teasingly. Trudy tried to get around them to keep hiding, but Nebora followed her all the way around Sol and caught her. "Got'cha!"

Trudy let out a squeal of absolute delight as Nebora spun her through the air. After one full revolution, Nebora lifted her up so Trudy could sit on her shoulder.

"Nebora!" Mira laughed. "Don't scare her!"

"I'm not!" Nebora grinned back. "She's having fun, right sweetheart?"

"Spin me again!" Trudy giggled.

And Nebora did, all the way back to camp where Loren and Gareth had returned to tend to the fire. They looked more confused than anything else, watching Nebora spin ever closer. She settled the girl down and began showing her what they'd gathered while Loren and Gareth stood to intercept Mira and Sol.

"No," Gareth hissed. "We can't take a kid."

"Where'd you find her?" Loren whispered at the same time.

"Her parents are dead on the other side of the watchtower. I have no idea where she came from except she said her town was gone." Mira shook her head. "I'm not going to leave her here alone."

Gareth scoffed and raised his eyebrows. "You want to take a little girl into the Barrens? You want to be responsible for that when we don't even know what's there?"

"She won't be here long," Sol interrupted and everyone stared at him. Mira was immediately crushed, eyebrows folded in despair. Loren was resigned, like he figured as much and Gareth stared at Sol with something close to disdain. "The scourge is around her heart." Sol's hand went to his chest and he drew a spiral across his tunic. "I don't think she'll last the night."

"Good. Ow!" Gareth held his arm where Mira

had punched him. "Fuck—what was that for?" He glared at her, but she wouldn't meet it. She didn't look at anyone as she pushed past them and headed for camp. Gareth huffed. "I'm not wrong, you know. What did she think was going to happen?"

"Shut up," Loren said and Gareth glared at him. "Just shut up for once."

Gareth straightened his back, lip curled, and bodily pushed past Loren as he followed Mira back to camp. Mira had sat down and Trudy was immediately a rapt audience when Mira revealed her lute. Gareth sat at the far side of the fire, facing away from them as he continued to rub his arm. Mira's lute sang into the dark, her voice energetic as it followed along with a soft tale about a girl who was a secret princess. One of Celena's favorite tales she'd whispered to Sol over countless nights.

In an instant, the camp became warm and inviting despite the dark looming around them. Reality buried deep enough, they could ignore it. Yet, for some reason, Sol's legs refused to join them; he couldn't get Mira's despair out of his head.

"I..." He swallowed and Loren looked at him. "I didn't mean to make her sad."

"I know," Loren said. "Come on; let's give the little girl a good last night." He smiled gently and brushed his knuckles up against Sol's. "Try to smile for her. She doesn't seem to be in pain, so let's help her forget the dark."

If only the dark would forget her. Sol wasn't even sure why the thought voiced itself in his head, but he let it stick there as he followed Loren.

The night quickly became bright and wholly different than the nights preceding it. The cheer they'd lost and left on the roadside returned and Sol was glad to see it, even if it was fake. After the secret princess tale ended, Mira strummed her lute faster and began loudly singing a humorous ballad that sent Trudy rolling with laughter. Made Nebora pull Trudy up to dance with her. Loren even joined in, bringing Sol with him, and the four of them danced with one another until the song ended. Gareth even stopped glowering after a time and showed Trudy his knife throwing skills, never once missing a target she pointed at. He even let her try, stringing together soft, encouraging words despite her throws never going far. When Trudy finally spent her energy, Nebora regaled her with tales of wonder, words suffused with fantasy that made the tale too big to believe, but Trudy swallowed it up as irrefutable truth.

It was endearing seeing how full of life and wonder she still was. How much everyone hid the doubt and darkness in their own hearts to see her smile and help her forget reality. Help themselves forget what was coming.

The night wound long with stories and their voices drowned out the winds from the Barrens. Sol would have forgotten about the dark as the campfire blazed on, if he hadn't felt it stirring within Trudy. Like it wanted to dance with their good cheer. Like it remembered what the star must have known before she was taken to the spire. Before long, Trudy's energy waned, and she curled up against Nebora's lap with a blanket someone retrieved at some point wrapped around her to stave off the cold. Nebora hummed a lullaby for her, fingers gently stroking her hair. She was asleep soon enough, a soft smile on her lips like she truly was at peace.

Everyone else was quiet. Even Nebora's humming softened into the ghost of a whisper. Their awareness of the darkness made the silence almost too heavy to bear. Sol felt for the scourge. It hummed against him, loud, but through it, he heard her the way her heart was beating so slowly.

"You can't take it out?" Gareth asked suddenly.

Given his refusal to bring a child with them at all, the question stunned Sol. He blinked at the knight. "Pardon?"

Gareth waved his hand at the girl. "The *scourge.* Can't you do something?"

"No." Sol tightened his cloak to hide how the denial made him tremble. "Human bodies are so tightly put together, any attempt could put her in a great deal of pain if not outright kill her." He recalled how Gareth's arm had twisted back in Arcridge and shuddered. Gareth flexed his hand in his lap. He must have remembered too. "I'm sorry."

Nebora sighed. "It's rotten."

It wasn't that Gareth cared about the little girl; if she survived, there was the matter of what to do with her. Likely, he'd asked at all to see if he could extract his own scourge. Save himself from his own demise. It was coming no matter what they did and even he realized it. Every single dead body found on the roadside reminded him of his mortality. No matter how strong he was or what convictions he still held, he would die. Sooner, rather than later.

Sol doubted he could do anything to help Gareth now, even if he'd wanted to. The scourge was wound too deep inside him.

The soft smile on Trudy's lips made it feel like everything was right regardless of the truth. That her parents weren't dead around the corner. That she would wake up in the morning back home, wherever it was. Sol wondered where they'd come from, why they'd come here of all places instead of heading toward the capital, and more importantly how they'd survived this entire time. Answers would never come. Asking her was out of the question. It was too close to the reality they wanted her to forget. That they wanted to forget themselves. Besides, all she'd ever known was the dark—she hardly looked older than ten.

At least she was smiling. It wasn't the terror or screaming like those against the gate.

Once more, Sol concentrated on the scourge within, and this time, he found nothing. His body stilled of its own accord and he didn't like how the realization left him chilled. Just like that, she was gone. Her breathing had ceased. Her heart had stopped and rested quietly against the scourge dying within her.

He was watching her so intently, wishing everything was exactly as it wasn't, that he hadn't noticed the others watching him until Mira touched his arm.

Words stuck fast in his throat until he cleared it. "She's gone," he whispered.

Nebora checked as well, pressing her head against the girl's back. When she came up again, she was frowning. "She is. I'm glad we found her at all. Made her warm before, you know." She exhaled and gathered Trudy up in the blanket. "We should give her and her parents their last rites before the scourge does anything with them."

"I agree." Loren stood. "There's enough loose wood to make a pyre. I only wish we could help those against the gate the same."

The pyre didn't take long to set up, even when Gareth took some of the fire away to see if he could melt those frozen at the gate free. Flames did nothing but accentuate the horror and he tossed the torch back into the growing blaze. Nebora and Loren had bundled Trudy between her parents and they lit up in a fire so bright, it washed the entire courtyard in gold. Mira held Sol's hand, but she remained silent and didn't look at anything but the flames.

Sol didn't know what to feel. Trudy and her parents' lives were cut short for reasons they'd never had a hand in. It was tragic, but that was true of *everyone* that died because of the scourge. Except the scourge *was* the fault of humans. Revenge enacted against those alive at the wrong time. Alive when the scourge broke free. It would continue just like this until someone broke the cycle.

Sol shuddered and refused to acknowledge the phantasm watching him past the wall. He emptied his mind of promises and emotions the best he could. It wouldn't matter. Didn't matter. The cycle would end, one way or another. He promised.

Yet after the pyre dulled and they'd buried the ashes in a shallow grave to sleep below the earth, he was restless. Damning thoughts filling his head with what ifs until they all landed on Loren. On Mira. There were no answers to the thoughts. All Sol could do as he and Mira crawled into the same tent to rest was stare at the dark until he was sure it stared back at him.

✦

MORNING CAME AFTER EXHAUSTION DREW SOL tight. No one spoke much. Mira's gaze lingered on the ash the pyre had left behind, like she wanted to talk about it, but she never raised her voice.

Sol's body hurt as he moved and it was only when they were packing their belongings together did he realize what was hurting. The lines along his skin. He checked his wrist and his stomach dropped.

The line had cracked, spiderwebbing fine lines across the inside of his arm. No one had mentioned his face, so it must have been fine there, and he quickly hid his arm so no one saw. The reason why likely didn't matter. He was simply coming apart like all stars did at the end of their journey with no one to keep them together. It was inevitable, yet he was afraid.

Despite the desire otherwise, they picked their way across the dead bodies to get over the gate. Gareth led the way, his back stiff as he went, Mira kept her eyes closed the entire walk over—mouth moving in silent apologies—Nebora kept her back straight too, and Loren brought up the rear after Sol.

Sol hated touching the bodies. He heard their voices deep in his mind as his fingers grazed them. Anguished cries as the scourge dragged the life from them. The brief flash of their families, lingering memories wishing to be relived. Never again. Ten years waiting to find a witness of some kind. Ten years suffering and the scourge eagerly shared it with Sol as though it was proud.

He was only glad when he touched the other side of the wall and the sensation ceased, although he wasn't sure if he liked this side any better.

Like its namesake, the land was barren, the ground white as snow caked the land. Legends said this land was once warm and bright, but when the First Umbral Cycle came, it grew so unbelievably cold and thrust the lands around it into winter no matter what time of year it was. A squall blew around them now, snowflakes like little icicles across his skin, and in the distance, there were chunks of ice as far as the eye could see. All untouched by human-kind, left barren and dead since the First Umbral Cycle. It must have been an ocean at some point as frozen waves receded in the far distance, blown away from the very center, and revealed the spire within.

The Onyx Spire. The reason Sol was here.

Howling winds swirled the snow into spirals around its dark, shimmering façade. This side of the wall with nothing to hide behind, Sol could no longer deny the spark of life held aloft high above like a beacon of hoped. It saw him too, its bright flame like a star in the darkness, and another shudder worked through Sol.

"This is it," Mira whispered and huddled deeper into her cloak.

Nebora nodded. "I see now why they call this place the Barrens."

The world here was quiet and dead in ways the other side of the wall wasn't. Even the scourge glistening beneath the sheets of snow didn't hum. It was like it waited, a rapt audience, for what Sol was going to do.

Loren touched Sol's hand, making him jump. "That's the tower you need, right?"

There weren't any other buildings on the horizon or anywhere else beyond the walls, but Sol appreciated Loren asked. "Yes," he said. "That's the Onyx Spire."

There was no mistaking it. Not the way it shimmered from the light above or the way the scourge made it as black as the stone it was named after.

Loren removed his hand and another one touched Sol instead, but he dared not look down to look because it was a sensation at most. The previous star's fingers were light, barely there, but she tugged his skin. Sol wanted wrench his hand away, but then she began whispering. Soft honeyed words once again brushing up against his cheeks.

"Help me. You promised."

He had. He couldn't deny it. With a deep breath to let the ice-cold air fill his lungs, Sol took the lead. There was no one else, after all, and he let her hand gently guide him for the path the first star must have made centuries ago. Her voice continued murmuring along the winds, words too soft to hear, but he understood her all the same.

"I'm here," he whispered in reply, so quietly that no one heard him but the wind. "I'm finally here to save you."

"We carried her across the emptied ocean,
until she could deny the voice no longer.
It called her so softly on the wind, like a friend,
and finally, to the chapel it brought her."

—Fragment of "She, Born of Starlight," Anonymous

THE ROAD WAS WINDING, AND IT WASN'T HELPED BY the gusts obscuring their vision with swirls of snow. The chill sliced through Sol no matter how tightly he held his cloak and he wondered if he'd ever feel warm again. The emptiness didn't help the stray thoughts. Ridges and overlooks peered over the muted landscape and the crystallized scourge blackened the ground beneath the snow.

Despite the darkened sky wrapping the frozen waves in the distance, the land was a blinding white. It shimmered against the light the phantasm released above the tower, even leaving a sheen along the air itself like a specter. Perhaps it was meant to tempt travelers off the path, but Sol dashed the thought aside. Travelers would never have made it this far. Nor had they reason to come unless they were with a star.

Or had a death wish.

Sol focused on walking. The shimmering afterimages the phantasm lifted from the ground couldn't tempt him to lead everyone astray. He put one foot in front of the other and ignored all else but the path forward.

He didn't know how long it was, silence growing taut between them as the echoes of their boots crunching the snow filled the air, but he was drawn back to the reality of his body when his legs began to throb. As a headache wormed its way behind his eyes. Exhaustion reared its ugly head, leaving the pain all too evident. The cracks must have gone further up his arms; pain stretched all the way to his shoulders now. All he wanted to do was forge on—it couldn't have been much farther now—but as soon as he acknowledged his mortal body, the spell of unrealness was gone. He began tilting too far in one direction. Loren caught him before his legs gave out, the touch making him jolt. Nebora finally sighed from his other side.

"Let's make camp." She stretched her arms and cracked her neck. "Can't tell how late it is, but I'm don't think we're going to make it before it's night. I'd rather us face whatever's waiting in there well-rested."

There were murmurs of agreement among everyone and Sol bit back from insisting they continue. His mind was frayed, his vision dizzy, and any attempt to continue would end badly. He acquiesced. Maybe closing his eyes would help dull the pain. Although, he doubted he'd actually sleep. Not with how close they were.

No one moved and he realized everyone watched him.

"Well?" Gareth crossed his arms. "There anywhere safe here?"

Right. Safe. Sol probably was, now that he thought about it, but perhaps they wouldn't be out in the open. The scourge watched them too closely. Too quietly. Sol swallowed, easing his fingers along the bruises all but faded from view, and peered across the land anew. Barren. Empty. Lonely. He wondered how it must have looked when the first star arrived. Had she seen an ocean with sparkling waves beneath a warm sun? Or was it cold and dusted with snowflakes as it was now?

The more he thought of her, the more he caught sight of the forgotten footpaths she'd once taken. Her soft footsteps led him through the snow, magic impressing itself along her path, and it hummed. Different than the spire; this one instilled hope in his heart.

Her magicked footsteps led them up to a nearby ridge overlooking the emptiness below. There was a buried firepit of a journey long forgotten with flecks of her magic upon the buried logs still. Unfortunately, the sky remained black above them. No stars to whisper soothing words to Sol. It would do all the same.

"Here," Sol said, his voice lost against the howl of the wind. He peered out and followed the bends of the land as it sloped downward toward the spire. Closer than he thought and he swallowed. "This should be good enough."

"There it is." Gareth had come up beside him, an arm's length away that Nebora immediately filled. A twist of annoyance curled Gareth's lips and he crossed his arms. "At least we know we'll be there tomorrow. Maybe by midday or earlier if the gusts subside." His breath was a white plume as he exhaled. "Finally."

Thankfully, there was enough wood buried in the firepit to blaze it anew. It fought back the chill the best it could and Sol resisted the urge to put his hands directly into it to feel the heat. Food was spread between them—dried meats, some preserved fruit Nebora had found at the gates, and stale bread. Sol couldn't find his appetite. His gaze continually drew toward the Onyx Spire. It watched them and he watched it in turn.

What if he left in the night? It wasn't far. He'd make it; the star would make sure. No one would have to know. No one would have to feel the end upon them because they'd be fast asleep. The thought snapped as Sol remembered the frozen faces up against the wall, how they were in such stark contrast to the calmness Trudy had found in her own passing. Two contradictory deaths at the hands of scourge. Not to mention all those they'd found on the roadside. He couldn't be sure which would happen to them. Would they wake to see the world swallowed up? Or would they simply cease to be and not even realize it? Both answers chilled him too much and fear kept him from leaving by himself.

Mira was strumming her lute again, the chords hesitant and subdued. She'd been so quiet since last night, eyes downcast and sad, and Sol wanted her back. The warm voice attempting to melt the growing silence. Nebora hummed with her, scant words from her lips following the beat—ones Mira had penned. Sol wanted to hear it all, everything she had from start to finish even in its unrefined state, but he didn't voice the plea.

Because it didn't matter.

Gareth finished his food first and left to secure the perimeter. Not that there was anything here; everything but them was dead. No scourge would attack with Sol here. They were his guests into the star's tomb. Yet, the scourge in Gareth had grown restless. Maybe walking helped.

"Sol?" Loren's soft voice broke through the silence Sol had been listening to as he tracked Gareth's movements. Loren had been trying to get his attention for the last minute and he watched Sol softly. "You good to sleep in my tent tonight?"

To be fair, Sol *had* been sleeping in Loren's tent the entire time, he'd just had Mira with him instead of Loren. Not this time, it appeared; she'd already gone into Nebora's tent with her. Maybe she needed sisterly warmth. Sol certainly couldn't provide it.

"It's fine."

They stayed together at the fire, watching it dance as it threw embers into the sky, until Nebora returned and settled beside Sol. Gareth came back shortly and when he sat, Loren cleared his throat.

"I'll take first watch," he said.

"Second," Nebora called.

"Third." Gareth stood back up, dusting off his pants, and didn't linger before he went to his tent. The flaps shut tight, sealing him off, and there was the telltale thunk of his armor coming off for the night.

"Fourth?" Sol tried, but Nebora shook her head.

"Squishies stay in tonight," she said. "Don't know what's out here. I'm not risking it."

Not risking another attack from Gareth was closer to the truth. The knight was certainly in a mood tonight, but Sol didn't mind skipping watch to avoid it. Sol nodded slowly and Nebora returned to her tent. As the flaps closed, murmured words filtered forth and Mira giggled softly from within. The rest of what was said was too quiet to hear beyond the crackling fire and Sol wasn't going to try and eavesdrop.

Alone with Loren, Sol hesitated. He was almost tempted to stay with him and the fire, but then Loren touched his arm.

"Sleep," he said. "I'll be fine. It's calming out here."

It *was* calm; there was a certain sense of finality so close to the spire, but Sol knew his finality differed from Loren's. Nevertheless, Sol nodded and entered Loren's tent to curl up in the furs he'd come to know so well. With his cloak tight around him, he only hoped he found warmth somewhere.

He never did and neither did he find sleep. Sol shivered, trying to stay still, but his body was so cold.

The pain down his arms had magnified, itching like his skin really was coming apart again, and he clamped his arms tightly across himself to try and prevent it. Maybe it was in his head. Maybe it was the voice worming its way through the dark.

"Come to me," it said, so clear and distinct.

His bones hummed with it, singing through the cracks in his skin just to reply. Sol held himself tighter and shut his eyes tight. His skin couldn't split open now and reduce his sad journey to an end right then and there. Nothing would be finished. Nothing would end. Another star would simply fall and continue the cycle, hearing Sol's own sadness. He begged for sleep—for oblivion to block out the sound and the pain. But in the focused dark, he instead saw a pyre.

The image stopped him outright and he picked himself up. Flames flickered against the hazy castle courtyard around him where bodies stood, their faces and details blurred, and all eyes were trained on the pyre. Sol's body was moving toward it before he could tell what was happening and he effortlessly slid through everyone like they weren't even there. He climbed atop the wooden plinth and found himself already laying against the flames breaking his skin.

Except it wasn't him. It was his star scourge as it

lay still within Celena.

It was her body lying in the fire, wrapped from head to toe in snow white linen. They were finally burning her to send her back to the earth. Embers drew high around her as a funeral song hummed through the air, making a melody with the crackling fire. Her bones crumbled before long. The crystallized star scourge cracking all the same. Glimmers coating her from the inside out that no one could see turned into embers. Stars once born in her veins left to die because that was what scourge was. The end of a star.

Yet, there was still no warmth. Even as he pressed himself close to her. Not a flicker, even as her body was consumed. He wanted a sign—something soft and true—he could hold onto that was the quintessential her being released upon her death, but it was already gone. He'd never get her back. Not her smile or her laugh. Not her warmth. Not the way her fingers gently stroked his hair.

She was gone.

He blinked, ripping himself away from the image as his star scourge burned, and he sucked in a real breath. Ice-cold air washed down his throat, reminding him what was real, and tears dampened his cheeks. Everything around him felt too real at once; the furs, the howling wind outside, the way the firelight danced against the tent—everything. He squeezed his eyes shut, breathing in and out to forget.

It worked until he heard movement coming toward the tent.

He hurried to wipe his cheeks as Loren pushed the flap aside to come in. Nebora busied herself outside with a hum and the aroma of coffee carried into the tent.

Loren only caught Sol looking after he'd taken off some of his leather armor and settled his sword down. He smiled sadly. "Ah, can't sleep?"

"No." Sol averted his gaze, searching for a plausible reason. "I'm cold."

"Yet you have all the fur and blankets," Loren teased and reached over to tuck Sol in tighter. For a brief moment, Sol's mouth betrayed him and smiled at the attention, but he immediately bit it back.

"No," he said and Loren paused. "It's not the lack of blankets. I just... I can't get warm. More won't help if I simply don't let off enough heat."

Loren paused, considering it, and gently felt Sol's forehead with an ungloved hand. The skin was warm. Sol wanted it to stay there. Or against the cheek Loren felt next, but he took it away too.

"You really *are* cold." Loren watched Sol, green eyes twinkling in the dim light, and laid himself beside Sol with space between them Sol wished wasn't there. "Do you know why? Were you this cold before?"

"I'm a dying star," Sol said. "I suppose I'll just grow colder." He held out an arm and peeled the sleeve back. The line was still cracked with thinner ones webbing out like roots along the length of his arm. Loren brought it closer and ran his fingertips over it. The gentle touch sent goosebumps across Sol's skin.

"I don't know why it's doing this," Sol said to cover his reaction. "I dreamt I-I saw Celena's pyre. M-Maybe it's because of that. O-Or maybe it's simply because we're so close now. I hear it all the time now—the scourge in the spire."

Loren kept hold of Sol's arm, but gently rolled the sleeve back down. "Is there anything that would help?" He turned on his side so he faced Sol. "What did Celena do before?"

"What do you mean?"

"She held you together when you made your body, right? You said the lines were thicker because she was late in keeping you together. She must have done something. This looks like you're coming apart again."

Sol hadn't thought of it like that. The pain along the lines and his joints did indeed mirror how he'd felt so long ago when Celena had been taken away from him. It had all changed when he was within Celena's embrace; his skin had resumed sewing itself together.

"Let me help," Loren whispered. "What can I do? I don't want this to happen to you." He hadn't let go of Sol's hand, like it was a lifeline keeping Sol together.

Loren was warm. Impossibly so. Alike Celena, but also entirely different in what emotions it sparked in Sol's heart. And, like Celena, he wanted to help. It wouldn't matter, but Sol wanted to pretend it would. He hesitated for a single breath, watching Loren's eyes in the dim light, and then tucked himself beneath Loren's chin to press himself as close as he could.

"Could I have this?" Sol whispered as Loren stiffened. "For one night?"

At first, Loren's fingers tightened with a grip too unsure to read, but then the rest of his body relaxed. He rested his other arm across Sol and gathered him closer.

"Of course. All the nights you need." Loren drew the pile of furs closer, tucking it around them both, and never once let go of Sol's hand. A tether to real warmth, reminding Sol it existed, and bit by bit, Sol began to forget all about the chill. All about himself falling apart.

"You're warm," Sol found himself whispering as he rested his head against Loren's chest. "I can hear your heart."

Loren chuckled and Sol liked how the sound reverberated through him. "I'm surprised."

"I can hear lots of things," Sol said. "Whispers from the spire. The hum on the scourge. Your heart. I don't think mine beats the same anymore." He trailed off as Loren put a careful hand to Sol's chest. The touch made his pulse race and Loren chuckled.

"I can still feel it," he said softly. "How are you so sure it's not the same?"

Sol's cheeks warmed. "Perhaps it's because of you." The words sounded too bold aloud, especially when Loren raised his eyebrows. "W-What would your life have been if the scourge hadn't come?" Sol blurted out the question to hide his sudden embarrassment.

Loren paused, gaze searching Sol like he didn't understand.

"I-I asked Mira a while ago," Sol added quickly. "She said she-she might not have left home. M-Maybe on her way to be wed instead of traveling. I'm... I'm curious."

Loren's confusion melted. "Oh," he said and glanced away. "There wasn't much for us in Yarrow, so that sounds like what was expected of her. We'd pair up, have kids, continue village traditions." He inclined his head, hair wisping across his forehead. "Maybe if you were smart, they'd gather funds to send you off to one of the castle sanctioned universities we used to have before the scourge, but more likely no. Never enough funds—pretty sure it was always a lie. They needed all the hands they could get." He adjusted his arm across Sol, hand brushing up against Sol's hip until he decided to rest it higher on his back. "Wasn't much of a life, to be honest."

"You didn't like it?" Sol asked.

"I was sixteen." Loren shrugged. "I slept around and didn't care about anything beyond that as long as I had fun. Only when my father died—when I dragged Mira out of all that—did I feel like life was something I could lose." He frowned and sighed. "I honestly don't know what I would have done if the scourge hadn't come. I wasn't smart enough to leave. I wasn't *good* at anything but sleeping around, minding the animals, and mending cloth."

Sol waited, hoping for more, but he'd trailed off. Sadder than Sol thought he'd be. "Would you change anything?"

"I don't know." Loren's face shifted so subtly, Sol wasn't sure if it was a smile or not. "If I changed anything, I might not have met you." He gently brought Sol's hand between them and kissed the knuckles. The act made Sol shiver, but not from the cold. It was a sensation not altogether unwanted. "I think that in itself is worth it."

Once more, Sol's lips betrayed him with a smile. How many now had Loren invited since they met? Sol wanted to memorize each and every instance, even if there was too many to count. He brought Loren's hand closer and kissed it on the knuckles the same, never breaking eye contact. "Were you serious before?" he whispered. "Asking me to travel with you?"

"I wouldn't have said so if I wasn't," Loren said. "It's lonely on the road. Even with Mira and we know how much she chatters." He chuckled and Sol stifled his own laughter. "But she might want to stick with Nebora and learn how to scare people like her. I just want to go somewhere that isn't here."

Somewhere that wasn't here.

There was a sudden urge deep in Sol's core. Something light and weightless dispersing within him despite the hesitant voice inside telling him this very human feeling was a lie. It was a downfall. He ignored it and lifted his head to softly press his lips to Loren's.

The moment stilled for perhaps an eternity, or,

more likely, a single second, before he received a gentle kiss back. When they parted, Sol found Loren watching him so softly, a question on his lips. Sol couldn't resist answering it and kissed Loren again.

And again, and again until all he felt was the warmth of the hungry kisses shared between them. So warm and all encompassing; stealing the world away until they were the only two who'd ever existed. Sol hardly noticed his fingers tangling in Loren's hair to push him closer and he hardly cared when Loren reciprocated with the hand firmly behind his own head. He never wanted to lift his lips from Loren's. He wanted to feel them all over his skin and wanted his own to do the same to Loren.

The warmth between them simply grew until it was so overwhelming, the chill never existed. The world became bright and fuzzy because of Loren's touch and it made everything else disappear. All Sol's body—his entire being—wanted was to taste Loren, share with him all the warmth he could manage on his own, and never let him go, even if the world ended.

Sol might have kept it up too, urged Loren's hands underneath his tunic and tempted his own beneath Loren's, if he hadn't needed to breathe. If reality hadn't dragged him back down, reminding him the soft warmth was fleeting. But *what* a fleeting moment it was.

"Thank you," Sol whispered while Loren peppered his cheek with softer kisses. "For everything. For looking for me when I looked lonely. For watching out for me. Checking to make sure I was alive. For just... being with me."

Loren paused and tilted his head. "Don't make it sound like this is the end," he whispered, gently brushing Sol's hair back. "We've got a world to see, don't we?"

Sol wanted to believe Loren. He tucked himself against Loren's neck so he didn't feel compelled to kiss him again to forget the aching reality. Hide his indecision beneath their shared pulse. Hide everything that may happen in the bliss of Loren's touch.

"I'm glad I met you." The words spilled out without conscious thought and he wished they hadn't sounded so sad.

Loren gently ran his fingers through Sol's hair and trailed the same hand down from Sol's neck to the small of his back. A jolt of pleasure dispersed through Sol with it there. Loren pressed Sol tighter against him and Sol happily curled up as close as he could.

"I'm glad we met too," he whispered and kissed Sol's forehead. "We've got a big day tomorrow. Try to sleep, for me."

Maybe Sol could, tucked inside Loren as he was, tasting him on his lips. He had to try. Sol shut his eyes and focused on the complete warmth that was Loren of Yarrow beside him. Hero, despite his insistence otherwise. His presence, his entirety was a grounding element even as the darkness threatened to pull Sol apart. He breathed the man in deep, memorizing all that he was, and concentrated on the heartbeat within. The one free of scourge.

Sol never wanted to move. He wanted to stay there until the gods themselves awoke and the world truly ceased to be.

"Crusted in salt shimmering like crystal,
*   the chapel ribboned colors like a shell.*
Inside, the voice led her.
*   Tempted her like a spell*
to peer into the end of all things,
*   what darkness humanity keeps quelled."*

—Fragment of "She, Born of Starlight," Anonymous

MORNING HERALDED THE STARK REALITY OF everything. Promises but forgone memories in the fuzzy dark. Over a meager breakfast and the rest of their coffee, they agreed to only bring the barest necessities, leaving the tents and most of their belongings tucked inside them. The walk shouldn't take them more than half the day and after everything—*After the end*, Sol thought distantly to himself—they could return here. Nothing had come in the night, no sound had stirred, and nothing had moved but the push and pull of the wind. Mira insisted her lute stayed with her and Sol was glad no one told her to leave it behind. It was part of her.

The trek was a slog even though they could see all the way to the Onyx Spire. The wind ripped a biting chill through their cloaks and pushed Sol and Mira as though they were paper. Nebora pulled her arm tight across Mira, keeping her steady, and Loren did the same with Sol. The motion ignited a soft warmth deep in his stomach, reminding him of last night, and he wished to return there to pretend the night had never ended.

Wishes weren't answered. He buried the desire as far as he could. Soon, it wouldn't matter.

Gareth trudged on in front, some sense of dignity keeping him upright even against the harshest gust. The veins in his neck had grown dark and the more Sol studied him now, the more he felt the wrongness welling up inside. It was a testament he still stood as straight as he did. The scourge was closer to the surface than ever and sung softly as the spire guided it.

They came upon the base of the spire sooner than Sol was ready for. He peeked out from beneath Loren's cloak and his stomach practically turned sideways. They were really here. The end.

The obsidian black spire jutted out of the land like a spear thrust into the ground from the darkened sky above. The phantasm of the star blazed high above, sheathing them in its flickering ethereal hues, and Sol heard the star herself. Not words, but a deep sound Sol hadn't heard since he'd fallen. A reverberation stars made against the emptiness between one another. A drone making his bones shiver. What once lulled him to sleep in the cosmos now filled him with dread. Making it so nothing felt right underneath its weight.

The entryway to the Onyx Spire was covered with a sheet of scourge reminiscent of glass, but it must have once been opened as a long black stain extended from the spire and down the road. The windows had been blown out long before, each one letting scourge spill over the edges. It created ribbons as it fell to the ground, snaring itself in place, and resembled a spider's web. Higher and higher, the scourge linked back to the spire, never once moving in the wind.

In fact, the squalls and gusts had stopped altogether. *Everything* felt like it had. Hushed while it waited to see what would happen here in the center of the dying world.

Whispers spilled from the tower, so many more than Sol expected and his heart sped simply listening. Lives upon lives of stars ending right here in front of him. Echoes of who they'd been was all that was left.

"What *was* this before?" Mira asked, her voice quivering. Sol couldn't tell if it was from her teeth chattering because of the cold or if it was because she was scared. No one answered her and she glanced at Sol. "It had to be *something*, right? The bard tales never say anything about this. Just that it's an onyx-black spire."

Sol swallowed and straightened his back. "Inside is a well. It's supposedly the center of the world," he said. "The point where the world meets and where it drifts away." He glanced at the frozen waves crowning the horizon. "This used to be an ocean."

As he formed the words, he saw it as it once was. The image reached out through eyes not his own. Bare feet on a summer day in the waves. He picked his gaze up; there was no spire then. He held out a hand and a sheer, white sleeve dipped down his arm, revealing skin covered in stardust. The waves trusted him and fled until they uncovered a small chapel of salt and coral. A happy sigh left his lips, a soft song, and he turned. Companions were there, but fuzzy. Faces not real. Gone to the flow of time. But in them, he felt familiarity. Friendliness. Trust. They would never harm him, not after the years spent together searching for this moment.

Sol blinked, jolting back to his own body, and the whispers let him go. The first star had been here when it was so warm and bright. His world slotted painfully back into place. The salt and coral chapel became a spire of scourge once more, jutting into the sky covered in never-ending darkness. The star above was a halo of light, burning as a dying flame.

And she whispered to him once more, words almost lost behind the pulse pounding in his ears. *"Don't be scared,"* she sang so softly as her phantom fingers traced his cheek. *"I'm here."*

"Why did the first star even come out here?" Nebora's voice drowned out the star.

"She heard something," Sol whispered. "It drew her here."

Gareth glanced at him, eyebrows in a tight line. "Do *you* hear it?"

Yes. No. Sol refused to answer and stepped onto the scourge darkening the road. It ignited through his weary legs, pushing through him with a hymn of so many stars mixed together, each voice sad and forlorn. Every step he took closer was a new verse and it lit up as glittering ripples beneath his feet as he neared what was once the doorway, now thick with scourge like it protected what was inside.

He pressed his hand to the center and the song shivered into the door. It pulled itself apart like roots and allowed him entrance.

Sol breathed out and faced Gareth.

"I hear a cry no one else does and it has led me here," he said and Gareth stiffened, the scourge in him quieting.

Sol didn't bother elaborating and walked inside.

It was small, black walls closing in around him while crystallized scourge hung from the ceiling like ribbons. The ground resembled black glass spiraled with stardust, creating the only light source in a haunting white glow. Each arm of the spiral led to the exact center below a dome that must have been the top of the coral chapel in the past. Now it was slick with scourge glittering like stars above, watching. In the center of the room, where the spirals met, was a raised dais with three steps leading up to it, each one crusted at the edge with glowing crystals. Upon the dais was what resembled a low well, the sides barely above Sol's waist, and the edge of that had been crusted the same. It would have been beautiful if Sol hadn't known the truth.

Right there was where the scourge began. Where the whispered truth gurgled below the surface. Right there was the end.

Sol's legs carried him up the well, following the path so many other stars have walked, and he peered inside. A pair of milky white eyes stared skyward, empty of all things.

Until her gaze flicked to his.

Their eyes locked and in hers, the world shifted. Days and nights flew by as colors and streaks until it came to a sudden halt. He lifted his gaze to the entryway. Flickering light spilled inside from a torch held aloft by a traveler and then *she* strode inside. The star before him. Her skin the same warm brown as his, dusted with the same white freckles, and her white hair was drawn over her shoulder, braided with pale ribbons. Even decked in cloaks and furs, she was as radiant as the stars above with a smile that made the world glimmer.

She turned her smile to her companions coming in behind her, only to be met with a blade so sudden, even Sol flinched. Everything went black. Her last memory died so quickly and suddenly, there was no time for a prayer. No time for a cry. She'd trusted them—Sol felt the betrayal deep in his heart—and her cry echoed across two centuries. She didn't understand. The ones who'd made it home became heroes, lauded until their dying breath on a lie that they were as pure as could be as they stuffed her decapitated body and severed head into the well.

Because she was disposable.

And then, the world shifted again, another hum in Sol's ear stringing him along. Time bled by in spurts until he saw the star who'd loved his prince as the stories sang. Tall and lean, he looked ever the warrior his escorts were. His white hair had been shorn across one side and braided along the other. With him was the wrapped body of the prince, Sol knew it intimately across time, and the young man had already breathed his last just like Celena. The world hadn't been worth living without him, so the star had gone into the well willingly as he held the wrapped body of his prince close. His escorts left with heavy hearts to a world filling with light, but after a time, the star's absolution wavered. The prince's body began to dissolve in the dark. First went his funeral wrappings. Then his skin and hair. Then all his muscles and tissue until only his skeleton remained wrapped up in the star's arms. And even then, the skeleton turned to dust, leaving the star truly alone in the dark he'd willingly entered. Loss and fear gripped him so absolutely until the well held his sadness no longer.

So many stars found the same fate. Willingly or otherwise. Again and again, trapped in the well, alone, desperate, and it tore them apart. All to bring light back to the world. One which proved again and again it didn't deserve it because it never learned. The memories ceased flying past Sol, leaving him with but glimpses of all the smiles and cries the stars left behind, and the first star came back into view. She stood beside him as she peered over the well created from white coral. The rest of the chapel retained its color, but the closer it came to the well, the more bleached it was. Soft dappled light shimmered through the windows, making the first star positively aglow beneath it.

Her eyes were trained on something inside. The well full of pitch-black darkness as though light was swallowed up and devoured within. Nothing inside but a whimper.

She gazed into the dark, listening, and those she loved, those she trusted as she set off on a pilgrimage across the land, forced her inside despite her screams. The sound echoed through the memory, rippling it into pieces, and Sol could do nothing but watch as the blurred shapes forced her into the dark. Humanity couldn't bear the weight of their own darkness coming alive below their very world, so they made her confront it for them because she'd come curious enough to help. To help save them from something deep in the dark they didn't understand. Could hardly even hear. Just felt deep in their hearts. They made her face it all alone and never returned as it consumed her, flesh and mind.

The scourge *was* her, just as it was every star after her. She began it all. Her cry as her body ripped apart from the unseen monster became the fleeting whispers carried by the wind. Sol watched as everything she was spewed forth from the well, screaming with her terror and her pain, as it overtook the coral chapel. The spire formed, glittering against a dying sun as the sky darkened with her rage. Everything she touched—everything she saw—became a blackened shell of itself.

She cried and cried for a witness to her betrayal. For someone to save her.

And then came another star, glittering across the skies.

Stars fell to help their brethren, only to trust humanity and believe in human emotions. Only to be betrayed just like the first. Or left to face the dark alone when no one should. Stars never quite realized what every human being would choose until it was too late. Always a star's death if it meant humanity would live and flourish.

Humanity never learned. Humanity continued to turn a blind eye to the stars it ripped apart. Humanity who buried stars in the dark. Humanity who *allowed* the cycle to continue on and on so long as they never had to confront their own darkness.

Sol took in a ragged breath, finding his lungs starved for air. Someone had said his name. He blinked and the present fixed itself around him, tearing him away from the stars of the past and giving him the star of the present. The one his hand was touching as its eyes watched him. It was her head. All that was left. Her body was long gone, eaten alive by the dark humanity refused to acknowledge as their own doing. He gently scooped his arms into the well and pulled her free.

The skin had sloughed off her skull, leaving white eyes forever open. Her hair was blackened from the scourge clinging tight to it like crystals. Sol's hands shook. This was the voice who cried for his help. The one he swore vengeance for because few humans were kind. She deserved more than they'd given her. She deserved to live. They deserved to rot.

Except *they* were already dead. Her vengeance would never touch them, only humanity so far removed from those who had destroyed everything she was and buried her so she became vague and pretty. Name and who she was lost to time.

It was always like this. A cycle continuing on and on in which humanity had no interest in stopping. Sol would be no different if he didn't break the wheel. His wants didn't matter. Only the promise he'd made upon his fall.

Trembling, he faced everyone. They watched him in silent shock, eyes wide and fixed on the head of his sister star who humans had killed two centuries ago.

"This," Sol spoke, "is what they did to the star before me. *This* is what they do to us. We are not your saviors. We are simply *material*." Tears glinted at the edge of his eyes. "Nothing more than a means to an end because humans will never confront their own darkness. You wall it off. Then you kill us and shove us into the well to buy you more time until our sadness—our decay—reaches a singular point, it explodes. She trusted her heroes and they cut off her head so she'd be easier to shove inside. They killed her and smothered her so they didn't have to face their own rotten hearts." He gently laid her head back in the well and shut what was left of her eyes. "Through your own misguidance does the cycle continue!" He whipped back to face them and they still did not move. "Your bard songs have no room for stars because we are disposable. Your cries are *not* the reason we're here; it is our own."

His voice cracked as he stared at Loren. His sudden resolve wavered beneath the gaze of the man who warmed the cold nights with just a smile. A simple touch fluttering through him. Scourge hummed through Sol's body in response, reminding him of everything he'd felt, blazing hot and raw through him, chasing the softness away. He had to continue; even he knew it. Tears ran down his cheeks, hot against his frigid skin. The cycle had to end on his terms or it simply wouldn't.

"I will *not* be your bleeding heart," Sol said, barely able to raise his voice as he tore his gaze away from Loren's. Part of himself begged him to reconsider, but the scourge inside and out drowned it out. "This will end here as I promised her it would, no matter my thoughts."

The scourge sang a hymn so absolute around him, it filled his entire body until it no longer felt separated. Until he himself felt born of scourge. Warmth ignited beneath his skin, reminding him of the star he'd been, and it coalesced as a single point inside his chest. Even as his own thoughts wavered— even as he whispered *no*—the star's rage built inside him. Because he would be her weapon. The scourge hanging from the ceiling bent toward him, the very gravity in the spire pulling everything so taut, like it would explode as soon as it touched him. The entire spire shook and laughter from the star bubbled out of the dark until it was all Sol could hear. Light built behind Sol's eyes, blurring everything before him out as a haze, until it all stopped at once.

A white-hot pain pierced his chest.

Everything fell silent and still. Sol blinked and looked down. His tears sparkled past the knife protruding from his chest.

"It began with her curiosity made manifest
with the voice humanity ignored, where darkness pervades.
Taken inside the dark, though not by her own choice,
but one we'd made for her because we were afraid.

And this will remain buried until the end of time,
of how our star, our lovely star, was betrayed."

—Fragment of "She, Born of Starlight," Anonymous

"**H**ER MAJESTY KNEW THIS WOULD HAPPEN," Gareth's voice rose above the panic roaring in Sol's ears. The knight stood proud, undaunted, as everyone faced him with unabashed shock.

White sparkling blood bloomed across Sol's tunic. He tasted it in his mouth. Coppery and warm. No. He blinked and more tears fell. Not like this.

"She *knew* you'd turn on us. The dull, uninspired star." Gareth moved, the metal of his boots clinking hard against the floor. Loud and real. Sol needed to get away—needed the knife out—but Gareth was in front of him too soon. "I just had to wait for it." He ripped the knife free himself and Sol staggered forward with it, catching himself on Gareth. More blood spilled on the ground between them and Sol's vision blurred.

"If *this* is what it takes to give us our lives back, so be it." Gareth's hand caught Sol's neck and pushed him upright, forcing Sol to look up at him. He had his sword out. When had that happened? Gareth's expression emptied of everything else but disdain. "You don't belong here."

A crossbow bolt whizzed between them and Gareth leapt back, releasing Sol's neck. Gareth turned, eyes wide, and Sol caught himself on the edge of the well. Mira loaded another bolt and Nebora and Loren flanked her, weapons drawn. Gareth threw an arm out in front of him, tossing his cloak over his shoulder.

"Fucking heroes from *nowhere*! She sent you as filler—you were never meant to get *this* far. I let you come all this way!" Gareth's voice slurred with a discordant hum. "You will die here if you want it so badly and no one will remember you!"

Another bolt went flying, but he saw it coming and pivoted, gritting his teeth. This time, Nebora charged after it, raising her axe high. Gareth jerked his sword upward to deflect her assault and sparks flew as their weapons clashed. He pushed her off and quickly made space between them Nebora was all too eager to fill with another swing. Sol lost them to a sudden haze of darkness as blood spilled out of his mouth in a sharp cough. It spotted into the well below, snaking inside as a ribbon of white.

No. This couldn't be it. Tears spilled over his eyes again.

"Sol—Sol, listen to me."

He picked his head up, taking in a gasping breath. Loren was right there on the dais with him. One arm steadying Sol, while keeping his other hand pressed against the wound. The scourge rumbled below them, whispers angry and warm, and shot up around them. It shoved Loren back and echoed a snarl through the spire. Mira tried to catch Loren, but her weight was no match against his; they clattered on the ground together and her crossbow went flying. Loren quickly picked himself up, gritting his teeth, and this time when the scourge rose to push him back, he endured.

"*Please*," he said, voice straining, and forced himself forward. The scourge tried to rip him back as hooks snaring his clothes, but he shucked it all off. "We didn't want this for you. We didn't know. I swear—*Sol*—I won't leave you here like this."

The way Loren said Sol's name each time made

him shiver. Made him want to believe. Sol shook his head as more tears ran down his cheeks. His conviction died. He couldn't do it. Not with how Loren stared at him, desperate. Not after the kisses he'd memorized to take into the dark oblivion. Sol opened his mouth, but all that came out was another gasping cough as blood and scourge ripped through his throat. He vomited it into the well until the entire thing swirled black and white below him.

It was enough to make the well overflow, letting scourge bubble over the sides. It slopped to the floor in heaps and formed hands to charge Loren again. Sol tried to stop it, but his concentration was too slow and his own hands useless as the scourge bled through them. The scourge persisted, screaming an unholy war cry that echoed above Nebora's and Gareth's own battle.

Loren held his sword out in front of him. The scourge bisected itself like ribbons upon the blade and the sensation ghosted through Sol. By the time he had himself back, the scourge was charging for Mira. Loren realized it too late to shield her; she flew back a second time from the force, screaming, and hit the back wall hard. She crumpled to the ground and Nebora whipped around, eyes wide. Gareth took his opening; his blade jutted into her side, slinging her blood across the floor.

Nebora retreated, gritting her teeth, and again and again she did the same as Gareth gained the advantage. His eyes had grown black from scourge and it writhed inside his body to augment everything he was. Strides became quick and purposeful and his strikes powered through any defense. Nebora withdrew, narrowly dodging each slice. It cleaved through the wall. Even the floor. Everything from strength that wasn't his. Loren rushed him, but he was no match. Gareth shucked him off like an insect and as Loren slumped against the dais, Gareth raised his blade high. Sol threw all his focus into the scourge inside Gareth to make him stop.

The sword did, but not for the reason Sol wanted. Gareth had stopped it all on his own and stared at Sol with eyes bleeding scourge down his cheeks. A wicked smile twitched across his lips. He kicked Loren out of his way and advanced too quickly. Sol tried to make the scourge around him rise—shield him—but his betrayal was too stark. It'd let him die so the star could use him as a puppet for her vengeance if he wasn't willing. Before Gareth could strike, another crossbow bolt shot between them, and Gareth snarled as he faced it. Loren threw the crossbow aside to dodge the counter, and dragged an alert Mira behind rubble for coverage. Gareth's sword lodged itself into it, unable to slice all the way through thankfully, and before he could pull his sword free, Nebora brought her labrys down on his scourge-infected arm.

The first slice didn't take off the arm entirely, but Gareth screamed. The skin began ripping itself apart as scourge forced itself out of its prison, and Nebora struck the arm again, cutting it off entirely.

And the scourge and screaming didn't end there. As though been given permission, the scourge tore Gareth's skin apart along every single vein. It vibrated, humming a song so wrong and violent as first his arm came apart. Then his legs. Then his throat as scourge spewed forth with the gurgling scream. The rest of his body followed suit, ripping apart his tunic and armor like it was tissue. Each split was a violent spray until he was finally silent and still on the ground.

Dead.

The scourge freed from Gareth scurried across the spire, sparkling bright with flecks of his blood, and more and more spilled from the well to join it. The previous star's head came up too, splitting open to free more shimmering scourge, and it began to whirl around Sol. Protection. A cage. He couldn't stop it. No one could absolve her anger except for him and the scourge would force him. He shook his head. He couldn't do this. He picked his gaze up again and found Loren's. Words failed. The plea for help became silent in his throat.

But Loren heard the silence. He pushed Mira into Nebora's arms to stand.

Loren's blade sung through the air as he drove himself through the scourge trying to wall Sol off. The scourge bristled at a human's intrusion and redoubled its efforts; it tore at his arms, cutting deep welts across any exposed skin, and then stole his sword entirely. Through it all, however, Loren forged on, eyes never once leaving Sol's.

"Sol," he said again in the way that made Sol's heart sing. "Sol—I promise you. I won't leave you here alone. I won't. We have a world to see."

Everything else was gone in the back of Sol's mind as he listened to Loren's soft voice. Not alone. A whole world to see. More tears spilled down Sol's cheeks. The scourge tried ripping through them again in a panic, desperately screaming at him that all humans told lies—flashes of evidence bloomed through Sol's thoughts unwanted—but Sol held onto the lie and tried to push through. He was too weak. The scourge ripped him back by snagging his hair in fistfuls, making white hot pain shoot throughout Sol's whole head, until it had fashioned a twisting wall between him and the rest of the room. Loren cried out in pain. So had Nebora and Mira. The scourge was too thick to see through. It was absolute.

This was it. The end and Sol could do nothing to stop the star from using him to enact total revenge. All she needed to do was wear him down. Get inside. Then they would all die.

Unless—

Every time a star went into the well, the scourge went away. It all ceased, just like that. A new sacrifice calmed everything and allowed the previous one to move on. Light returned and humanity prevailed. It could save them.

Tears washed down Sol's cheeks anew. He was falling for the same lies, the same emotions he promised himself he wouldn't, but he desperately didn't want Loren to die.

"If I go into the well," Sol called out and all the movement in the spire slowed as though to listen, "this all stops. I'm sorry." His voice cracked even as he tried to level it. "I wanted to go with you, Loren. I really did."

The scourge screamed, buzzing so loud in Sol's head, he thought for sure it aimed to tear his thoughts apart until he stopped the foolish decision. Darkness overflowed the edges of the well, so much of it, Sol wondered if he would even be enough to stop it all, but he had to try. The pain in his chest made him grit his teeth as he threw one leg over the ledge, and then the next. All he had to do was let go and plunge in after all the other stars before him.

Until a broken sword cleaved its way through the wall of scourge and Loren threw himself inside after it. He tossed his blade away and before Sol could react—push him away to protect him or plunge himself into the well to end everything—Loren looped his arm around Sol's waist and yanked him off the well. They clattered on the dais together, and once more, the scourge began turning like a whirlwind around them. Her voice was still in his head. Tearing his thoughts apart until he remembered the promise. Until he let her have everything he was and more.

Loren cupped Sol's cheek with a bare hand. It silenced her voice. Blossomed warmth between them. Sol blinked; Loren was protecting Sol from the scourge winding around them with his own body. The man's breathing was uneven and weak, the arm keeping him steady was shaking, and he looked ready to pass out. But he didn't. He smiled sadly and it was then Sol noticed the damp tears on his cheek.

"You are not disposable," Loren whispered. He drew Sol upward and pressed him close. "I promised you we'd see the world. I will not leave you here to sacrifice yourself."

Sol shook his head. Promises didn't matter. "I'm a dying star." The blood was thick on his lips. "There's nowhere for me to go. For me to do." He traced Loren's face with trembling fingers to memorize it. To take it with him into the dark. "This is all there is for me." He'd meant to convince himself of the fact, letting Loren go, but the words left him hollow. Cold. He pulled himself out from beneath Loren, but that was as far as he could take himself. Not with the way Loren watched Sol as he steadied himself. Sol tore his gaze away and stared into the infinite darkness deep inside the well. What would be his tomb.

"I..." He choked on the words and covered his mouth. "I—I don't want to die, Loren."

It came out quiet and weak, a silent prayer for another resolution. Another ending. The inside of the well shimmered as his tears hit it, as his blood continued to ribbon downward. Starlight spread out like galaxies inside and he shook his head. This was it. The end of his tale where all he'd become was vague and pretty. A dull, uninspired star and that was it.

Scourge flared anew, cutting him off from Loren once more, and desperate pleas and damning whispers filled his head. The previous star's voice was lost to a haze of so many others reaching out. To console him because he cared too much. To damn him for falling for the same human feelings all other stars fell for. He didn't care. This was his decision alone. To save those he loved. Even if it meant the end of him.

Loren forced himself through the squall of scourge a third time and caught himself on the edge of the well. Sol finally saw what the scourge had done to him for daring to care for a dying star; his cloak was in tatters behind him, pieces of his leather armor was torn beyond recognition, and his arms and face bled with so many cuts and welts, it was a wonder he still stood.

And yet, he never wavered. Kind eyes forever trained on Sol without malice or blame. He gripped Sol's shoulders. "Let humanity die and rot," he whispered. "You are not disposable. I will not leave you here alone to endure this. To die for us when humanity doesn't even care." He pulled Sol into a hug so suddenly, even the winding scourge slowed like it was in shock.

Until it stopped outright when Loren kissed Sol. The whole room did. Even though they were both bloodied and broken, Sol wanted so badly to melt into Loren. Ignore everything else and stay here with him.

It lasted a single moment before the scourge

twisted faster, making them part. The cries of count-less stars before Sol came down on them. Each one demanding revenge so absolute, the world would have to be swallowed up tenfold to absolve them. There was no other way.

Except Sol didn't want it to be the end. Be it as absolute revenge snuffing out the life from the world or the end of his own life to renew it. He wanted to live the promise Loren had made and this was his choice. Loren pressed him closer, arms tight across his back, and his lips found their way to Sol's cheek this time.

"Nebora!" Loren threw his head back, shouting. Sol couldn't see her through the spiraling scourge. "Take Mira and *run*!"

"No!" Mira screamed and then cried out. "Nebora put me down! Loren—no!"

"This better not be the end!" Nebora shouted. "Do you hear me, Loren?!"

Mira's cries to be put down and the sound of Nebora running became distant before they were drowned out by the roar of the scourge. The cries of the stars realizing all their machinations and plans of revenge was for nothing. Dying here as a whimper with no one to absolve their final wishes. No one here to grant them the oblivion of a new sacrifice.

"I promise you, Sol." Loren's voice anchored Sol

as his arms tightened around him. "You will never be alone."

The darkness wrapped around them, cocooning them inside scourge glittering like stars. It really felt like they were up high in the cosmos by the time it ceased. Sol pressed himself as close as he could to Loren and listened intently, trying to find his heart. The one thing true and right in a world grown dark. The scourge forced itself into Sol, crystallizing in his lungs as it stole away the pain. It made the world so distant and faraway.

If not for Loren's arms tight around Sol. Reality persisted. Helped him breathe.

Loren's absolute touch kept Sol from splitting. Pieced his mortal body back together as it began to fray and tear. Kept him whole as his own star scourge pushed out all the rest so he could heal. Even as the scourge screamed at him—begged him—to let it remain. To let the world meet its end. Sol would not. The stars would rest. He begged them to let go in return, squeezing his eyes shut.

His body became fuzzy and empty, the scourge within his own veins quieting to a dying whisper, and Loren's touch tethered Sol to his mortal body. Entwined their hearts together to the world he'd sought to end.

Whatever the scourge did now wouldn't matter

because Loren would never let him go. In turn, Sol never intended to let Loren go. Even if light itself winked out of existence because of this selfish choice they'd both made, stealing the world away in a whimper, even if it all fell to darkness for this one single thing, Sol didn't care. Loren's heartbeat was loud and sure in the dark. He was forever warm even as the deepest chill encroached. Even if the whole world was swallowed up because of Sol's inaction, his resolution here would not waver. The world had years to find a solution; he would not be the sacrificed star. Nor would he be the harbinger of a star's revenge. The cycle would end here and now.

As long as Sol was with Loren, wrapped in his arms—in their shared pulse—nothing else mattered.

— "Sol of the Cosmos" by Mira, the Swallow's Yarrow

IN THE DARKEST PIT OF THE DARKEST NIGHT stretched too far across the land, there came a shooting star. It lit up the sky so completely, the lands below glimmered in the wake of all the colors left behind. The searching star soared above it all and traveled across villages and towns awash with flickering embers for signs of life. At first, all was silent as though perhaps it all had ended. But then the star heard the song it searched for.

The bard's voice sung from sleepy taverns awake late into the night and she regaled humanity with the tale of a star just like the one falling now.

How he had loved a princess so brilliant and bright who died before her time. How he had fallen in love with a hero so humble and kind, he shied away from being called such. And of the darkness they trudged through to revive the world.

The star was long gone before it heard the end of the tale by her own voice, but more and more, bits and pieces arose from the towns not snuffed out in darkness. Echoes of the tale she'd left in her wake as she and the warrior woman at her side traveled so everyone knew the tale regardless of those trying to find blame in the very same tale to use against them. A story retold again and again of hope, of loss, of a single choice to live taken by one fated to die. Of cycles broken as righteous anger released, resting finally after years of torment despite the scars made deep into the land still filled with the dark.

The star continued its trek across the lands, watching for someone to catch it as the stories foretold, but perhaps, the world didn't truly need it. Perhaps it could remain a visitor simply passing by. No one stood poised, even if they noticed it passing overhead. A little wave was all the star received and it wished it had hands to return the human gesture.

What had drawn the star's attention this night had not been a cry for help like its brethren had whispered about, but rather two heartbeats curiously entwined. One the star knew as a friend gone from the cosmos. The sensation was so curious and warm, the star had to see it for itself.

The two heartbeats were loud and sure as they walked the world together as the story promised, leaving glittering footsteps in their wake as they themselves traveled the dark. A dark which uncoiled as they passed. Bit by bit, like embers of a soul put to rest. There was hope here now. A finality where the wounds would not be repeated. Of this, the star was sure.

The star need not fall tonight and rejoined the sky, letting its colors cover the world below it. In the moment it flung itself back into the cosmos it had been born in, the sun peeked out across the horizon. With it came a cascade of colors blooming through the dark. One of many new dawns the world saw as each day went by after all the cries fell silent.

Just like it was promised in the legend whispering high and low through the lands once swallowed up in the night, the two heartbeats traveled the world, hands tightly clasped, and following them was the light.

Acknowledgements

Writing is still something I am too used to doing alone, but it's never truly alone! There are always people in my corner.

First of course, is my mom and Miranda, my two first readers who will absolutely read something immediately hot off the presses, even if it desperately needs an edit job. After them comes Aowna for always being kind and efficient with feedback and then Menoa who made me feel like this project was my next one (I hope Nebora continues to be your favorite). Then is Monster Manor writing community I've somehow found myself in who always make me feel like I'm home even if I'm too shy to talk a lot. And finally, to my shy supporters who always seem to be there in the shadows.

I'm sure there are more names, but as usual my brain is scattered and I haven't yet come up with the idea of keeping a running list.

The final thanks are aimed at you, dear reader! Thank you for taking a chance on my slow, somber dark fantasy and I hope you enjoyed reading as much as I enjoyed writing.

About the Author

S. Jean (she/they) is a queer sci-fi & fantasy author writing whatever strikes their fancy at any given moment. When not writing or dreaming of what to write, they can be found dabbling in game dev and drawing!

For more information, visit: https://sjean.carrd.co/